RULE OF VAMPIRE

DUNCAN MCGEARY

RULE OF VAMPIRE

DUNCAN MCGEARY

www.dragonmoonpress.com

ISBN: 978-1-988256-94-8

Dedicated to the Farewell Bend Writer's Roundtable.

CHAPTER 1

She didn't want this. She smelled his blood flowing only inches away and she pushed against him, but he refused to let her go. He was forcing himself on her. She could easily have broken his grasp, but now she didn't want to. His blood was too near, his frenetic movements too much like prey. Her instincts overwhelmed her reluctance.

The blood that slid down her throat tasted sweet, just as the boy had seemed sweet at first. But there was also a bitter aftertaste.

She held him tight as he struggled, as she felt his life drain away. An overwhelming sadness washed over her.

This wasn't how she'd wanted the evening to end.

***

Jamie had been longing for the company of someone her own age, someone nice and cute and fun. Actually, she would've settled for someone grumpy and dorky, just as long as he could converse like a normal human.

It was the Fourth of July on the beach in Crescent City, California. The sands were crammed with locals and tourists. At ten o'clock, the fireworks would start. The locals were bundled up, equipped with lawn chairs and coolers and stacks of driftwood prudently collected earlier in the day. The tourists were realizing too late that wood was scarce, that fires on the beach weren't easy to start, and that they hadn't brought enough clothing. Some of the out-of-towners were huddled together, crouched over tiny fires, trying desperately to extract warmth from the tenuous flames.

The moment the Pacific Ocean quenched the setting sun, Jamie glided open the sliding doors of her motel room and walked barefoot down to the cresting waves and waited, the freezing water washing over her toes, sucking them down into the sand and then washing over her feet again and again until they were numb.

She wandered alone among the crowds of people, trying to remember what it had felt like to be one of them. It was as if she was a shark swimming through schools of fish. Most of them sensed the danger and shied away from her, moving out of her path.

Even at the height of summer, the wind off the ocean was penetratingly brisk. Jamie couldn't feel it. To her, the cold was but a tickle. But she wore a hoodie, because wearing something warm was expected of her. And she wanted desperately to fit in.

The young men had come bounding down the beach like puppies and she had turned away, not sure if she was ready to flirt with so many high-spirited males. One lonely boy— that, she could handle, but not this pack of half-drunken frat boys, hooting at every female they saw. Two or three girls had attached themselves to the group of guys, though they looked a little young to be out carousing.

Calling them frat boys was maybe elevating them a bit above their station. Here on the Northern California coast, the local schools were mostly community colleges. Still, they wandered these beaches like young men wandered all beaches in the summer, looking for fun and action.

One of them broke off from the others and approached her, almost shyly. He was slender and dark, with a cute upturned nose and black-rimmed glasses. He was dressed warmly, which probably meant he was a local, because out-of-towners always underdressed, thinking "beach" and "California."

"Hi," he said. Up close, he was even cuter than she'd hoped. She could see that he was trying to think of something else to say, but she rescued him by giving him a bright smile and echoing his greeting.

"Hi…"

"My friends and I are building a bonfire down the beach, and we have some wine. You're welcome to join us."

How could a girl resist? Jamie thought. *Well, easily, actually.* There was a time when she would have been a leery of such a proposition. But when the girl in question was more dangerous than a dozen strong men put together, it wasn't such an outrageous suggestion.

She walked down the beach with the dark-haired boy to join a rowdy group of young people gathered around a fire. When she walked up, the guys all stared and the girls glared at her. Jamie so outshone them that they nearly faded away. She'd always been pretty, in a girl-next-door sort of way. Her red hair and freckles had always attracted their fair share of attention. But now her baby fat was gone, and the sharply angled bones of her face made her beautiful instead of simply cute.

She focused her attention on Stuart, the boy who had first approached her. He seemed to be the leader of a core group of four guys. There was Pete, who was burly and loud and thought he was funny; Jimmy, who was quiet but watched everything that happened; and Greg, who was friendly and easygoing, and the one who probably held the others together. The rest of the group was assorted hangers-on.

Jamie had learned that she could blend in when she wanted to. But while the others became accustomed to her as the novelty wore off, to Stuart, she became ever more scintillating and attractive.

Their group had built the biggest fire on the beach, and that attracted more and more people until numerous friends and strangers mingled, their social interactions smoothed by the wine. Jamie drew Stuart away from the others, little by little, up into the sheltering logs and rocks. She saw him shiver and impulsively hugged him, even though she knew her skin would impart little warmth.

He froze, as if he wanted this closeness but was afraid to try anything. When she broke off the hug, he was blushing, and she thought, *What a sweet boy.*

A couple of policemen came toward them, a Mutt and Jeff pair, and she smiled at them. "Not supposed to have bonfires," the short, fat one said by way of greeting. But it was a halfhearted remonstration.

Jamie looked up and down the miles of beaches, where there were dozens of fires, and laughed. The taller policeman looked chagrined.

"So how's that workin' for ya?" she asked.

"It's hopeless," the taller cop said, grinning.

To her surprise, however, Stuart took offense. "What are you hassling us for?"

She turned to him and was astonished to see his face red and his eyes glaring. She was suddenly reminded that he was probably still a teenager.

"Because your fire is bigger than anyone else's," the shorter cop answered just as belligerently. *Uh oh,* Jamie thought. *Immediate escalation.* "Like it's in our face."

"So, what? You're going to arrest us?" Stuart shouted.

Jamie was pulling at his arm, trying to calm him down. "It's all right, Stuart. They're just giving us a warning—it's their job."

As Stuart and the shorter cop faced off, Jamie and the tall cop looked at each other, and it was obvious they were thinking the same thing: *much ado about nothing*. Both of them turned toward their companions and pulled them away, trying to get them to relax. Stuart went off to stand by the fire, and the shorter cop threw up his hands and stomped down the beach.

"I'm Officer Jurgenson," the tall cop said, looking sheepish. "Robert," he added, and then seemed surprised to have said it.

"Jamie," she said, and smiled at him. He was actually kind of good-looking, with dark hair that was graying at the temples, a cleft chin, soft brown eyes, and a kind of weary dignity. This was the man she'd rather spend the evening with, she realized. Someone a little older and more mature.

He winced and pressed a hand to his side.

"Are you OK?" Jamie asked. She'd found that as a vampire, she could sense flaws in humans, could tell when they were sick or injured. It was in her nature now to prey on such weaknesses.

"Just pulled a muscle, I think," he said.

She nodded, though she knew it was more than that. *None of my business,* she thought. *Too bad. Such a handsome man.*

"Well, enjoy the fireworks," he said cheerfully. He walked away, and she watched him go. He turned around and winked at her.

She sighed and set about trying to smooth things over with Stuart. She didn't want her entire evening to go to waste. Slowly but surely, she coddled and reassured him until he was back to his calmer self. Again, she drew him away from the others, and soon they were sitting in the dark together.

They chatted about little things; later, Jamie couldn't even remember what they had talked about. It was enough for her, at the time, just to be talking to another person. He was a younger guy than she ever would have dared flirt with when she was alive, but she was finding she didn't much care about human judgments and restrictions anymore.

She might have rewarded this young man if the evening had kept progressing the same way, but then the fireworks started, and they fell silent except to echo the *oohs* and *aahs* they heard up and down the beach. When the last shimmering fragment fell into the ocean and those around them started packing up to go, it was as if someone had flipped a switch. Perhaps Stuart had guzzled too much wine while they'd been staring into the sky.

He didn't lean in toward her, inviting a kiss, as she might have wanted. Instead, he grabbed her, turned her around, and began biting her neck. She winced and almost laughed aloud at the thought of this human biting her in the neck. *Do vampires get hickeys?* she wondered.

He is just overeager, she thought. She gently pushed him away, but that seemed to anger him, and he grabbed her harder than before.

"Stop," she said. "Go easy, Stuart. I like you."

He didn't say anything, just came on stronger than ever. His playful fondling became insistent and he used his strength to pin her down. The look in his eyes, glinting in the moonlight, was cold and calculating.

"I've been playing your little game all evening," he growled. "You play hard to get, but I noticed you managed to ditch the others…"

"I just wanted to tal—" she started to say.

He put his mouth over hers and began thrusting his tongue into her mouth. Her eye widened as she wondered if he was going to puncture his flesh on her lengthening fangs.

Then it was too late. Maybe he would've backed off, maybe he wouldn't have. But she'd gotten a taste of him, and it had been too long since she had fed.

Jamie was surprised by how sweet his blood tasted. He

struggled weakly, his efforts already undermined by the bottle of wine.

She had taken only a few swallows because she'd thought that wine didn't affect her. Now she was finding out that, transmuted by a victim's blood, the effects of wine were magnified and deepened. Underneath it all, she felt sadness at this poor boy's fate. He was a young man, rash in his actions, who would never grow up to learn wisdom. Perhaps he would have broken off if she'd protested enough, if she'd been the young woman she appeared to be. Perhaps he would've come to his senses. But now she would never know.

She left him on top of her as she drained him, his body dead weight. There was sadness permeating her hunger, but for a few moments, there was anger, too. Too many times, when she'd been a living girl, men like this had forced themselves on her. She'd almost come to expect it. But now she had the strength and power to do something about it.

Somehow, even as he was dying, Stuart summoned enough strength to cry out, "I'm sorry!"

Jamie faltered, her fangs receding into her jaws without her being conscious of it. *Finish it!* she heard Horsham say in her mind. Her Maker's voice was insistent. *You must finish it!*

"Are you all right, miss?" she heard someone ask. Over Stuart's shoulder, she could see the Mutt and Jeff cops returning. They'd heard his cry and had mistaken it for hers. "Is this guy bothering you?"

Stuart moaned and she pushed him off her. He rolled a couple of inches until he was facedown in the sand. Jamie got up calmly. "He's had too much to drink," she said.

"You better get his nose out of the sand," the shorter cop said. He hurried over and turned Stuart over. There was blood all over his neck and down his chest. She'd bitten the artery, as she'd been taught, and the blood began spurting up toward the policeman, who cursed and fell backward. The boy was going to bleed out in seconds. All that wonderful sweet blood going to waste.

"What the…?" the tall cop cried. "What's going on here?"

Jamie was backing away. She could try to explain, but what was the point? They weren't carrying firearms; there was nothing they could do to stop her.

She turned and ran, and she knew that to the two cops, it would look as if she had disappeared into the darkness.

CHAPTER 2

"Terrill has been found," Hargraves intoned as if it was gospel. He had the appearance of a 10-year-old boy, and it was always slightly humorous that he was so serious. "Horsham is dead."

Fitzsimmons met this news with a kind of glee. Council meetings had been entirely too tame and routine lately, as far as he was concerned. They were meeting in an old, staid financial firm in London, but it was still a far more modern meeting place than the drafty castles they'd been meeting in for most of their history, much less the bare caves of their first meetings. As far as Fitzsimmons was concerned, this was the first bit of interesting news to be brought for their review in what seemed like centuries.

He was about to say "Good!" when Southern beat him to it. Southern could always be counted on to react first, without thinking. He was a tall, aristocratic man who had added gray streaks to his beard and hair, though his face and hands were without blemish. He was one of the richest men in England and in the news often, so he'd taken the trouble to create the façade that he was aging like a normal human

Fitzsimmons preferred to stay in the shadows. He looked ordinary in every way: brown hair, slightly overweight, medium height, a forgettable face. It wasn't by accident. He'd cultivated that look for millennia.

"That's good news," Southern said. "Horsham dead and Terrill found. I presume the two items are related?"

Everyone knew that Horsham had hated Terrill and had

been searching for him for years to exact revenge.

"It appears so," Hargraves said.

"Then Terrill did us a favor," Fitzsimmons said. "We were going to have to take care of Horsham one of these days anyway. He was culling the humans a little too vigorously for our safety."

"Yet," interjected Peterson, ever the legal scholar. He was the rare vampire who had been bitten when he was an old man, and he'd never totally lost his fussy-old-man ways. "Horsham wasn't doing anything illegal."

Fitzsimmons turned to his colleague and raised his eyebrows slightly, as if to say, *When has that ever stopped us from doing what is necessary?*

There was barely a quorum for this meeting: five members out of the ten total. Even that many attendees was rare these days. Yes, it had been entirely too boring for entirely too long.

But a quorum is a quorum, Fitzsimmons thought, *and that means decisions can be made.*

"I vote that we approach Terrill for membership in the Council," he said. "I believe Partridge has wanted out for some time now. In fact, I can't remember the last time he attended a meeting."

"Terrill won't come," Susan Clarkson said. The four male vampires turned toward her, surprised she had spoken. It was ever so enlightened of them to have voted in a female vampire, but they didn't really expect her to contribute.

"And why is that?" Fitzsimmons asked, though he already knew. *Better it comes from her,* he thought.

"Terrill refuses to feed on humans," she said. Her face was blank and it was hard to get a read on what she thought of this remarkable fact. She was a Nordic blonde, classically good-looking, but she was so cold that her looks could only be admired from a distance.

"How very odd," Hargraves intoned, and the rest of them laughed.

"Nevertheless," Fitzsimmons said, "he is among the oldest of us, and we could perhaps benefit from an alternative viewpoint."

"Is it true that Michael was his Maker?" Peterson asked. Though he appeared older than the rest of them, he was barely more than a baby vampire himself. He'd been voted onto the Council because he was so much more conversant with modern ways than the rest of them.

"So it's said," Fitzsimmons answered. *Hogwash,* he thought. *Michael is a myth.* "If so, imagine how wise his advice will be."

"What? That we should become cow lickers?" Southern scoffed. "I'd rather you drove me out into the middle of the desert and left me there to burn. Nevertheless, I second the motion. We need some new blood, so to speak. All those in favor?"

All of them raised their hands but Peterson, which was more or less meaningless because he pretty much voted against everything, for reasons no one could discern.

"What if he won't come?" Clarkson asked.

"I move that we appoint Clarkson to bring him back, by any means necessary," Fitzsimmons quickly followed up. Good for her. She was following his instructions exactly, though she wouldn't be expecting this last bit of inspiration.

"Wait," she began to object, but it was already too late. The others were raising their hands, even Peterson, and she fell silent. For once, her countenance took on some emotion as she shot Fitzsimmons a poisonous look.

"Terrill must learn that he is one of us," Hargraves said. "He has been free too long."

They all nodded in agreement, and again Fitzsimmons felt a moment of giddiness.

This was going to be fun.

"Shall we eat?" Hargraves asked.

Though they were meeting in an office of a reputable bank, it was a back room where few, if any, employees ever wandered. If they had, they would have seen an odd table in the middle of the room, with a concave surface, narrowing at one end, where there was a drainage hole. A medical student might have recognized it as an autopsy table, if he was observant enough to look past the polished oak and the carvings of what appeared to be gargoyles on the thick legs.

At the center of the concave depression, there was a bundled-up object that occasionally, throughout the meeting, had twitched. Now Hargraves removed the covering to reveal the vampire beneath, naked, her mouth covered with duct tape, her hands and feet bound. She was short and blonde, and a little chubby. Fitzsimmons was pretty sure he'd seen her around the offices.

"What did she do?" he asked idly.

Peterson picked up the mallet and the wooden stake in front of him and said, "Rule number one, I think. Consorting with a human." It really didn't matter. The Rules were just an excuse, and most everyone knew it. Certainly no one on the Council had any illusions.

Peterson shrugged and put the point of the stake over the captive vampire's heart. She was screaming at the top of her lungs through the gag, but they'd gotten so good at this that it came out as no more than a loud hum.

Peterson brought the mallet down without fanfare. The stake had been sharpened so that it slid easily between the vampire's ribs and into her heart. The Council members watched as the life went out of her eyes. Blue blood welled up around the wooden stake and started to drain away.

They leaned over and sank their fangs into her soft body, tearing away mouthfuls of her flesh. Their faces took on a blue glow as the vampire blood covered them. Human blood was great, but vampire blood was addicting.

In the back of Fitzsimmons's mind, he knew that they had gone over the edge, that vampires were intent on consuming each other. The Rules of Vampire—which had been created by Terrill to save their kind—were instead going to be their downfall.

CHAPTER 3

Bend, Oregon, was becoming a city—or so the residents told themselves. But to Terrill, it was still a quaint little town. It wasn't so big that he could fail to notice the three black Cadillac Escalades that had begun following him around. They had windows with just enough tinting to allow a vampire to survive in the daylight.

But why would they be following him? As far as he knew, Horsham had been his last enemy, and Horsham was gone forever: finally and most definitely gone.

Terrill sighed. He'd been enjoying himself for the first time in ages. Sylvie really seemed to like him, though neither of them was brave enough to use the word "love" just yet. The word had almost slipped out of him a couple of times as they luxuriated on the grass in the afternoon sun, holding hands, her head on his chest where the silver cross was fused to his skin.

The wounds had healed around the cross, and it was simply part of him now. Occasionally, Father Harry would ask him to stand up and show his cross to the congregation, as if he was a prize bull. The congregation liked Father Harry enough that they were overlooking his increasingly bizarre sermons about demons and hellfire. After all, Father Harry was a bit of a miracle himself, as he'd been shot in the belly but survived the carnage that that maniac Horsham had inflicted on the police station.

The townsfolk accepted Terrill as an odd but likeable eccentric. He volunteered at the Catholic soup kitchen most days and had become a trusted friend and confidant to many of the homeless. Crazy or addled or drug addicted, it didn't matter: he embraced them all.

He was loving life. Because it *was* life. He was alive, his heart was beating, and who would've ever thought that would happen? When the sun beat down on his head, at worst, it gave him a sunburn. He sometimes missed his old strength and speed, but he didn't need it. He certainly didn't need his ability to see in the dark, because most nights he was home in bed, with Sylvie.

He'd once been vampire, but no more. He was immortal no longer. He could die tomorrow, and it didn't bother him in the least. He was content.

So why were they following him?

Terrill approached one of the Escalades at a stoplight, but the SUV sped away. *Well, that's fair,* he thought. Throwing open the door wouldn't have been healthy for the vampires inside. He'd wait until evening and see if they'd talk to him then.

He walked home most days. St. Francis, one of local Catholic churches, was downtown, and he and Sylvie had settled in a home on the west side. It was an outrageously expensive house for being so tiny, and it was a long stretch to call it a Craftsman-style cottage, but Sylvie loved it and that's all that mattered to him. Terrill was wealthy beyond anyone's imaginings—but even Sylvie only had clues about that.

He was ready to give all that wealth away. He was just trying to figure out how to go about it. Turned out that giving away money effectively was almost as complicated as earning it in the first place—not that he'd really had to work at it. Time had been on his side. "Compound interest is a vampire's best friend" was the phrase that was often used, and Terrill believed he'd probably coined it himself, long ago, so long ago that he could barely remember it.

His memory of the long, bloody centuries was fading, thankfully. He was feeling more the age of his human body, in his mid-thirties, tall, lanky and dark, and slowly gaining a potbelly from all the home-cooked meals. He'd noticed his first genuine gray hair a few weeks ago, and wrinkles and spots were appearing in strange places for no apparent reason.

Sylvie was slowly teaching him modern ways. She was barely old enough to drink, though her working life had mostly been spent in one brewpub or bar after another. Her hair was glossy black and thick and curling, her eyes were wide and dark, her nose was long and narrow, and when you took her in parts, she should have been ugly, but she was gorgeous in an oddly put-together way.

She greeted him at the door, and he could tell from the look in her eyes that she'd been thinking about her sister and that she was going to ask him The Question. One thing about Sylvie: you never had to wait for her to get to the point.

"Have you found Jamie yet?" she said without preamble.

He wasn't sure why she had such faith in him, faith that he could find her sister. Jamie was a vampire and he'd once been a vampire, and that was connection enough for Sylvie. But even more importantly, he was Jamie's Maker. And it was true that he could probably guess some of her moves: she'd go somewhere that was mostly cloudy and overcast, she'd want to blend in, and she probably wouldn't have taken public transportation, so she couldn't have gone far.

Of course, she could've stolen a car and be all the way across the country for all Terrill knew, but he sensed that she was near—probably in Oregon or one of the neighboring states. She was a baby vampire, without a mentor, and she'd want to stay close to home.

But his real ace in the hole was his connection to the street people who passed through town. They had a tendency to keep moving and to be aware of all the hiding places. They went unnoticed and yet were everywhere, observing everything.

Grime had mumbled something about "I...ge...er...," which Terrill had translated as "I'll get her." And that was good enough for Terrill.

Meanwhile, old Perry had made it his job to ask every transient who passed through St. Francis about Jamie, and they answered him when they wouldn't have answered Terrill or Father Harry. No matter how much the two of them were respected, they weren't of the brotherhood. Perry was a lifelong hobo and knew everyone.

Jamie's looks—red-haired, freckled, and gorgeous—were unusual enough that Terrill thought there was at least a chance she'd be noticed, especially if she was trying to hole up in less-reputable places—and she was probably going to gravitate toward many of the same places where the homeless congregated.

Terrill snapped out of his reverie, aware that Sylvie was staring at him, waiting for his answer. "Not yet," he told her. "The last time anyone saw her, she was heading south, so I've been asking a lot of questions about areas to the south of us. I don't think she'd go *too* far south, though, because she'll want to stay in the shade."

"Let's go," Sylvie said. "We'll head down Highway 97. Stop in all the little towns. Ask around."

Terrill nearly laughed. Finding a vampire in the dark was nearly impossible even when you knew she was there! But he just shook his head. "Let's wait until we get a sighting."

"Harrumph," Sylvie snorted, and walked off to the kitchen to prepare dinner—which was about the best response Terrill could have expected.

He went to the picture window and pulled aside the curtains. A black Escalade sat in front of his house, as if inviting him to come out.

So he went.

CHAPTER 4

The SUV's door flew open as Terrill walked down the front path. There was a woman with short blonde hair and icy blue eyes sitting in the passenger seat, waiting for him. She wasn't smiling; she wasn't scowling. Her face was carefully neutral.

"Are you looking for me?" he asked.

"Yes, Terrill. We need to talk. Get in." Her voice was deep and mellow and hypnotic. He almost obeyed without thinking, but with an effort, he pulled back.

"Stop it," he said. "I know your tricks."

"Of course you do," she said. She frowned, and it was as if the skin of her face was feeling the force of frown muscles for the first time, as if it was virgin territory. "You are a vampire."

"I *was* a vampire," Terrill said.

"That's impossible," she said. "Once a vampire, always a vampire." The frown remained on her face.

"Oh? You've been following me for the last few days. How do you think I walk around in the sunlight? You're close enough now to hear the beating of my heart, to smell the blood coursing through my veins."

She didn't answer.

"What do you want?" he demanded.

Suddenly, she became conciliatory. "I'm not your enemy, Terrill. I have nothing but respect for you and your views. In fact, I voted in favor of asking you to join the Council."

Terrill didn't trust this any more than he had her original no-nonsense approach. He just stared at her. For a moment, he had to struggle to remember what she was talking about. "The Council of Vampires?" he said aloud as the memory came back. He started laughing. That bunch of meddlers! He'd barely been aware of their founding and had pretty much ignored them ever since.

"Things have changed, Terrill," the woman said. "My name is Clarkson, and I think you'd better listen to me."

Something in her tone caught him short, and he stopped laughing.

"Get in the backseat," she said.

To his surprise, he did. He didn't think he'd been charmed, but he wasn't absolutely certain. As the SUV pulled away from the curb, Terrill suddenly remembered that he was human and these were vampires, and he was completely defenseless. *How interesting that I'm not afraid,* he thought. He could die at any moment, but he felt calm, whereas all those centuries that he'd been immortal, he'd been afraid of losing his life. *How very strange.*

"You may not know it, Terrill, but your Rules of Vampire are now the law among our kind, enforced by the Council," Clarkson said.

"The vampires I knew would never stand for that," he said.

"The vampires you knew are mostly dead, many of them at the hands of the Council. We're no joke, Terrill, whatever you might think."

How ironic, Terrill thought. He'd first formulated the Rules of Vampire as a lark during World War II. Vampires had been disappearing at an alarming rate, so he'd tried to construct some guidelines for them to follow, to help them survive. But though they were called rules, they'd really always been suggestions:

Rule 1. Never trust a human.

Rule 2. Never leave the remains of a kill, or if you must, disguise the cause of death.

Rule 3. Never feed where you live.

Rule 4. Never create a pattern. Kill at random.

Rule 5. Never kill for the thrill. Feed only when necessary to eat.

Rule 6. Never steal in the short term; create wealth for the long term.

As if she could read his mind, Clarkson smiled. Again, the creases on her smooth face seemed almost unnatural. "We've come up with a few more since then, most of them just corollaries. All of them enforced, punishable by death."

Terrill supposed it was possible. He had been in hiding for decades, living by a code that was even more severe than his original Rules, one that had made the Rules moot: he had refused to kill humans. He'd been out of the loop for a long time.

"You want me to join you?" he said.

"It has been decided by a vote of the Council," Clarkson said.

"And if I refuse?"

She turned around in the front seat and her blue eyes sought his, making sure that he was paying attention. "You can't refuse, Terrill. The Council has become all-powerful. Every vampire would turn against you—and those you love."

They were pulling up in front of his house, and as the Escalade slowed, Clarkson's eyes went to the kitchen window, where Terrill could see Sylvie whistling as she fixed dinner.

"But I am no longer vampire," he protested. "Surely you can see that I'll be of no use to you."

"I'm sorry, Terrill. Truly, I am. But I'm afraid that if I returned and told the Council that you have miraculously turned human, they would be even more determined to have you in their power. You'd best return with me and make your case to the full Council."

To his surprise, Clarkson let him get out of the SUV. She

got out with him and stood next to him on the sidewalk. She was nearly as tall as he was, and her posture was impeccable. She might have been a Greek statue, pale and lovely in the moonlight. He glanced toward the kitchen window and saw Sylvie staring out at them.

"I would rather you came willingly," Clarkson said. "I'll give you a week. If you want to talk to me, I'll be staying downtown at the Oxford. I hope you'll make the right decision, Terrill. You..." Unbelievably, she blushed. "You've always been my hero."

She got back into the Escalade and snapped an order at the burly driver, and they shot away.

Terrill walked slowly up the path. Sylvie was waiting at the door. She didn't say anything; she just took him in her arms. She'd wait for him to explain if he wanted to, or let it go completely if he didn't want to.

Later that night, it all poured out of him.

CHAPTER 5

ENGLAND, 1250 A.D.

"I always called you a bastard, Terrill. I don't know about the rest of these lads, but I never thought you were anything but a bastard. It's not my fault if you didn't take me seriously."

Terrill stood in his soiled clothing in front of his resplendent friends, too shocked to move as they laughed.

"Tell you what," Peter Martel continued, "if you want to buy us a round like you always did in the old days, we'll let you sit down."

The old days? Terrill wondered. He'd been drinking with these fellows only the week before. He'd been one of them…or so he'd always thought.

"I've bought you drinks every night of the week for years," he said in a dull voice.

"Indeed. Why else do you think we associated with a bastard?" Martel asked. Everyone at the table laughed some more—and then, worse, they started talking about the tournament as if Terrill wasn't there.

The Tournament of Chalize. He'd shown up at the castle for his placement, hoping for an early joust, thinking he might be able to win his favor back by winning the grand prize. Instead, the local authorities had asked him for the papers proving his nobility.

"Papers?" he'd repeated, not quite understanding. "You know who I am."

"No, sir. We do not," the fat man behind the table had said.

At this, Terrill had backed away, stunned. He had stumbled over a wooden plank and landed on his back in the mud. And he had heard laughter: laughter from servants who, only a short time before, wouldn't even have dared to look him in the eye.

Now, he turned his back on his former friends and headed over to the stable. Somehow, he wasn't surprised to find that his horse, William the Conqueror, was no longer there. "The duke's widow took him away this morning," said the stable boy. There was sympathy in the lad's voice, the first sympathy Terrill had heard since he'd been turned out of his lodgings the day before.

It began to sink in. He was a bastard. He'd always been a bastard, but he'd also been the duke's only male offspring, so he'd been indulged and coddled all his life. Oh, he hadn't been allowed to live with the family; the duchess wouldn't permit that. But other than that inconvenience, he'd never been without privilege. More importantly, he was realizing belatedly, he had never been without coin.

The privilege had meant nothing. The coin had meant everything.

Why didn't I see it? Why didn't I plan ahead? Terrill thought bitterly.

Because he had never had to plan ahead, he realized; he had always been provided for, his bad behavior always excused. He'd walked away from debts knowing that they would be paid.

Even as he thought this, Terrill saw big Jeremy walking his way with a grim expression. The officious fat man, the mayor, and his brethren the town council, thought they ran the town, but it was Jeremy and his thugs who really had the final say. Terrill didn't wait around to see what Jeremy wanted. The previous day, he'd placed some large bets on certain participants in the tournament, knowing he himself was unlikely to win it all. Now, as Jeremy undoubtedly knew, he could never pay up.

Terrill ran.

He remained in hiding for weeks, doing odd jobs, even begging. He had no skills, he soon discovered. None at all—except drinking. His once-fine clothes turned to rags, his hair grew shaggy, and he began to stink. He slept in barns, sometimes even in the open.

The only people who would feed and shelter him were the very poorest of citizens, people he had once barely noticed existed. They lived on a plane below the servants, below the tradesmen, below the yeoman farmers. They'd always been in the background, bowing to him. Now they looked on him with sympathy and gave what little they could share.

After one particularly wretched couple gave him some bread, Terrill broke down in tears. He'd been sitting by the side of the road, watching them with pity as they passed by, but it was they who took pity on him, giving him the last of their food. As they walked away, he buried his head in his hands and cried.

"What's the problem, son?" he heard someone say.

Terrill looked up to see a man standing over him with his hand outstretched. He took the offered hand and the man raised him to his feet.

"Come with me, young man, and we'll talk over some drinks," the man said.

The stranger led Terrill to a tavern that was little more than four walls and a mud floor, and sat him down at a rough-planked table.

The man looked young—not a wrinkle to be seen—but he had gray hair and a gray beard. His eyes were bright, curious. He was dressed in the finest of clothes, but he wasn't noble, Terrill sensed; instead, he was one of those men who made their own wealth without the benefit of a privileged family.

Once, Terrill would have looked down on such a man, but now he had nothing but admiration for the fellow.

Four drinks later, he was telling the man that. "I was a fool. I thought I was a nobleman when I was but a bastard. The only reason I was accepted was for my money. I wish I had it to do over again. I would give to the poor instead of the rich."

The man—he'd said his name was Michael, but had given no family name—looked at Terrill intently. "I am in need of an assistant," he said. "I'll pay you well and you'll be fed and clothed."

"I would be honored," Terrill said.

They didn't make it to Michael's home that night. In the darkness of a country lane, Terrill sensed the man come up behind him. He felt a sharp pain in the back of his neck, and then nothing.

***

Terrill woke inside a dirt hole. There were planks over his head, and he could see sunlight through the thin cracks between them. He put his fingers through one of the gaps, and it was as if someone had cut into them. He yelped and pulled his fingers back. In the dim light, he could see that they were blackened, as if they had been burned. They certainly hurt as if they had been burned. He groaned, but after a few minutes, the pain receded and his fingers appeared to be healed.

Being stubborn, Terrill tried again, with the same results. So he stayed in the hole for the rest of the day, wondering if he'd been buried and left for dead, or if perhaps he *was* dead and the fire outside was hell.

When the light faded, he slid the planks aside and sat up.

Michael was sitting on a log a few feet away, and met his eyes.

"What did you do to me?" Terrill asked.

"I've turned you into a creature of the night, who lives on blood; who will burn in the daylight; whom God has forsaken, and who is shunned by mankind."

How is that different from what I've been? Terrill wondered. *Hiding at night, stealing from others, forsaken by all.* He accepted Michael's explanation right away. For one thing, he could feel it in his blood: he wasn't tired anymore, but he was hungrier than ever. It was no more disconcerting than finding out that he wasn't a noble, wasn't rich, but was a bastard and destitute.

"You will be stronger and faster than any human, but you must understand how to handle these new powers," Michael said. "I will teach you the rudiments. It will be up to you to learn them—or not."

Later that night, Michael led him to a pasture that contained a single, scrawny cow. "I purchased this for you," he said.

Overwhelmed by hunger, Terrill fell upon the unfortunate beast. The savagery of his own behavior amazed him. He didn't just suck the cow's blood; he tore the animal apart, and he delighted in its pain. When he was finished, he looked over at Michael. "You purchased it?" he asked. "Why didn't you simply take it?"

"Should I deprive a poor man of his livestock?" Michael asked, looking at him curiously. "Don't you remember what you said last night? About pitying the poor?"

"That was last night," Terrill said.

Michael looked disappointed, but not surprised. "Perhaps someday…"

Disappointed or not, over the next few weeks, Michael was true to his word and taught Terrill to survive. Terrill learned that there were things he should do if he didn't want humans hunting him down: avoid contact with humans as much as possible, try to feed only when necessary, and destroy all evidence. Move along after a kill. Try not to kill in the same way each time.

"One last thing," Michael said one night. "If you follow these suggestions and live long enough, you will need money. You can accumulate wealth by investing small amounts and leaving it with the bankers. You'll forget about the investments, and then one day find that you're rich."

Terrill nodded. When Michael left, Terrill didn't try to stop him. The whole time the gray-haired man had been with him, he'd had to hold himself back. He'd never seen Michael kill a human, only animals, though he hadn't stopped Terrill from tracking down Peter Martel and his former friends and dispatching swift and brutal justice.

After they parted, Terrill saw Michael every few generations. It was as if the older vampire was checking up on him periodically. Each time, Michael—who by then was legendary among the other vampires—went away again.

Terrill tried to live as Michael had suggested, quickly seeing the wisdom of his advice. He began to think of Michael's suggestions as rules, though he didn't formalize them as Rules of Vampire until hundreds of years later.

CHAPTER 6

Jamie stayed in her motel room for a full day and night. She turned on the radio and TV, but there was little local news of any interest. The town newspaper was a weekly and wouldn't be out for another few days. She had no way of knowing what had happened to Stuart.

Was he dead? Had he Turned? Were they looking for her? *What would Horsham do?* Jamie wondered. He'd only mentored her for a few days, but she'd been so overwhelmed by the bloodthirst that she'd barely paid attention to him. He'd mentioned something about Rules of Vampire—but then, he'd also scoffed at them. She was pretty sure one of the rules was something along the lines of "Get out of town, fast."

Jamie was broke. The motel was going to kick her out any day now. She had nowhere to go. Thinking about that, she would have broken down and cried if she had still been human. But to her amazement, she was unworried. She'd deal with whatever came. She was stronger and faster than any human; better equipped to survive.

The next day, it was cloudy and raining, and Jamie ventured out, protected by her hoodie. She walked to the local market and glanced at the headlines on the front pages in the newspaper racks, but there was nothing about a murder in Crescent City. A cop car drove by and slowed, but then kept going.

She went into the store and looked around. When she'd first run away from home, she'd survived mostly by shoplifting, and the skills came back to her automatically. She lifted a box of

L'Oreal hair color and was out the door before the clerk even knew she was there. She hunched her shoulders and walked back to the motel. By the time darkness rolled around, she was no longer a redhead, but a blonde.

It was hard to hide the freckles, especially with her extremely pale skin, but when she looked in the mirror, it seemed to her that she was a completely different woman. *Even Sylvie wouldn't recognize me now,* she thought.

She felt a twinge. *Sylvie…*

Why did she still care? Her sister was part of her human existence, and that Jamie was dead. She found that she had few fond memories of her father and mother or her friends—and certainly not of Richard Carlan or any of her other loser boyfriends. She had almost shoplifted a box of black hair dye, but an image of her sister had come to her and her hand had plucked the next box over. *I should have stayed in Bend, no matter the consequences, and watched over my little sister, just like I always have.*

But she remembered her Maker, Terrill, looking at her in pity. She couldn't stand it. She'd run away, intending never to look back.

As soon as it was dark, Jamie went out make the rounds of the local taverns, most of them playing country music, which she couldn't stand.

She was sitting at the bar in one of them when a man moved close to her. He drew up a stool, turned toward her, and gave her a dazzling smile. She instantly distrusted him. There was something strange about him. She couldn't help herself—she sniffed, trying to get a whiff of his blood.

He looked amused. It was as if he had noticed her sniffing and knew what it meant. The bar was loud and noisy and smelled of spilled beer and whiskey, and Jamie couldn't quite get a read on him.

At first, she thought he was a slender and fit old man, because his full head of hair was pure silver. But when she looked at his face, she couldn't see a single wrinkle. Based on his appearance alone, he wasn't older than his late twenties.

To hell with him, she thought. She turned away.

He had the effrontery to laugh. "Come now, you're here to pick up a man. Don't I fit the bill?" he said lightly.

"Screw you," she said.

"If you'd like."

"Yeah. Clever. Go away."

"As you please," he said. He looked disappointed—but in a mocking way. *Yeah, I don't need this type of guy,* Jamie thought. She sent out "Stay away!" signals for most of the rest of the evening. Finally, she calmed down.

She shouldn't have been hungry already, but when a cowboy tried to pick her up, she let him. She took him out behind the bar and let him lift her dress; then she said, "No, show me your money first."

He slapped her and pushed her against the wall.

She tore his neck out without a second thought, drinking his blood in as messy a way as possible; anything to drive away the human part of her. *Sylvie would want no part of me.*

She ate his face and his fingers, then threw up. When she was done retching, she ate the rest of him.

***

Jamie woke in the bathtub of the motel room the next morning. Someone was pounding on her door. In a few moments, unless she missed her guess, the motel manager—who was a pencil-necked creep—would use his key to barge in. She turned on the shower, and as soon as she had washed off the cowboy's blood, she got out…just as the manager opened the door.

She stood in front of him, naked, and smiled.

Jamie wanted to tear off his face, but instead she let him push her back onto the bed. He was done in seconds, it seemed. After he left, she got back into the shower and washed and washed until the hot water turned cold, and then she stayed there and washed some more.

***

The next night, Jamie went to an all-night diner and waited for the inevitable proposition. This time, she took the man's money, not his life. She checked out of the motel she'd been staying in and walked a mile down the road to the next cheap motel. There seemed to be no end of them on the highway that ran along the beach.

***

"Out, lady. We don't allow your kind here."

"What are you talking about?" Jamie asked. She was standing behind the motel room door half-dressed, which didn't help the situation.

"You know what I'm talking about. Get out of my motel, you slattern!"

Slattern? She almost laughed at the fat little motel manager. When she'd first moved in, she'd had a nice chat with the man, who had proudly announced that he was a writer and that this motel gig was just something he was doing to earn money until he got discovered.

"I haven't done anything," she protested.

"Yet!" he shouted. "I know your kind. I saw that man go into your room last night...and he wasn't the first!"

She sighed. She really didn't want to argue. It was time to move on anyway. Problem was, her latest john had snuck off without paying, and she was broke.

"One more night?" she pleaded.

"I want you out by noon or I'm calling the cops." He stomped away.

She got dressed as fast as she could, wishing she had time to take a shower, because she could still smell the alcohol and cigarettes of the john on her. Her clothes needed washing; her backpack was falling apart. She caught a glimpse of herself in the mirror. *Slattern, indeed,* she thought.

It was twelve-thirty by the time she closed the motel room door behind her. She saw a police car pull into the alcove by the lobby. The two Mutt and Jeff cops from the Fourth of July got out. The tall cop glanced her way and hesitated, then followed his partner into the office.

Robert Jurgenson, Jamie thought. *You handsome man.* She was ashamed, suddenly. She didn't want him seeing her this way.

She hoisted her backpack and hurried off in the other direction. It started raining before she had walked more than a few hundred yards. *Perfect,* she thought. Her sandals splashed into a puddle, sending mud up her shin. *Just perfect.*

All my problems would be solved if I used my speed and strength to prey on these humans, she thought. *It would be so easy. Just take them and kill them.*

But Terrill had shown her that being a vampire didn't mean you had to be a monster. He'd imposed a rule upon himself that he wouldn't kill humans. Perhaps Jamie would have followed the example of Horsham, who hadn't given a damn, but the image of her little sister always seemed to glimmer at the sides of her vision, as if Sylvie was with her every step of the way.

Jamie didn't want to kill, but she couldn't always help it. She wasn't that strong. The bloodlust would overwhelm her, and she would come to herself with a dead man in her grasp and little memory of how he had gotten there. It was pretty clear what her trigger was: an abusive or aggressive man. No women, no children; and any man who acted with respect toward her was usually safe.

So far, though, all her victims had been losers—there had been very little money in their pockets, or anything else of worth. She needed to find herself a rich abuser type, but she was looking so...so *slatternly* that she was unlikely to attract such a man.

Jamie walked down the highway, trying to figure out how she was going to book a motel room with no credit card and no money down. It would be nearly impossible, unless she found a manager who could be paid in a different way.

The rain was bad enough, but when the clouds started to part and blue skies appeared, she hurried her pace. She hadn't yet reached the next motel before the sun burst out from behind a cloud and shot agonizing rays of pain onto her. She staggered and cried out. She stretched the fabric of her hood with her vampire strength, just short of tearing it, shoved her hands into her pockets, put her head down, and kept walking.

CHAPTER 7

The undergrowth on the Northwest coast is thick, growing into dense hedges and lining every vacant lot. As the sunlight became brighter and seemed to saturate the air, invading every gap in her clothing, Jamie started looking for shelter; any kind of shelter.

At the edge of a muddy, cracked parking lot, she saw a small hole in a thatch of blackberry bushes. She ducked into the hole and crawled deeper in, feeling the thorns catching at her hoodie. Whatever animal had created this tunnel used it often, for it widened the further she went.

When she emerged on the other side, it was as if she had found a fairyland. It took her a few moments to realize she hadn't accidentally entered someone's house. Except for the fire pit at the center of the clearing, it looked like a shabby but genteel living room. She looked up and saw planks and tarps. The walls consisted of branches woven so thickly that they looked solid, and the floor was a mishmash of carpet pieces. It felt comfy, warm, and inviting. It was both dry and out of the sunlight. Jamie immediately relaxed.

Then she noticed the three men sitting comfortably in chairs on the other side of the "room."

"I'm sorry," she said. "I didn't know anyone was here."

"No one is," the eldest of the trio laughed. "We don't exist. This is the land of the forgotten."

She didn't know what to say. The men didn't seem alarmed, just curious. They were rough looking, bearded and longhaired, with tattered clothes, but Jamie had developed a sixth sense for how threatening men were, and she felt nothing but goodwill from this bunch.

"Sit down, make yourself comfortable," the old man said. "I'm Billy. This scrawny fellow is Cam, and the guy who can't stop staring at you is Patrick."

"I'm Jamie," she said. She almost felt like curtsying, and she had a memory of introducing herself to her first-grade teacher.

Billy got up from his wicker chair and motioned her into it. He went over to one side of the enclosure, where there was a small table laden with plates and cups. He poured some coffee into one of the cups and handed it to her.

"Welcome, Jamie," he said. He sat down at her feet companionably.

She waited for them to ask why she was there, but they continued a conversation they had apparently been having before she arrived, about whether LeBron James was as good a basketball player as he thought he was and whether Jordan could've taken him apart.

She found herself nodding off. Here, among three strange men, she felt the safest she'd felt since she'd been Turned.

***

The next morning, they fed her some scrambled eggs and bread toasted on an open fire. Jamie had found that she could eat human food, but didn't really need it as long as her bloodthirst was satisfied. She ate the breakfast politely, but turned down seconds.

When she was done, Billy got up. "Come with me," he said, and started crawling out of the tunnel. Jamie looked through the small gaps in the walls of branches and tried to ascertain whether the sun was shining. She couldn't tell. She trusted in fate and followed the old man out.

It was a typical Crescent City day: overcast, drizzling a slight rain that you almost couldn't feel but that would eventually soak you to the bone if you didn't seek shelter.

The old man took her to a thrift shop a few hundred yards away from their hideaway. He introduced her to the manager, Marc, who let her come in and pick out a wardrobe of warm clothes. She filled a garbage bag with clothing items.

Then Billy took her about half a mile down the road, onto a side street that was rarely traveled by cars. A soup kitchen had been set up, and men, women, and children were seated at picnic tables, being served a warm meal. The drizzle had stopped and the clouds were dispersing. The coastal winds would clear the sky of cloud cover by noon, and Jamie started getting anxious.

As if he could sense her alarm, Billy led her back to his home.

"Me and the boys are heading north for rest of the summer," he said after they had crawled through the tunnel and were standing in the "living room" again. "We always wander up to Bend, Oregon, this time of year. But you're welcome to stay here as long as you want, Jamie."

It was then that Jamie realized what Billy had done for her. He'd shown her how to survive.

Jamie hadn't cried since she'd been Turned, even when she'd left Sylvie behind. But now her eyes filled, and she put her hands to her face. The three men patted her on the back awkwardly, which only made her cry more.

She watched them leave, hoisting their backpacks and smiling. After they were gone, it was as if someone had cut the wires that had been holding her up. She fell into the tangle of blankets and sleeping bags the men had left for her, and it seemed as if she didn't fully wake up for days.

When she finally did wake up, she was ravenous: not for the food the men had so thoughtfully left behind, but for blood. Fresh, warm, living blood.

She tried to fight it. But without really being conscious of what she was doing, she dressed in the nicest clothing she could find in her new bag of garments and headed out into the night.

***

"That girl has had it hard," Billy said as the three of them exited their winter getaway. He'd felt almost like a father, showing her around; like the father he hadn't been able to be to his own children. "She's like a lost kitten or something."

"Yeah," Patrick said. "But did you notice underneath all that grime and smell that she's drop-dead gorgeous? I mean, what the hell is a woman like that doing down here?"

"You guys are fools," Cam muttered. "She's one of *them*. The night creatures. We're lucky we got out alive."

Billy laughed. "You are one weird motherfucker." Cam was always going off about monsters. Other than that, he was a great guy, fun to be around. But every once in a while, he started spouting that kind of crazy talk.

It was dark by the time they reached the edge of town and stuck out their thumbs. "Should've left earlier," Cam muttered, "instead of babysitting some monster."

"Jesus, Cam, give it a rest," Patrick said.

A pickup went roaring by. It was huge, with a double cab and a long bed.

"The bigger the truck, the smaller the dick," Billy said as it passed them.

It slowed down and backed up.

"I take it back," Billy said.

There were two young men up front and two more in the

backseat. "Jump in the bed," the driver said, grinning. "We can take you as far as Cave Junction, at least."

Billy and Patrick moved toward the back, but Cam stayed rooted to the spot.

"No way," he muttered to Billy, loud enough for everyone to hear. "Can't you feel it?"

"Feel what, you fool? A free ride?"

Billy could see that Cam wasn't going to move, so he came back and spoke insistently into the motionless man's ear. "We'll be in the back. If they get out of the cab and start moving toward us, we'll skedaddle, OK?"

It was starting to drizzle again. Cam looked miserable; the rain seemed to be falling on him harder than on everyone else, and his hair was dripping down his forehead. He gulped and followed Billy. Patrick put out a hand and helped them up.

The pickup shot out of there without warning, throwing the three men into the bed. Cam nearly went over the side. "Told you so!" he shouted.

They headed up the highway, but just before the Oregon border, the truck veered off onto a gravel road. Billy and Patrick exchanged alarmed glances. Cam's face turned white, and he stared back down the highway stoically as if to say *Told you so* again.

The driver slammed on the brakes and they slid for a couple of dozen yards on the loose gravel, sending the pickup sideways and nearly throwing all three of them over the side this time.

Before the wheels even stopped moving, the men in the passenger seats were flying out of the doors and rushing toward them. To Billy's eyes, they were a blur, they were moving so fast. He didn't wait to see what would happen, but sprang over the side and ran for the trees. He wasn't as old as he looked. He cultivated that appearance for just such situations.

He ran into the woods and desperately looked for a place to hide. He was an expert at hiding places; he'd spent his whole life seeking them out. He practically dove at the base of a tree, knowing instinctively that there was a tree well beneath the thatch of leaves. In seconds, he had concealed himself.

One of the men had followed him, but he'd been a screen of trees when Billy made his move and was turning around and around in the clearing, searching intently. His eyes looked as if they were glowing, and Billy surmised that the creature could see in the dark. Cam had been right. *Monsters.* Billy realized that he wasn't really surprised, that he'd somehow always known things like this existed.

Now the monster was sniffing, as if he could smell Billy. He turned toward the tree and Billy froze, but then he moved on, and finally, he angrily shook himself like a dog that had just lost a fight. "Shit!" the monster said, and ran back toward the pickup.

Stay where you are, Billy thought. *Don't fucking move.* But he heard Cam screaming, and before he knew it, he was digging himself out of his hole and crawling back toward the road.

He lay flat on the ground and watched helplessly.

They'd pushed Cam and Patrick against the truck and were standing in front of the two quivering men as if soaking in the fear their victims were radiating.

The driver of the pickup stood a little off to one side, as if he enjoyed watching his friends, almost as if he was supervising them. He was slender, with floppy brown hair and black-rimmed glasses. "They're all yours," the driver said. "You won't believe the rush."

The smaller of the other two guys turned toward him. "What do we do, Stuart?" he asked.

"You eat them, dumbshit."

The biggest of the attackers moved first, closing in on Patrick, who screamed as loudly as he could, as if he was actually expecting someone to hear him and save him. His scream was cut off as the monster bit into Patrick's neck and tore out his windpipe.

Meanwhile, Cam had sunk to the ground, and even from this distance, Billy could tell he had voided himself. The other two monsters—vampires, for that's what they were, Billy finally admitted to himself—fell on him from either side, and Billy saw chunks of flesh flying into the air. Cam didn't make a sound.

Billy couldn't watch any longer. He crawled back to the tree well and hid for the rest of the night, alternating between shaking, crying, and cursing.

But through it all, he vowed revenge.

CHAPTER 8

Terrill had barely closed the front door behind him when he shouted, "I've found her!"

Sylvie appeared from the kitchen, her face lighting up. "For sure?"

"She's in Crescent City," Terrill continued. "She even used her own name."

He'd been serving up stew at the soup kitchen in St. Francis when Perry appeared at his side and said, "You need to come with me."

Terrill handled the ladle to one of the cooks and followed Perry into the dining room. An old guy was sitting by himself in the corner. Terrill slowed down, sensing that the man had recently experienced some kind of trauma. *I hope it wasn't Jamie,* he thought. *No, what am I saying? I hope it was Jamie!*

The story came out of the man reluctantly. His name was Billy, and it was clear that he didn't trust anyone in authority, even someone at a soup kitchen. But Perry kept murmuring reassurances, and eventually Billy came out with it. Jamie, as it turned out, was only incidentally involved.

The story was as bad as anything Terrill had ever heard. These vampires were wild, completely untrained. It was probable that Jamie had created them, by not taking the proper precautions, by breaking Rule Two: Never leave the remains of a kill. It was all the more reason to find her and bring her home.

"You're saying she's one of them?" Billy said, scowling. "This Jamie girl?"

Terrill thought about how to respond. "They "—he had nearly said "we"—"aren't all the same."

"They suck blood, right?"

Terrill nodded.

"Then they're all the same." Billy said. "They all need to die."

Terrill didn't bother to argue. The cross on his chest seemed to grow heavier all of a sudden, as if his body was remembering its old existence. Vampires were exceedingly rare. Billy and his friends had been unlucky. The chance of him ever running into another vampire was unlikely.

Terrill went to Father Harry and asked for the afternoon off.

"What you're doing is voluntary, remember?" the priest said.

"I didn't want to leave you in the lurch."

"Go!" Father Harry boomed. "Tell Sylvie! Quit wasting time!"

So that's what Terrill had done.

Sylvie was ready to leave that moment, without packing, without any planning whatsoever. Terrill sat her down at the kitchen table.

"You need to be prepared for things not turning out the way you hope," he said.

"What do you mean?"

"I mean she may not want to come back. She may not want my help." Terrill had been so focused on the search that he'd been putting off thinking about what would happen when they found Jamie. All he could really offer was to mentor her, to advise her, to keep her safe.

He wondered what he would do if she refused to stop hunting people. In all of vampire history, Terrill knew of only two vampires who had voluntarily quit killing humans: himself and his maker, Michael. Both had been very old vampires when they'd made that decision, with centuries of feeding behind them.

Jamie was a baby vampire, and the bloodlust was always strongest early on. She wouldn't be able to help herself. If Terrill enabled her and she continued killing, then he'd be as guilty as she was.

"But you can keep her safe, right? Tell her how to survive?" Sylvie was asking him.

"Yes, Sylvie," he said. "But survive to do what? What if she wants to continue killing? You want me to help her then?"

She shook her head, and he could tell that the ramifications weren't sinking in. Of course Jamie would stop killing, she was probably thinking. But Sylvie didn't know what it was like. There was no way for her to know—she'd never felt the hunger.

I'll figure it out on the drive down, he thought. *There's got to be a way.*

Terrill was loading up his Toyota when he saw the Escalade down the street. He sighed. He'd waited until late in the evening in hopes that they'd give up, thinking that Sylvie and Terrill had gone to bed around midnight, as usual. Obviously, that hadn't worked. He walked toward the SUV and Clarkson got out to meet him.

"Trying to escape?" she asked.

"You said you'd give me a week," he said. "Can you give me ten days? I should be back by then."

She was blank-faced. It was impossible for him to tell what she was thinking. "Why?" she asked flatly.

He told her about Jamie, how he had become her Maker, and about the battle with Horsham.

"She got bad advice," Terrill said. "I need to help her."

"She's alone?" Clarkson asked. "Without anyone mentoring her?" Terrill knew that this was one of the reasons the Council of Vampires had been created in the first place. Untutored vampires were a danger to everyone: they showed little judgment or caution. Rules of Vampire didn't mean anything if there was no one to teach them to.

"All alone," Terrill said. "And not doing so well."

Clarkson stared off into the distance, then seemed to come to a decision. "I'm going with you," she said.

Terrill felt a chill. Who knew what the Council would do to Jamie? She was probably breaking every Rule in the book. "That isn't necessary," he said.

"I insist."

As Sylvie and Terrill drove out of town, he looked in the rearview mirror and saw two black Escalades following close behind.

***

Without stopping, it was a five-hour drive to Crescent City. Once or twice, Terrill accelerated and tried to lose the Escalades, but it was no use. It was a stupid thing to do. If he got in an accident, the consequences for him and Sylvie could be dire, whereas the vampires behind him would regenerate in minutes.

Crescent City was the kind of place that Terrill would've gravitated toward when he was still a vampire. It wasn't safe to hunt human prey there, for it was a small town, and small towns tended to notice strangers and strange occurrences. But in his later existence, when he'd subsisted on the raw flesh of animals, it would've been a good hiding place. It was usually overcast, with lots of thick vegetation.

Billy had reluctantly given them directions to his hideaway. It was still dark as they drove into town. Terrill decided to stop at a diner and have breakfast. He was still learning that he needed to refuel his human body with food a few times every day. If he didn't remind himself, he'd forget. He'd start to feel faint and Sylvie would scold him.

Sylvie and Terrill sat at a table near the windows. Clarkson came in after them and sat down next to him, followed by her three goons, who sat at the next table over. She didn't say anything, just watched as Sylvie and Terrill ordered ham and eggs. Terrill thought he saw her curl her lip, but that was probably just his imagination.

What's she been doing for food? he wondered. She and her crew had been in Bend long enough to need to feed, but Terrill hadn't heard of any mysterious disappearances there, so she was probably going to a local butcher and buying raw meat. He knew from experience that that made most vampires cranky. He smiled to himself.

He had checked the weather before they left, and the forecast had said that Crescent City would be enjoying one of its rare sunny days. Sure enough, as they were finishing breakfast, the sun started to peek over the coastal hills. Clarkson and her men were looking more and more uncomfortable. They got up abruptly and moved quickly to the Escalades with their dark-tinted windows.

Got you! Terrill thought.

"You ready to see your sister?" he said as soon as Clarkson's blonde head disappeared into her black SUV.

"Yes," Sylvie said. She looked a little nervous, and Terrill wondered if she was finally realizing the difficulty of what they were about to try to do.

"I need to explain something to you," he said. "Clarkson represents an organization that we don't want anywhere near Jamie..."

As they drove toward the hideaway, he explained what he wanted to do. Sylvie didn't question his plan. When they pulled up to the parking lot, he got out. Sylvie got into the driver's seat and drove away.

Terrill watched as the two Escalades pulled into the parking lot and stopped. It appeared that their inhabitants weren't sure what to do next. After a few moments, one of the SUVs pulled out and followed Sylvie.

Part one of the plan was a success. He went to the entrance in the blackberry bushes and started crawling through them. It was too bright outside for Clarkson to follow. She could only watch from behind her tinted windows. In Terrill's back pocket was a pair of gardening clippers he'd brought from home. He'd known that he'd have to get away from the Council vampires from the moment he'd heard about the hideaway.

He entered the little room inside the thatch of bushes. It was exactly as Billy had described it. There were signs of habitation, but to his great disappointment, Jamie wasn't there…which made no sense. The sun was shining brightly, as promised: that had been part of his plan. So where had she gone?

He stood there at a loss, wondering what to do next. Behind him, a hidden door built of branches, which had blended in with the rest of the enclosure, opened. He turned to see a silver-haired, young-looking man walk into the "room" and stretch out his arms as if offering a hug. "Terrill, the first of my progeny," the man said. "I can't tell you how proud I am of you."

"Michael?" Terrill breathed, not believing his eyes. "You're alive?"

"Of course I'm alive!" his Maker said. Michael didn't look any different than he'd ever looked: he was still eternally young and eternally gray. He had a modern haircut and up-to-date clothing, but his eyes still held the same mix of wisdom and craziness. "A strange way to put it, of course. I'm not really alive at all, am I? But you are, dear boy! Impossible as it is to believe, you are a living, breathing, heart-pumping human being. I very much want to know how you accomplished such a thing!"

CHAPTER 9

FRANCE, 1653

"It's time for you to Make some offspring," Michael said. Every few decades, Michael would stroll back into Terrill's life. It was always an occasion for celebration. Several hundred years had passed since Terrill had been Turned. They were in France, but speaking English, to the disgust of everyone around them.

Terrill had lost count of the drunken victims he'd consumed, so the comment came drifting through a haze of alcohol. *Make some offspring?* he thought woozily. *Not this again!*

Michael was always going on about it, but Terrill had never desired to be a Maker. He didn't want to spend weeks, months, or even years—depending on how much he wanted his progeny to survive—tutoring a baby vampire. Most didn't last long anyway. Their instincts to kill and consume were too strong, and no amount of training could make new vampires cautious.

Whenever Michael would reappear in Terrill's life, he would insist that Terrill start to create his own offspring. Over the last several decades, Terrill had gravitated to Northern Europe, where there were plenty of small kingdoms in conflict that tended not to exchange information about strange disappearances.

"Two strong vampires can watch out for each other," Michael insisted. They were sitting in a large tavern in the center of a medium-sized town. The area was just populated enough for them to be anonymous.

"So why did you leave me on my own?"

Michael laughed. His silver hair glowed in the candlelight.

His skin was flawless, like marble. "I could see you were going to do well without any help from me. And I am too old now to be bogged down. No companion can ever know all that I know. I find it frustrating."

"I'm getting pretty long in years myself," Terrill said.

"Yes, which is why I haven't given up hope for you yet."

"What do you mean, hope? Hope for what?"

Michael looked ready to say something, then shook his head. "Not yet. Someday, I may tell you, and on that day, you'll understand."

Terrill downed a goblet of red wine. He had poured in a little of the blood of his latest inebriated victim so he could feel the effects of the alcohol. "You just told me I'm all right on my own," he said. "So why should I want to create progeny?"

"Look at it this way: it can be an experiment," Michael said. "You get to watch as they develop."

"So that's what I am to you? An experiment?"

"Indeed. You've developed in some interesting ways. Not what I expected, mind you."

"Sorry to disappoint you," Terrill groused, slamming down his empty goblet.

Michael ignored Terrill's outburst. "For instance, what do you think of the barkeep?" he asked.

Terrill looked over at the tall, gloomy man behind the counter. He was dark and lithe, with short black hair and scars on his face. "Horsham? He's all right, I guess. He keeps a clean establishment—and best of all, he keeps the fighting down."

The closest that Terrill had ever come to being caught was during a general sweep of a province after a brutal tavern brawl had spilled into the streets. Since then, he'd tried to find more upscale taverns, ones with reputations for harmony.

"I heard he was a captain of the Free Rangers," Terrill

continued. "Got tired of the warfare, took his earnings and bought this bar."

"Have you ever heard of such a thing?" Michael asked. There was a strange intensity to the question.

"No, now that you mention it. Most Free Rangers never get to spend their wages. They're addicted to war, and the only way they stop is with a blade in the gullet."

"Don't you find it interesting that Horsham walked away?"

"I suppose." In truth, Terrill was starting to get bored with his own existence. For the first time, he wondered what it would be like to have a friend. Before he'd become vampire, he'd been a most sociable fellow. Until recently, he hadn't much missed that, but now…

That was the problem with following the Rules. They kept you safe, but at the price of a boring, humdrum existence. Sometimes Terrill wanted to break the Rules just to see what would happen—to be challenged by the danger of doing something stupid.

So far, he had resisted the impulse. He had seen others go that route, and it never ended well.

Michael changed the subject, but Terrill's thoughts kept going back to the idea of having a friend, someone to share experiences with. His eyes wandered over to the mercenary veteran behind the bar. Someone like that wouldn't have to be trained to fight. He'd already know how. He'd be canny and wary, which were the biggest challenges for new vampires. Perhaps…

"Did you hear me?" Michael was saying. "I must go."

"Good," Terrill said, then laughed. "Sorry. I mean, I'll see you again in another decade, or whenever you next pop up."

Michael nodded gravely. "Let us hope." He walked away without another word.

Terrill poured another dollop of alcohol-laced blood into his goblet and took a sip. The drunker he got, the more appealing the idea of a companion became.

He eyed the barmaids. That might be even more interesting. But undoubtedly, even as a vampire, a woman would want him to be constant—and Terrill had no intention of foregoing a variety of feminine companionship—whereas a friend wouldn't care whom he dallied with.

Terrill was still sitting there at closing time. "Time to go, fellow," Horsham said, standing over him, frowning. His look said, *Are you going to give me trouble?*

Terrill smiled and staggered to his feet. "Farewell, friend. You run an admirable bar."

Horsham's eyes followed him out the door. Terrill's bonhomie hadn't sounded quite genuine, apparently.

***

Terrill stood in the darkness of the alley, invisible to passersby. He still wasn't sure he wanted to do this. On the other hand, the idea of getting up the next night and the next and doing the same things he'd done for a hundred years didn't sound appealing, either.

Think about this! he urged himself. *Come back tomorrow when you're sober. There is no hurry.*

But he knew he'd never do it sober—and he trusted the wine. He came to his best conclusions under the influence of wine.

What does it matter? the colder vampire part of him asked. *If I don't like it, I can abandon him. Let him try to survive on his own. Or I can eat him. Why should I care?*

But something inside Terrill told him that if he committed to this, he wouldn't walk away so easily. That was strange. For most of his existence, he wouldn't have given the slightest consideration to the welfare of another. What was different about this?

Then it was too late for second thoughts. Horsham was locking the back door of his tavern in the dark of the alley. Terrill found himself moving swiftly, walking up behind the barkeep as he locked the door.

And then something happened that had never happened before in all of Terrill's long existence. The man turned swiftly and plunged a knife into Terrill's heart.

The cold steel seemed to freeze his heart for a moment, as if the organ wasn't sure it could survive the assault. But the knife was metal, not wood, and Terrill pulled it out of his chest and leaped toward Horsham.

Again, the man surprised him. Horsham grabbed a cudgel that had been hidden near the door and started bashing Terrill over the head with it. Stunned, Terrill fell to the ground, holding his hands protectively over his head, feeling the bones in his arms break as the cudgel rose and fell repeatedly. His head slammed into the cobblestones. He tried to move, but he felt paralyzed.

The knife was back in Horsham's hands and he was standing over Terrill, screaming. "You thought you'd catch me off guard, you black-hearted scum! I figured you out from the moment I saw you. You are unholy, an abomination!"

The knife sawed into Terrill's throat, and that finally spurred him into action—one of the few ways to kill a vampire is to cut his head off. He pushed the man away, and Horsham went flying. But instead of being stunned or running, Horsham went on the attack again.

Terrill felt the knife enter his body again and again. It hurt, it weakened him, but such blows couldn't kill him. He grabbed the barkeep by the throat and began to choke him.

"Don't kill him," he heard someone say.

Michael came out of the shadows and grabbed Horsham from behind, pinning his arms. "Now, Terrill!" he said. "Suck his blood!"

Terrill sank his fangs into the helpless man's neck.

Three days later, in a cheap room at a nearby inn, Horsham reanimated, one of the rare victims who returned as a vampire.

Horsham never let Terrill forget that he had needed Michael's help; that he hadn't taken him down alone.

CHAPTER 10

Jamie waited impatiently for dark, pacing the small enclosure. She'd put off feeding for too long. Now she wouldn't have the luxury of picking her prey; she'd just have to grab some random guy. She hated that. She hated killing, but at least she could try to rid the world of the rotters.

She heard scurrying behind her and turned to see a small squirrel poke its head under the branches. It looked at her in alarm.

She was on it in less than a second, astonished at her own speed. She raised the screeching critter to her mouth without a second thought and sank her fangs into its body. It tasted awful, but it slaked her bloodthirst. She sat down in one of the wicker chairs and thought about that for a while.

She had heard Horsham mention scornfully that Terrill was drinking the blood of beasts, but for some reason she had never thought of that as an option until now. Human blood was what she wanted, so human blood must be what she needed, she'd thought. But was it possible she could live off of animal blood alone?

Her mouth was befouled by the taste of the squirrel. It was like eating a spoiled hunk of meat might have been when she'd been human. She wondered if she would get sick.

Truth was, she just didn't know enough about being a vampire. She remembered how helpless, how out of control she'd been before Horsham took her under his wing. But what if everything he'd taught her was wrong? Horsham had told her that all vampires were the same; that their human memories were meaningless and would quickly fade; that vampires had no empathy for humans, only for their own kind.

It was Terrill who was wrong, he'd said. Terrill was an abomination.

But what if it was possible to be vampire and not kill people?

She laughed as she realized how ridiculous that sounded.

I am a vampire, she thought. Terrill had made her so. By killing her. So much for Terrill being morally superior.

When darkness finally fell, Jamie felt that she had resolved her quandary. *I am a vampire,* she repeated to herself. *I am a vampire.*

***

She was running out of lowlife dives to try. It was becoming clear to her that she was going to have to leave this town soon, as much as she loved her little hideaway. Too many abusive boyfriends and husbands were mysteriously disappearing, though strangely, no one seemed to be reporting it. Still, someone was eventually going to catch on to the fact. Officer Robert Jurgenson was going to remember that incident on the beach and put two and two together.

There was a bar downtown she hadn't tried, a little more upscale than most of the places she'd been. She dressed in the best clothes she had, but when she got there, she still felt a little out of place.

As soon as she sat down, she sensed someone standing next to her table. She looked up with a tacked-on smile to see Officer Jurgenson smiling down at her, as if thinking of him earlier had summoned him. He was wearing khakis and a dress shirt and looked like the man of her dreams.

"May I sit down?" he asked politely.

Jamie was speechless. All her usual patter abandoned her. She didn't want to be phony with this man, but she wasn't sure she remembered how to be genuine.

He ordered them drinks, whiskey sours, before she could stop him. "Is that OK?" he asked, as if belatedly worried that he'd been too forward.

"Fine," she said. "My favorite."

"You dyed your hair," he observed.

"I wanted to start having more fun," she said, flipping her blond locks, and he chuckled.

Then they just sat and looked at each other for a while. The silence was awkward, and yet...it wasn't. It was as if both of them knew that they'd be chatting away like old friends in no time, and they were savoring the moment of introduction for as long as possible.

When the drinks were delivered, they touched glasses and both took a sip.

"So...I might as well get this out of the way," Jurgenson said. "That night on the beach—why'd you run away?"

"What did Stuart say?" Jamie asked. Jurgenson hadn't arrested her; he hadn't even seemed disconcerted to see her. *So obviously, I'm not in trouble,* she thought.

"He said he cut himself and fainted, and that you were trying to revive him. I thought the kid was going to die. In fact, the paramedics tell me his heart actually stopped for a few minutes. They had all but given up on him when he suddenly sat up, looking none the worse for wear. Which was pretty strange, considering how much blood he lost. Perkins told me, 'The IV transfusion seemed to flow into the kid as if he was sucking it up.' "

Why *had* she run away? What possible excuse could she give? Jamie thought hard, but couldn't come up with a plausible story. She was starting to get nervous when Jurgenson said, "You know what? Never mind. None of my business."

She smiled at him, no longer nervous, and let it go. "So, how long have you lived in Crescent City?" she asked, and off they went, chattering the night away.

***

"Can I take you home?" Jurgenson asked much later as they stood outside the bar.

"Not tonight," Jamie said, hinting that the night would come when she'd want him to. It was strange, how she had almost forgotten what she was. She'd started off the evening proclaiming *I am a vampire*, but ended it feeling more human than she had since…since she wasn't.

"OK." Jurgenson didn't look put out. He seemed to understand that the evening had been a smashing success and to be willing to go at whatever pace Jamie dictated. *My hero,* she thought.

Suddenly, he turned pale and bent over. Just like that, he was puking at her feet. There was blood mixed in with the whiskey sours.

"Jesus, I'm sorry," he rasped, still bent over. "That was awful."

"No, it's OK!" Jamie said, concerned. "Are you all right?"

"Yeah. Most of the whiskey went to waste, though," he said, trying to smile.

"No…I really mean it. Are you all right?"

Jurgenson was standing straight again, though he was still pale. Jamie saw a flicker of doubt cross his face. Then he sighed. "I can't imagine why I'm saying this. It's got to be the worst first date in history. But somehow I feel like I owe it to you."

Again, he hesitated.

Jamie had already figured out his secret, but she also sensed that he needed to say it. "Tell me," she said softly.

"Well, the long and short of it is…don't get too attached to me. I'm sorta dying. Stomach cancer."

Despite knowing this already, Jamie felt the shock of the statement.

"I feel like a total heel, getting to know you only to dump this on you," Jurgenson continued. "I think we'd better not see each other again. That would be totally unfair to you. As soon as you realize how devastatingly attractive I am, I'll been taking my charms away forever."

"Too late," she said.

He nodded miserably.

"Since we can't waste any time," she said, "can I go home with you?"

***

Jamie never went back to the hideaway. Jurgenson—no, Robert: he was Robert to her now—had been married before, and his ex-wife had left her clothes behind. "She ran off with some rich guy," he explained. "She didn't need them anymore." They fit Jamie perfectly.

She moved in that night.

"I'm a little weird," she said the next morning as Robert got up to go to work. "I usually don't get up until really late, and I go to bed really late, too. Is that all right with you?"

He laughed. "Darling, you never have to leave here at all if you don't want to."

While he was gone, she went around the house and removed the mirrors, and hid them in the back of the giant walk-in closet in the bedroom, the same closet the ex's clothing was in and which she'd already figured out he never entered. Now she just had to avoid being in the bathroom at the same time as him.

Within a couple of days, they had worked out a routine. Jamie didn't stir when Robert left for work, but was waiting for him with dinner ready when he came home. They went out after dinner, and when they got home, she kept him up a little later than he was accustomed to, but he managed to convey—in the best way possible—that he was good with their late-night gymnastics.

But on the third night, Robert was too ill to go anywhere, and he called in sick the next day. Jamie nursed him throughout the morning.

As he finally fell into a troubled sleep, it occurred to her that she had a solution to his problem. She could cure him—forever.

That posed a dilemma. She wouldn't "cure" him without asking.

And she couldn't ask without revealing what she was.

CHAPTER 11

"Where have you been?" Terrill exclaimed. "Everyone thinks you're dead."

"Good," Michael said. "Just as I wanted."

They stood in the middle of the homeless men's hideaway and stared at each other.

Again, Michael held out his arms, and this time Terrill hugged him. "You left me alone for a long time," he said into his Maker's shoulder. "None of the other vampires had the slightest notion of what I was trying to do."

Michael let him go and stepped back. "What did you expect? None of them have the experience we have. Most of them won't feel what we feel for a thousand years yet."

"Horsham never did," Terrill said quietly.

"That was disappointing, I admit," Michael said. "It's not just about age, apparently." He sat down in one of the wicker chairs and looked around. "So this is where your progeny is hiding?" he said, sounding curious. "Well, we've lived in worse places in our time, haven't we?"

Terrill could only vaguely remember those earlier years. When you became a vampire, you forgot being human, and it seemed that the opposite was true, too…though as far as he knew, he alone had made the change from vampire to human. *Or am I the only one?* he thought, looking at his Maker. "How did you get here in the daylight?" he asked.

"I have found that the older I get—thousands of years older than any other vampire I know of—the more I can tolerate the sun, though I must still be careful," Michael said. "I have to congratulate you, Terrill. I never even thought about becoming human again. I was simply trying to learn to be a more human vampire."

"It wasn't what I set out to do," Terrill said. "It just happened."

"No. It wasn't by mistake." Michael sounded strong, confident, and inspiring, like the Alpha vampire he had been of old. "You set out to live a moral life, and the moral life came to you. I always thought religion was a bunch of hoo-ha, but maybe there is something to it."

"Not religion," Terrill said, "but what religion teaches."

Michael stared at him as if to say, *I don't understand.* Then he shrugged. "I wanted to tell you, I really like your Rules of Vampire."

Terrill blushed. "I just codified what you and I always talked about."

"Nevertheless, very clever."

Terrill settled into one of the other chairs and they sat companionably for a while. Michael picked up one of Jamie's dresses off the floor of the hideaway and sniffed it.

"I met Jamie, you know. I liked her," he said. "Even as a vampire, she's got some of her soul left. I'm beginning to believe that the stronger the soul a human has, the more likely that as a vampire, they will behave decently. Maybe that's been our problem all along: we're Turning the dregs of humanity, and thus they become the dregs of vampire society."

Again they sat in companionable silence. *How strange,* Terrill thought. *It's just like old times, even though it's been hundreds of years since we last saw each other.*

But things *had* changed, and they couldn't afford to be just sitting around. Terrill cleared his throat. "They'll be expecting me back," he said, but what he really wanted to say was, *Why are you here, Michael? After all this time, why are you here?*

"So the Council of Vampires has finally approached you," Michael said, and the tone of his voice made it clear he was at last getting down to business.

"Finally?" Terrill echoed.

"It was inevitable. I've been waiting for it. If only you hadn't been so damn good at hiding yourself, it would've happened a long time ago. Even I lost you for a time. If it wasn't for Horsham, you might still be in hiding."

"You *want* me to join the Council?" Terrill asked.

"Yes," Michael said, "but not for the reasons they think. They've taken your Rules of Vampire and perverted them. What you and I never realized is that to those without a soul, without a smidgen of conscience, the Rules are only legalisms, excuses to manipulate others. Vampires have always avoided giving such powers to other vampires—but the Council has grown so strong that they're slowly taking over."

"Would that be such a bad thing?" Terrill asked. "If they enforce the Rules, how can that be a bad thing?"

"Rule Five," Michael intoned. "Never kill for the thrill. Feed only when necessary to eat."

Terrill nodded.

Michael raised his eyebrows as if to say, *See the problem?* "What does that mean, exactly? It's a judgment call—and if you have no judgment, then anyone can be guilty of breaking Rule Five, and anyone can be innocent of breaking it, too."

"True," Terrill conceded.

"Or take Rule Four: Never create a pattern. Kill at random," Michael continued. "Again, what does that mean? What is a pattern? What is random?" He waved his hand in the air. "Any of the Rules can be interpreted in any way the enforcer wants. You and I understand what these Rules mean, because you and I *care* what they mean—we want them to work. They come from inside us; they're not enforced from the outside. Without that inner guidance—what humans call ethics—the Rules don't mean anything. Worse, they can be perverted to evil ends." Michael laughed ruefully. "And we vampires don't need any excuses for that."

Michael stood up and waited for Terrill to stand as well. "You're the only one who can stop them," he said gravely.

"What can I do?" Terrill said. "I'm only human."

"Well…about that."

Terrill felt a chill. "No," he said.

"You can't fight them as a human. Only as the old Terrill, the most powerful living vampire, can you fight them."

"Don't you mean second-most powerful vampire?"

Michael smiled at him. "I wonder. And as far as they know, I'm dead. There is no way around it: you must become vampire again. Vampire…and something more. I've been researching this for centuries, Terrill, and I now believe that you were not the first to have made such a conversion. Long, long ago, there was another. The other vampires couldn't stand to see it, and they tried to Turn him back. But he emerged as something different: a hybrid, stronger than both species. He kept his humanity, he could walk in the daylight, but he had all the powers of a vampire. Only thus can you defeat them."

No, Terrill thought. *I'd rather die.*

"You have no choice, Terrill," Michael continued sternly. "They'll force you to join them in any event. But you'll be powerless, a figurehead—the great Terrill, the Maker of the Rules of Vampire, giving his approval to all of the Council's actions."

Terrill shook his head, still resistant. There was another option, and he was prepared to take it. He could give up his life and be thankful for the time he'd been granted. He was mortal.

He never wanted to be vampire again.

Michael watched him sadly. "Don't you understand? The Council will take Sylvie. That's their edge. They know that you love her. You're human now, Terrill. If you were vampire, you might be able to walk away. But not now—not from the woman you love."

So it was that Terrill gave up his life a second time.

CHAPTER 12

Stuart figured out what he was pretty quickly. When he walked out of his house the next morning into the sunlight, his skin started crinkling and turning black, and then the pain hit and he dove back through the doorway with a yelp, startling his parents, who were sitting at the breakfast table.

He got up, hiding his face, and yelled, "I'm going upstairs to play video games!"

In his room, he watched his blackened, blistered skin slowly smooth out and return to a whitish hue—paler than he remembered, but normal-looking enough. It took longer and was more painful that he would've thought. In the movies, the vampires just sort of reverted. You didn't see the pain or the time it took. And you couldn't tell from watching movies how strongly the bloodlust would overtake you.

Thank God he was a big horror movie fan, though. It surprised him, how easily he accepted what had happened to him. Maybe thanking God wasn't right. Maybe he should be thanking the Devil. In any case, Stu readily accepted his new condition—no, he *reveled* in his new condition.

He sat there on his bed, getting hungrier and hungrier. He idly wondered if he should go downstairs and…well…eat his parents. Then he pondered why he would consider doing such a thing and feel so little guilt.

He also discovered that all his old doubts were gone: Was he good-looking enough, smart enough, and cool enough? Was he going to flunk algebra? Was he going to be able to find a girl to go to prom with who measured up to his standards—and those of his friends? With the disappearance of these doubts, Stuart's conscience also seemed to fade. It was more a logistical problem, this eating of parents, than a moral problem. He needed a home base to hide out in during the day and his parents were paying the rent, so he'd let them live.

At sunset, Stu headed out the front door without a word. He spent the hours of darkness exploring his new abilities. He found that he could scoot up to the mansions on the hills above town without being seen and look in the windows at the popular rich girls as they undressed, and they couldn't see him.

He got within inches of a number of pedestrians, who also couldn't seem to see him if he didn't want them to. It was a matter of moving away from where their eyes went and into the places where their eyes didn't go. He could smell their blood, and some of them were sweet and some were sour and some were diseased, and others were just begging to have their blood sucked.

He was quick and silent, and when he idly wished he could move a boulder to get a better look at Sandra Carpenter as she practiced her cheerleading moves in the nude, he tried it and found he was able to lift it out of the way with ease.

At four in the morning, his hunger overwhelmed him, and when he stumbled across Jim Harker walking home from a bar, he grabbed the old man and dragged him into the bushes. When his victim began to shout, Stuart grabbed him by the throat and crushed his windpipe.

As he sucked the dead man's blood, Stuart regretted killing him so quickly. He'd gotten a hint of a taste of living blood, and it had been far tastier than what this corpse provided.

Next time. There are going to be many next times, he thought with satisfaction.

The next day, he slept in, ignoring his father's reminder that he needed to find a summer job and not laze around the house all day. He did laze around the house all day, and when his father came home that afternoon and started to reprimand him for it, Stuart simply looked him in the eye and the human stuttered to stop and backed away.

Stuart waited near the window, watching for the sunlight to fade. It seemed to take forever, but finally the rays coming through the window lost their sting. He got up, got dressed, and headed out the door before his parents could see him.

He repeated many of the activities he'd engaged in the night before, but he was already losing interest in the girls his own age. He wanted someone more like that woman—that vampire—Jamie. Someone mature and sexy and willing. She'd led him on all evening there on the beach, and when she'd tried to slow him down, it had made him angry and he'd tried to force her.

He admitted that to himself. As a vampire, he could see that he'd been a weak human. He had deserved to be taken down. He shuddered to think what would have happened if those two cops hadn't come along. He'd be dead meat, just like old man Harker, whose dull eyes had become even duller as he died.

Stuart was, if anything, hungrier than he'd been the night before, but again he saw it as a logistical problem. Killing citizens like Harker, who was a pharmacist as well as a drunk and pretty well-known around town, was going to be noticed.

He wandered down to the beach where, during the summer, the homeless gathered like flies. He picked off an old bag lady who had wandered away from the others and sucked her dry. She tasted slightly better than Harker had, but only because she was still alive while he was draining her.

As the blood flowed down his throat, Stuart remembered leaving Harker's body looking almost untouched by the side of the road, and it occurred to him that in the movies, the dead sometimes came back. When he was done with the old lady, he idly twisted her head, tore it off, and threw it into the bushes. Let her try to come back from that!

By the third night, Stuart was bored. And he was lonely.

He visited his friends, one by one. He found them in bed and crawled in with them. Pete was properly freaked out and tried to smash his face in. He was the strongest guy Stuart knew, but he was like a little child compared to Stuart. Stuart left him dead, his lifeless eyes staring at the ceiling, a look of disgust on his face.

Greg screamed like a little girl and almost slithered away, he was so small and wiry, but Stuart caught him crawling out the window and bit into his thigh, and found that he could drain a human from any part of their body. When he was finished, he picked Greg up and arranged him on the bed, glassy eyes staring in horror.

Jimmy woke up and then just froze. When Stuart started sucking on his neck, Jimmy said quietly, "Please don't." Stuart left him faceup on his bed with a puzzled expression on his dead face.

All three of them were waiting for him when he went out the next night, and he took them down to the beach, where they each picked off a homeless person. Stuart decided to go upscale and grabbed a tourist. Her blood was clean and fresh, and he knew that his homeless-eating days were over.

They piled into Stuart's pickup and went roaring down the coastal highway. All three of his progeny were still hungry, so when they saw the three hitchhikers, they stopped.

One of the vagrants got away, but Stuart wasn't worried. Who was going to believe an old bum, anyway? Especially if he started shouting about vampires and stuff.

His buddies all stayed at Stuart's place the next day. His parents didn't object. They seemed to be afraid of him.

Stuart loved that.

CHAPTER 13

Terrill stood at the center of the enclosure, his eyes closed. He could sense his Maker—who was destined to become his Maker yet again—stepping up behind him and felt him gently lift the collar of Terrill's shirt. Michael's fangs went in smoothly—no other vampire had had so much practice—and Terrill's life drained away.

His last thoughts were *Will I still be human? Or will I be vampire?*

And then he died a second time.

***

Terrill sat up, and it was clear from Michael's startled reaction that he hadn't been out for long. He didn't remember any dreams or nightmares. It was as if he'd simply closed his eyes.

He was in pain. He could feel the outlines of the cross fused to his chest, and he lifted his shirt to see his flesh blooming bright red around its contours.

Michael looked surprised. "Interesting. But maybe it's for the best, Terrill. It will be a constant reminder that you are like no one else, living or dead."

Terrill almost couldn't speak, he was in so much pain. He stood, lowered his shirt, and put his hand to his neck, his fingers feeling the two puncture wounds. He turned up the shirt's collar.

"Now," Michael said. "Here's what you must do."

***

"She isn't here," Terrill said when he finally emerged from the hideaway.

Sylvie looked disappointed. He'd called her on his cellphone and told her to come and get him. The plan to avoid the Council vampires by sneaking Jamie out of the other side of the thicket was useless for now.

"Should we wait for her?" Sylvie said worriedly.

"I'm not sure she'll want to see us. If she sees us waiting, she might not appear at all. No, I think we'll have to surprise her." Sylvie didn't seem to notice how distracted he was.

The two Escalades rolled up. The lead SUV's passenger-side window, which was facing away from the sun, slid down. Clarkson motioned for Terrill to come over.

"No luck?" she asked.

"She was here recently," he said. Clarkson's blank stare made him want to explain more than he needed to. "I could tell; there were women's clothes all over the place. Anyway, she was here."

"Well, on a day like this, she'd better be under shelter. Still…maybe she's moved up in the world again. You know, from homeless to whore."

Terrill saw Sylvie wince. "That was uncalled for," he said.

Clarkson looked contrite, but she didn't apologize. "What are you going to do now?" she asked.

"You said you'd give me two more days. We'll ask around; we'll come back tomorrow; we'll drive around and see if we don't catch a glimpse of her. It's not like the town is so big that it's impossible to track her down."

After Clarkson assented to their plan, Terrill and Sylvie drove down every road in Crescent City more than once, but found no sign of Jamie.

They waited until noon the next day, then swooped down on the hideaway and repeated what they'd done the day before.

This time, Clarkson questioned why Sylvie was driving away.

"I don't want to spook Jamie," Terrill said.

Clarkson glanced at the two huge black SUVs and shook her head. "You're up to something, but whatever it is won't work. You're coming back to London with me. I'll give you one more day."

Sylvie was getting more and more anxious. They spent another day driving up and down the roads, as if they expected Jamie to just magically appear. Since the sun was shining brightly, that seemed unlikely, but Terrill didn't say anything, because Sylvie seemed to need to be doing something, *anything*, to find her sister.

He grunted a couple of times when they drove directly into the sun, and she glanced at him curiously. "You OK?"

"Yeah," he said, gritting his teeth. "Must be something I ate."

She accepted that explanation. Terrill had still been trying to learn what, when, and how to eat human food, and sometimes he'd gotten it wrong. A little too much grease or a little too much spice, and his human stomach had rebelled.

The cross on his chest burned. It was as painful as when it had first burned into his vampire body, and this time the pain didn't fade. He'd taken off his bloody shirt the previous night, thankful that the weather was cool enough for him to cover the wounds with a sweater. His skin was red, raw, and festering.

"You'll always feel the pain," Michael had said. "It will always be a reminder of what you are."

Not that there was much chance Terrill would forget it. His strength and speed were returning. Sylvie had knocked a salt shaker off the table at the diner during breakfast that morning, and his hand had shot out and caught it before it fell more than a few inches. Thankfully, she was looking out at the ocean at the time and didn't notice. After that, he'd purposely tried to move more slowly, trying to mimic the way he had moved when he'd been human.

He had so much energy that after he and Sylvie made love that night and she drifted off to sleep, he got dressed and went for a run. When he returned, it was as if he hadn't exerted himself at all.

But there was one thing that didn't come back: the fading of human concerns, the loss of conscience, the constant vigilance, and the hunting for weakness in others—the soulless part of being a vampire.

He still loved Sylvie as much as ever. He still felt no desire to kill humans or feed upon them. On that second afternoon, he managed to get away for an hour and buy some raw meat at the local butcher shop, and he ate it for the fuel, trying to ignore how good it tasted, trying to ignore the memory that living flesh tasted so much better and human flesh tasted best of all.

By the end of the third day, it was clear that Jamie wasn't coming back. She'd disappeared. The Escalades followed Sylvie and Terrill back to their motel. He wasn't surprised when he heard the knock on the door later that night.

"I've given you all the time I can," Clarkson said. She didn't seem upset, but it was clear that there would be no argument.

"Please," Sylvie said. "Give us one more day."

"I can't. If I don't report back, they'll only send someone else, and I assure you, whoever they send next won't be so patient or gentle. You agreed to come with me after ten days, and your time is up."

"I'm not going," Terrill said. "Don't be too eager," Michael had warned him. "React just as you reacted to me."

"You have no choice," Clarkson said.

"Yes, I do. I can't go with you if I'm not alive."

Sylvie looked alarmed. "What? What are you saying?"

Terrill turned to her and took her in his arms. "I swore I'd never be part of that world again," he said softly. "I've been happy being with you, Sylvie. But I'm mortal now, and my time will come sooner or later, and I'd rather stay the way I am for a short time longer than risk becoming one of *them* again."

As Michael had predicted, Clarkson's immediate reaction was to move closer to Sylvie. Clarkson was several inches taller and loomed over her. The vampire didn't touch the girl, but the meaning was clear. "Sylvie is going, whether you come or not," she said.

Terrill hung his head as if defeated. *This is exactly the way it would've played out if Michael hadn't shown up,* he thought. *The only difference is, I'm no longer the weak human I used to be.* But the Council vampires didn't know that, and he had to hide it for as long as possible. It was an advantage they wouldn't see coming.

Michael had warned, "You mustn't tell Sylvie. She isn't as adept at hiding the truth as you are."

Terrill turned to Sylvie. "We have to go with them," he said dejectedly. "I'm sorry about Jamie, but she's managed to take care of herself so far."

Sylvie turned away. She'd go with him; there was no other choice. But it might take a while for her to totally forgive him. He wished he could tell her what Michael had said: "I'll look after Jamie, Terrill. As if she was my own progeny."

Sylvie walked over to the bed, crawled under the covers with her clothes still on, and turned her back to him.

"First thing tomorrow, we head back," Clarkson said. "There's a private jet waiting at the Redmond Airport."

She left without another word.

CHAPTER 14

"What are Council goons doing in a Podunk town like Crescent City?" Jeffers couldn't keep the disappointment out of his voice. They'd traveled all the way up here from L.A. in hopes of never seeing a vampire.

"Well, Jeffers," his partner shot back, "what are *we* doing in a Podunk town like Crescent City?"

Jeffers snorted. "Vacationing vampires?" He looked out the window at the ever-darkening skies of the coast. "Well, I guess they picked the right spot."

They'd been waiting for their seafood in a restaurant perched on the end of a pier. They couldn't see much of the ocean through all the rain, except for the white crests of the waves. A black SUV had pulled up outside and two tall, burly men in black suits had gotten out, looking up and down the pier.

Both Callendar and Jeffers had immediately realized that the new arrivals were vampires. The two agents had been chosen young for their jobs because they could both sense the supernatural. Since their recruitment, they'd been trained to recognize even more clues. But neither of them had been looking for action on this day.

"Whoa!" Jeffers said as the SUV's passenger emerged. Even in the gloom, her blonde hair stood out. She was as tall as the goons, but slender, and she moved with a natural predatory grace that told the two agents that she was a fighter. "Never mind the goons."

"What?" Callendar said. In the back of his mind, alarms

were jangling.

Jeffers was suddenly all business, his relaxed vacation persona dropping away. He dug out his cellphone. "I've only seen sketches of her, but unless I'm mistaken, that's Clarkson, the American representative on the Council. What's she doing here?"

Callendar tried not to stare at the woman as she entered the restaurant. Her eyes swept over the diners and passed over him, then came back to him as he busied himself with the menu. *Screwed that up,* he thought. But he hadn't been ready for anything to happen this week, not on the far northern coast of California. He was dressed in a T-shirt, baggy shorts, and flip-flops. His bulging belly, which was usually covered up by impeccably tailored suits, was hanging over his belt, his brown, thinning hair blown off his bald spots by the constant breezes. As a concession to the coastal weather, he also wore a yellow, fleece-lined hoodie. His weapon and cellphone were back in the motel room.

Jeffers was always more vigilant than Callendar: taller and trimmer, too, his dark hair always in place no matter the weather. Even on vacation, he was wearing slacks, a dress shirt, and a coat, and Callendar saw him surreptitiously adjust the holster at the back of his belt while he held the cellphone to his ear. "Hey, this is Jeffers. I'm thinking that I might head back early. I've been having some neck pain."

Callendar tried not to smile. Vampires could hear much better than humans, so Jeffers was using a crude code. Neck pain…nice.

"Yeah, I'm in Crescent City. No, in California. Callendar is with me. What? We're on vacation. Yes, together. Did you hear what I just told you?"

Jeffers's eyes drifted over to the vampires, passing over them casually. Callendar had managed not to look their way since that first awkward glance.

"We're staying at the Comfort Inn, Room 207. Yes, together, dammit! Right, we'll be waiting." He stabbed at the cellphone in frustration, ending the call. "Jesus, what an idiot!"

"Hollander?"

"I used to think getting him out of the field and behind a desk was a good thing. Anyway, I *think* the message got through."

They waited for their meal, trying to look relaxed, trying to look as though they were on vacation and didn't have a worry in the world. It seemed to be taking forever for their food to arrive. "Shall we get out of here?" Jeffers finally asked. But just then, the waitress appeared with their orders.

The chowder and shrimp were so good that they nearly forgot that only a few dozen feet away, three vampires were ordering a bottle of wine. When the agents finished their meal, however, the realization of that danger came back to them in full force.

They left the restaurant without looking back, though Callendar was curious to see if they'd been made.

"What do you think?" Jeffers asked as the door closed behind them.

"It's the middle of nowhere," Callendar said. "If we weren't expecting them, I doubt they were expecting us."

"Which raises the question, what the hell are they doing here?"

***

Inside the restaurant, Clarkson didn't see the two agents leave. Ordinarily, she might have realized who and what they were, but she was so troubled by her interactions with Terrill that she didn't even notice them.

Terrill wasn't what she had expected. He seemed so physically weak, so emotional; so human.

That had been a surprise. She'd never heard of such a thing, but the truth of it was undeniable—she'd smelled his flowing red blood, so unlike the slow blue blood of a vampire.

She hadn't told Terrill this, but her own Maker had also been his progeny, which kind of made her his granddaughter— though most vampires wouldn't see it that way. Other than one's Maker, it didn't matter to most vampires what relationship they had to each other. But Clarkson had studied Terrill since she'd first been Turned, trying to figure out what made him different.

There was an unexpressed uneasiness among most vampires that the two surviving eldest of their kind, Michael and Terrill, had started exhibiting unusual behavior, such as not feeding on their natural prey and disappearing for decades, even centuries, at a time. It mystified the vampire community—and there was the fear that with age, they too would turn soft. It was the equivalent of humans worrying about getting Alzheimer's.

For Clarkson, it was especially worrying, because she couldn't help but wonder if the weakness had descended from Michael to Terrill to her. Quite obviously, it had skipped her own Maker, who had been an especially clever vampire, a corporate raider who had been visiting his offices in the Twin Towers on 9/11. Not even a vampire could have survived that catastrophe.

But from the beginning, Clarkson had found herself feeling unexpected empathy for some of her victims, feeling sad instead of thrilled as the life blinked out of their eyes. She'd cultivated an icy, affectless demeanor to disguise the roiling emotions beneath the surface.

She'd hoped for answers from Terrill. Instead, she'd found a human whom she simply couldn't read, much less understand.

A human. She sensed that this development was historic and important, but she couldn't figure out the ramifications for the political waters she found herself swimming in. The Council had barely accepted her, and then only because she had been voted in by the large and wealthy American contingent. She found her fellow Council members to be backward and hidebound. Most of her time on the Council was spent trying to convince the European faction to join the modern world. They were technologically backward, though they had more than enough money to hire people to teach them about computers, smartphones, and other such marvels. But all the money in the world didn't help if you didn't know the right questions to ask...or didn't care.

Still, Clarkson knew better than to be fooled by the outside appearances of her colleagues. None of them seemed especially clever or dangerous, but none of them would have reached their positions without those characteristics.

She snapped out of her reverie, realizing that her two companions were waiting for her. "I'm going back to Bend in the other SUV with Holder and Simms," she told them. "I want you two to stay here and find this baby vampire, Jamie."

"Shall we bring her back?" one of the goons asked.

Clarkson pondered this. The young female vampire was without a mentor. She was probably out of control, breaking every Rule. She probably didn't even know the Rules. What would the Council want her to do?

"No...kill her. Kill her before she Turns anyone," Clarkson said finally. One thing she'd learned that always served her well: when in doubt, eliminate the problem and explain later.

She took a sip of her wine. She'd learned to like the taste of fermented grapes and always tried to make sure her victims were nice and drunk when she drained them of their blood.

"Don't say anything to Terrill," she said.

CHAPTER 15

His friends were out of control. He should've known: Pete had always been a loser and Jimmy and Greg were immature assholes

"Look, guys, we can't be leaving dead bodies everywhere," Stuart said one night when Pete showed up on his doorstep with blood on his lips. Stuart's parents turned pale and retreated to the TV room, which is where they'd stayed most nights ever since they had realized that their frighteningly changed son wasn't interested in watching any of his favorite programs.

Pete shrugged. "What can humans do to us? We're stronger and faster than any of them."

"Can't outrun a bullet," Stuart reminded him.

"So?" Jimmy asked, sounding genuinely curious. "That wouldn't kill us, would it?"

"We don't know what will kill us and what won't kill us," Stuart said, exasperated. "You want to try to find out? Besides, it would hurt no matter what."

"Got that right," Greg said. They'd been returning from one of their hunts when he'd been hit by a car (whose driver hadn't seen them, of course) and sent flying for what seemed a hundred feet in the air. He'd landed with a grunt, his arms all twisted, but had still managed to get up and run away. "I spent all day in bed before my arms straightened out."

"Besides," Stuart continued, "If we don't destroy the bodies, the victims will come back. We don't really want the competition, nor do we want a bunch of undead running around. People are going to start to notice."

As he had feared, he hadn't finished the job with his first victim. Old man Harker had wandered into the police station the next day, complaining that he'd been attacked. He'd looked near-dead, which wasn't unusual, and when he'd gotten belligerent, the cops had put him in a cell with an eastward-facing window and gone off to breakfast. When they'd returned to the station, they'd smelled a peculiar odor, as if someone was barbecuing, and found Harker's burned-up body curled up in the middle of the sunlit cell.

"I'm just saying, take it easy," Stuart said. "Try to pick off people nobody will notice are missing. Try to finish off the bodies. Don't leave any evidence." He wasn't sure why, but unlike the mostly fastidious vampires in the movies, when he fed on a human, he felt a ferocious hunger that wasn't satisfied until he'd consumed most of his victim's flesh. Pete was equally savage, while Jimmy just drained the blood, wiped his face, and walked away. Greg was somewhere in between, depending on who he was hanging out with at the time.

At first, none of them had gone anywhere without Stuart, but as the days passed, they were reverting to their old shifting alliances and associations. It seemed that no matter how sociable they had been as humans, vampires were loners by nature.

Stuart was already making plans to get out of Crescent City, and he wasn't planning to take his loser friends with him.

***

Despite his warning, their hunt that night quickly devolved into chaos. It turned into the Night of the Long Knives as each of them took revenge on their individual adolescent tormenters.

Greg was still angry with Jodie Fergus, who had dumped him in the ninth grade, and he crawled up the walls of her house like a spider and sneaked in her window. His vampire friends heard screaming, and then the lights went on, followed by the sound of a man bellowing. Finally, there was silence, and then Greg returned, covered in blood and laughing.

"Her dad tried to get in the way," he said, running past them. "I never did like the old bastard."

They heard sirens as they followed him into the woods. They stopped at the top of the hill, barely winded.

"You know, I always wanted to get back at Coach Wenders," Pete said. "Half the team was drunk that night, but because I was too wasted to run away, I'm the only one he kicked off the team."

"I don't think that's a good idea…" Stuart started to say, but Pete was already trotting toward a subdivision about half a mile away.

Coach Wenders was in good shape and put up a struggle. He broke Pete's nose, but other than that, he mostly managed to smash his own furniture before he was taken down for the final time.

Stuart walked over and looked at the mangled body. The coach wasn't going to revive, vampire blood or no vampire blood, but he kicked the man's head to an unnatural angle just to make sure.

Then it was Jimmy's turn. He told them about an incident that until then had been a secret: some of the football players had beaten him up once. This seemed like a great excuse to take out some of the big men on campus who had lorded it over all of them for years.

It turned into a real mess. The vampires found the boys at a kegger along with a hundred other people, many of them classmates. Before Stuart could stop his friends, they walked into the middle of the crowd and started attacking the three boys they had deemed the most guilty. Most of the others ran away, but there were still far too many witnesses to what happened next.

"Hey, Jordy," Pete shouted as he nearly tore off the arm of the only kid there who was bigger than him. "How about trying to show you're stronger than me now?"

"What're you doing, Pete?" Jordy screamed. Stuart had always liked the big guy, who was slow and more or less friendly with everyone, especially one on one. "We're buddies!"

Pete showed his fangs and Jordy fell silent. He still put up a fight, but it was like a three-year-old having a tantrum at his father. He was knocked about the clearing, landing on rocks and stumps, until he couldn't move. Then Pete moved in on him and started eating his flesh.

Greg was ripping one of the other boys apart with his bare hands, which, Stuart noticed for the first time, were sporting large claws. He looked down at his own hands, and as if in response to his thought, his fingers also turned into claws. *Huh. Didn't know I could do that.*

Jimmy had the third boy on the ground and was lying on top of him, quietly sucking his blood.

Stuart looked nervously into the darkness. He could see at least five people hiding, watching everything. With a sigh, he moved into the shadows and started stalking them, one by one. He was satiated after the first, but he kept pursuing the others until he had killed them all. He made sure they were well and truly dead.

That's it, he thought. *I'm getting out of this town.*

These idiots were going to bring every law enforcement officer within a hundred miles down on them.

CHAPTER 16

Jamie and Robert were dancing at the bar where they'd had their first date when his phone chirped. He glanced down at it and frowned. "It's the station," he said, and wended his way off the dance floor. Jamie followed. The police department usually left him alone at night, in consideration of his illness, so it must be something important.

"*How* many were killed?" he said, his voice rising. Even through the music, most of the other bar patrons heard him and faltered, staring. He turned his back, trying to concentrate completely on the conversation.

"I've got to go," Robert said to Jamie when he turned around again. "Can you catch a cab home?" He started digging into his pockets for money. He had figured out that she was broke, although he'd never asked about her finances. He never asked about her past at all. It was as if, since he had such a short time left, he had decided not to care about anything that had happened before they met and just wanted to squeeze what happiness he could out of every moment.

"Can't I go with you?" Jamie asked, and her voice was insistent: *very* insistent. She had vowed to herself not to use her glamour powers on him—not ever—but every once in a while (for his own good, she told herself), she let a little leak through.

Still, he was resistant. "From what they're saying, you really don't want to see this," he said with a frown.

"I'll stay in the car," she promised. "I'll wait for you." She didn't want to leave him. It was bad enough that he was gone all day and she couldn't follow him. She knew he felt the same way. Besides, if carnage had come to little Crescent City, she had a foreboding feeling that she had brought it with her.

***

Since Robert was the senior officer in the department and one of the few who had experience with homicides, they'd left a spot for his car near the edge of the crime scene. It was out on an old logging road, halfway up the coastal hills that loomed over the town: a small clearing with a campfire in the middle that still held some burning coals. Red plastic cups were everywhere, along with a couple of dented silver kegs. Logs and rocks circled the campfire, and many of them had been overturned.

There was blood everywhere. Jamie could see a mass of flesh on one edge of the clearing, and on the other edge, another ripped-up body with bones showing. Near the fire was a young man lying on his back, with wide-open, unblinking eyes.

Robert looked at her with concern and she smiled sadly at him. "Don't worry," she said. "I've seen some things in my time."

He looked at her searchingly and seemed to find confirmation in her expression. He shook his head, as if to say, *I really don't know you that well, do I?* "I can get one of the guys to take you home," he offered, gesturing at a couple of uniformed officers.

"No," she said. She looked at the sky and could see a glimmer on the horizon. Maybe she should take him up on his offer… but she needed to know what had happened here. She could guess: Stuart. She was afraid that he'd come back.

But more than one vampire was responsible for this bloodshed, and that concerned her. It was unusual for even one victim to be Turned. It happened maybe once in every twenty killings, and then only if circumstances were ideal, Horsham had told her. For more than one person to be Turned in such a short time was nearly unheard of.

Her instincts told her she had a few hours of darkness left, so she shook her head. "I'll wait, Robert. Do your thing."

He nodded, got out of the car, and was greeted by the short, fat cop who had accompanied him on the Fourth of July. The man's eyes widened when he saw Jamie in the front seat.

"What's *she* doing here?"

"It's OK, Jerry. She's a friend." Robert straightened up and seemed to transform into the embodiment of law enforcement before her very eyes. She shivered a little and wondered how long she could keep her secret from a man like this. More to the point, how long did she *want* to keep her secret?

"So what happened here, Jerry?" Robert asked crisply. "You said eight bodies. I only see three."

"The others are in the woods…" Jerry's voice faded as they walked away, but Jamie, being a vampire, could still hear him. "It looks like they were chased down. It's the damndest thing. Come on, I'll show you…" They disappeared into the woods, out of earshot even for Jamie.

White-suited crime scene techs were moving around the clearing, but no one was paying any attention to her. Without really planning to, she found herself getting out and investigating the bodies. She bent over each of them, sniffing.

She'd made it to body number three when one of the techs spotted her and hurried over. "What the hell are you doing? Get away from there, you'll contaminate the scene!"

"Sorry," she said, backing away. She'd found what she wanted. As impossible as it seemed, there had been four attackers. Something very unusual was happening here in Crescent City.

Jamie started walking back to the car, hoping that Robert hadn't seen her. She was passing by the undisturbed body at the center of the clearing when it suddenly sat up.

She couldn't help it: she let out a scream.

Robert and Jerry came running, along with every other cop within hearing distance. They all skidded to a stop as their eyes went from her to the young man, who was trying to stand.

The paramedics got over their shock, ran to him, and made him sit down again. "What's your name, son?" she heard one of them ask.

Robert watched all this with a frown. Then he turned and put his arm around Jamie's shoulder and led her back to the car. "I'm taking you home. Now."

She didn't argue. They didn't speak as they drove back to his house. She couldn't tell what he was thinking. Was he mad that she'd left the car? Or was he thinking only about how a victim the medics had declared dead had suddenly stood up?

If anything, Jamie was more shocked at this turn of events than Robert was. According to Horsham, Turnings were rare, even if you left a pristine body; even if that was the result you wanted. It was this, more than anything, that had kept vampires in check over the millennia. They could not reproduce any time they wanted or Turn whom they wanted, when they wanted.

Not only that, but—as in her case—it usually took a few days for the transformation to take place. But this...this had to have happened in the course of a few hours. She'd assumed from what Robert had told her that Stuart hadn't died, that he'd recovered. There hadn't been any other logical explanation for his coming to inside the ambulance.

But what if he *had* Turned? And what if it had taken only minutes?

What if the line of vampires Terrill had founded was unlike any other line of vampires that had ever existed? Starting with her, it seemed as though every victim who had been left intact had Turned.

What if vampires could pick whom to Turn on a whim? What if, unimaginable as it seemed, everyone who was bitten became vampire? There would be no controlling that, no hiding it. It would mean all-out war between humans and vampires, and while the vampires were heavily outnumbered and outgunned now, this could rapidly change the equation. Vampires would have to come out of hiding, and one side or the other would ultimately prevail.

It would change everything. All the sacred Rules of Vampire would go out the window.

CHAPTER 17

Southern's apartment was near the Thames, and he could see the London Eye from his balcony. He was one of the richest men in England and owned half of what he could see from there.

Sometimes he'd sit for hours, as if hypnotized, watching the giant Ferris wheel turn. Any species that could create something like that had its good points. He didn't hate humans, unlike some of his brethren. He rather liked them. He wanted to coexist with them.

He undressed slowly while Miss Hoyt lay on the bed, her eyes wide, making what Southern interpreted as appreciative sounds through her gag. Living among humans as he did, he couldn't afford to let her scream out during the incredible climaxes he was certain he would induce in her.

He liked the sex first, the feeding second. Some vampires liked it the other way around, but that was too messy for him.

He'd had his eye on Miss Hoyt for months. She worked in the front office of the bank where the Council met, a glorified receptionist She had no idea whom she was working for. She was an archeology buff, and he'd enticed her up to his room with an invitation to view the Royal Sigil.

The story he'd concocted was that the slab of stone with the blue flower of his family crest painted on it had been found during a construction project. In truth, he'd had it in his possession for generations of mankind. It was proof that his family had always been blue bloods, both figuratively and literally.

Miss Hoyt was tall and leggy, just the way he liked them. She had a rather horsey face, but who cared, especially since the gag covered most of her buckteeth. She was squirming, and he was anticipating a long evening punctuated by a frenzied feed, followed by a leisurely stroll in the early morning to dump her splintered bones into the river.

As he climbed on top of her, Clarkson's image came to him, as it usually did during sex. She was his colleague, his conspiratorial ally, but other than that, she showed no interest in him. As far as he knew, she'd never shown any interest in any man, woman, or vampire. But the colder she was to him, the more out of reach, the more turned on he was by her.

She'd sent him a coded message that morning. Not only did she believe that the legendary Terrill would join their side, but she'd also revealed the extraordinary, if not impossible, news that Terrill had become human again.

That was going to snag a fang in Fitzsimmons's plans to take over the Council by packing it with his followers. A pattern had begun to emerge: Council members who urged restraint were being charged with crimes, one by one, and being replaced by hardliners. It was clear that Fitzsimmons and his followers intended to take over the Council and use the Rules to enforce their will.

Miss Hoyt was squirming. *I'm probably taking too long,* Southern thought. Nothing like thinking about Council business to delay his satisfaction. He let himself feel the moment, and it was only a few seconds later that he shouted his climax and, at the same instant, bit into her neck. Her frantic movements slowed, then stopped, and then came that delicious moment when the blood turned a little cold.

He finished her off, wrapped up what was left in the bedsheets, and took a shower. He was getting dressed for his walk down to the Thames when there came a pounding on his door.

Southern had long ago created an escape route. If someone had started to break down the door, he would have jumped over the side of the balcony, slid down the rope he'd placed there, and been halfway down the block before the door was opened. But though the knocking was insistent, he didn't sense a threat.

He checked his watch. It was four in the morning, certainly not a strange time for a visit from another vampire. Did he have an appointment? Had someone mentioned coming by?

He unlatched the door, holding Miss Hoyt in a bundle in one hand.

Four of the Council's enforcers slammed into him, throwing him to the floor. The bedsheet containing Miss Hoyt's remains split at the seams and her bones rattled across the wood.

Southern didn't struggle. He'd seen how effective the Council's goons were at controlling their victims. He'd seen how this played out.

He wasn't the slightest bit surprised when Fitzsimmons walked in the door, followed by Hargraves and Peterson. The inner circle, Southern realized, though until that moment, he'd thought Peterson was on their side.

"You too, Peterson?" he said bitterly. "You're with them?"

"I'm with myself, Southern." The fussy old man was unusually blunt. "And whoever the winning side is."

Hargraves laughed in agreement.

Fitzsimmons rolled his eyes. "Not exactly the most sterling of motives, but I take what I can get." He walked past Southern and opened the curtains onto the waning night. "Nice apartment," he said. "It's got good 'fang shui.' "

He walked back to Southern and stood over him. "You're under arrest for violating Rule Three: Never feed where you live."

"I know what Rule Three is, you wanker!"

"Well, we don't want there to be any misunderstanding, do we? Is that Miss Hoyt?" Fitzsimmons asked, gesturing at the scattered bones. "I believe she works—that is, *worked* in our front office and was therefore out of bounds. Do you deny it?"

"Of course not," Southern said, suddenly feeling very vulnerable. This wasn't a borderline case: he'd broken a Rule, there was no doubt about it. "But you all do it. You've done it a hundred times!"

"Have I?" Fitzsimmons asked. "Strangely, there is no evidence of that. Hargraves? You guilty of anything? Peterson?"

Both vampires silently shook their heads.

"See," Fitzsimmons said. "You just think everyone is guilty because *you're* guilty."

"You won't get away with it this time," Southern said. "We're on to you and your clique. You don't have a majority yet, and I doubt you'll get away with killing the head of the opposition."

"You're probably right," Fitzsimmons said. He pulled a polished stake out of his coat. "That's why you were killed in an escape attempt, sadly. No one will doubt that, since there will be three Council members testifying to the fact. Right, Peterson? Hargraves?"

Peterson looked a little squeamish, but Hargraves looked like a 10-year-old child about to be given ice cream: a 10-year-old child with 100-year-old eyes.

Fitzsimmons knelt over Southern and placed the point of the stake over his heart. "Damn, I forgot to bring a mallet. Let's see...oh, there it is: your precious Royal Sigil! Hand that rock over to me, Peterson. That ought to work."

"Wait!" Southern shouted desperately. "I'll join you! Fuck the others—I'm on your side! I can tell you who all our agents are! I know things about Terrill you need to know!"

"My dear Southern," Fitzsimmons laughed. "There isn't a single thing you know that I don't already know." He was enjoying this little drama. Ordinarily, he let others do the hands-on dirty work, but he had missed it. And since there was no one to stop him, he had decided he'd dispatch arrogant old Southern himself.

He slammed the chunk of rock down on the stake. A fountain of blue blood sprang into the air, and Southern shrank before their eyes until he seemed to be nothing but skin, bones, fangs, and protruding eyes.

"You can have him," Fitzsimmons said, waving at the body disdainfully. Eating another vampire was a rare treat, and the enforcers fell on the body and started ripping into it. "Give me the keys to the car before you get them all bloody," he ordered. He turned to Peterson and Hargraves. "We need to get to the airport. I believe Clarkson will be arriving with our prize sooner than poor Southern expected."

CHAPTER 18

The private jet that was waiting for Sylvie and Terrill at the airport in Redmond, Oregon, was luxurious. It featured good-sized beds, but they were both too upset and anxious to try to sleep. Sylvie was a little calmer than Terrill, but that was only because she didn't know the stakes.

Terrill laughed grimly to himself. He knew the stakes well—they were sharp and deadly.

Once they were in the air, Clarkson sat down across from them.

"Now we can talk," she said, looking even more serious than usual. "I left the enforcers behind because I couldn't be sure whose side they were on."

"I don't understand," Terrill said. "What do you need me for?"

Clarkson cocked her head at him as if bemused. "You really don't know, do you? You're a legend, Terrill. When you disappeared from sight, you did something that no vampire has ever done, except for Michael, and you must know how he is regarded. You've nearly reached his level in the mythology of our kind."

Terrill shook his head ruefully. "By trying not to be vampire, I've become famous?"

"Most vampires can't imagine not feeding on humans—not even those of us who might like to try that. But you are also the author of the Rules of Vampire, which in your absence have become paramount."

"Still, I don't understand. Are you saying some vampires are for the Rules and some are against them?"

"No," Clarkson said. "Most vampires are for the Rules; only a small element wants to eliminate them completely."

"So what's the problem?"

Clarkson hesitated. "This is where it gets complicated. Some well-meaning vampires thought that if the Rules worked so well when they were voluntary, making them mandatory would be even better. The problem comes in the enforcement. How do you interpret the Rules? How strong do you make the punishments?

"Slowly but surely, the punishments have become more severe. At the same time, the interpretations of the Rules have become stricter, so that just about any vampire can be charged with violating one or the other of them. It has become political. It has become about power."

Terrill still couldn't understand what she was driving at. "So you want to loosen the Rules, make the punishments less draconian?"

"Personally, I think they should be made voluntary again," Clarkson said. "After all, those who break the Rules usually reap their own karma. But yes, most of the vampire community would like the Rules to be interpreted less strictly and the punishments to be less dire. However, the hardcore strict interpreters have been gaining more power by eliminating their opponents."

"Then why do they want Terrill?" Sylvie broke in. "They must know that he won't agree with them."

"That's true," Clarkson conceded, "and would be a problem for them if Terrill were able to say what he thinks. But they have you, Sylvie, so they think that Terrill will become their mouthpiece, their figurehead. They can broadcast to other vampires that the founder of the Rules of Vampire is in favor of strict enforcement."

Sylvie turned to Terrill. "You mustn't let this happen, Terrill. Not even for my sake. I won't have the deaths of so many on my conscience."

"These are vampires we're talking about, Sylvie. Why do you care?"

"You were a vampire, Terrill, and I loved you. Surely not all vampires deserve to die. But even more importantly, these are the bad vampires who are winning, Terrill. I don't want that on my head."

Terrill almost smiled. Bad vampires. Good vampires. She was sometimes so naive about the way of things. And yet... was she wrong? If it had only been the two of them, Terrill wasn't sure what he would have chosen to do. But Michael had advised him to play along until he completely understood what was happening. That way, the enemy wouldn't know about his newly regained powers until it was too late.

"If you don't agree with the hardliners, why did you come to get us?" Terrill asked Clarkson.

"For one thing, because the Council ordered it. My friends and I aren't yet strong enough to challenge direct orders," she said frankly. Then her steely expression softened a fraction. "But mostly, because I believe that you'll find a way out of this, Terrill. You always have in the past, and I have faith you'll do it again."

***

Clarkson left them and went to a table on the other side of the cabin, where she started doing paperwork. Terrill and Sylvie retreated to the small bedroom.

"Do you believe her?" Sylvie asked.

"I don't know who to believe," Terrill said. "I never expected the Rules of Vampire to be anything other than suggestions. I wrote them almost as a joke, like 'Here are some things that are so obvious they don't need to be pointed out, so I'll point them out for your amusement.' "

"What are you going to do?" Sylvie asked. "I really meant what I said, you know. I don't want you doing anything against your beliefs just for me."

"I'll go along with the hardliners at first," Terrill said, "until I figure out what to do."

Sylvie fell silent. It was clear she wanted to say something else, but was struggling with whether to say it.

"What is it, Sylvie?" Terrill asked gently.

"I know you're not human anymore," she blurted out.

"How can you know that?" he asked, surprised. He didn't believe his outward appearance had changed at all, though inside, he felt his vampire strength and powers returning. He could hear Clarkson's pencil scratching in the other room; he could even hear the pilots' conversation up in the cockpit.

"I love you, Terrill," Sylvie said. "And I know you. Your manner changed, as if you had suddenly gained more confidence. You don't react to things the same way. But more, your skin feels cold; your heart beats so slowly."

"They must not know," Terrill warned.

She snuggled into his shoulder. "I love you, Terrill. I know you better than anyone else ever will. They'll never find out from me."

He smiled, feeling strangely relaxed despite the danger. He leaned over and kissed her.

Quietly, they made love, not knowing if they'd ever have the chance again.

***

The jet landed at midday. Someone had set up a canopy that ran from the terminal to the plane. As the travelers disembarked, they could see three men—well, two men and what appeared to be a very adult boy—waiting for them. "That's Fitzsimmons, Peterson, and the little guy is Hargraves," Clarkson said. "I expected Southern, but maybe he sent Peterson instead."

As they approached the welcoming trio, Terrill rammed his hand into the railing. "Ouch!" he exclaimed, and held up a thumb with red blood welling from it.

He saw the Council member who looked like a boy, Hargraves, lick his lips at the sight of the blood. The point had been made: Terrill was human. The welcoming committee waited impatiently as Sylvie stopped, dug into her purse, and then wrapped a Band-Aid around his thumb. She looked up at him and winked.

Finally, the pudgy, middle-aged man Clarkson had called Fitzsimmons stepped forward. He took Sylvie—and quite pointedly, not Terrill—by the elbow and led her toward a waiting limousine with dark-tinted windows. "It's an honor to meet you, Terrill," he said. "I've been hearing about you since the moment I was Turned. Welcome to you, too, Sylvie. We aren't accustomed to human guests, so please tell us if we don't meet your needs." He turned to Clarkson. "I'll see you at the Council meeting tonight."

Clarkson's face was blank, as usual, as she nodded, but Terrill was now familiar enough with her to notice a hint of alarm in her eyes.

He had no choice but to follow the avuncular vampire into the back of the limo. As they pulled away, Fitzsimmons's eyes went to Terrill's injured thumb. "Sylvie takes good care of you, I see. Must not be easy, becoming human after so many centuries. You are so *vulnerable* now. Both of you."

Terrill and Sylvie exchanged a glance. The vampire had made clear, in his simple words, that he was threatening them.

"I mean, what vampire would carry a Band-Aid?" their host laughed, then watched out the window as the airport receded into the distance.

CHAPTER 19

Jamie woke before noon, which was unusual for her. She rolled over onto her back and smiled. She was still sore, which meant they had been so energetic last night that even her recuperative powers hadn't managed to catch up. They had stayed awake late into the night while Robert apologized again and again for subjecting her to the sight of the bloody crime scene. No matter how many times she reassured him, he seemed to assume it had traumatized her.

Well, if such concern led to that kind of lovemaking, she was going to make sure to be traumatized again. Maybe by the sight of a spider. Or a scary movie. Anything that would send her into the arms of her big, strong man.

She hugged herself. Sometimes she wanted to hold him so tight she was afraid she was going to hurt him. He was so vulnerable to her. She could smell his blood, of course, but she didn't want to drink it. Perhaps that was in part because she could smell the sickness in it, but mostly it was because the blood belonged to him, to the man she loved. She wanted him whole so she could have all of him.

There were voices coming from the living room. *Strange*, Jamie thought. *I thought he'd gone to work early.*

She rooted around the walk-in closet until she found a robe that was suitable for company and started walking down the hallway. Something made her stop halfway and listen.

"You drove all the way from Los Angeles just to visit me?" Robert was asking.

"We drove all the way here because it's a long way from L.A.," a man answered.

Another man's voice broke in. "Callendar and I needed to get out of town for a while. Our job was getting a little too stressful. Unfortunately, our job seems to have followed us, so we won't be able to stay long."

"Anyway," the first man said, "I'm so glad to hear that you've found someone. After my sister...left you like that, you deserved someone nice."

"She *is* nice," Robert said, and the genuine warmth in his voice caused Jamie's blue blood to flow faster. "It's as if we were meant to meet each other."

"Good. My sister didn't deserve you."

"Have you heard from her?" Robert asked. He sounded both reluctant and intensely curious. If Jamie's heart had been racing before, now it grew cold with jealousy.

"Running around Europe with her rich boyfriend, who is an insufferable snot, by the way. I'd so rather she'd stayed with you."

"Thanks, Bill. So...if you have time, I'd like to take you guys to a good restaurant tonight."

"We'll see, Robert," said the man called Bill. "Tell you what: Can I get back to you on that? We've come across a cold case we need to pursue."

"Anything I can do to help?"

"Well, as it happens, our case may be tied to your murders."

Jamie began to feel like she was snooping. She took a deep breath and swept into the room.

"There she is!" Robert said. "Jamie! I'd like you to meet my brother-in-law—that is, *former* brother-in-law—Bill Callendar. And his partner in crime," he hesitated and turned to the taller of the two men. "Sorry, I've forgotten your first name, Jeffers."

"Aaron," the man said. "Aaron Jeffers."

Both visitors turned around with big smiles…which immediately faltered and then faded away completely as they got a good look at Jamie. She stopped cold just inside the room as the significance of the looks on their faces sank in. Who *were* these guys, and how did they know what she was? How *could* they know?

The tall one, Jeffers, started to reach toward the back of his belt and then stopped. He appeared to be confused. Callendar also seemed paralyzed with indecision.

They don't know, Jamie thought. *They suspect, but they don't* know.

"I'm so glad to meet you," she said as cheerfully as she could. She continued on into the room, but instead of shaking their hands, she sat down on the sofa across from them. They sat down, too, looking perplexed and wary.

Robert remained standing, and it was clear that he could tell something unusual had happened but couldn't figure out what. Finally, he joined Jamie on the sofa.

Ordinarily, they might have continued to make small talk. Instead, Jeffers turned to the couple on the sofa and, looking straight at Jamie, said, "What do you know about what we do, Robert?"

"Do? You're Special Agents of the FBI."

"Yes…but as it happens, we're kind of *special* Special Agents. We seek out unusual cases, cases that don't have logical explanations. Much like the case of your eight dead teenagers and the spate of other murders and accidents your town is suffering."

"So, serial killers, spree killers; that kind of thing?" Robert asked. "Well, obviously, we could use your help."

"No," Callendar said. "There's more to it than that."

He'd been toying with a glass ashtray on the end table, and suddenly, he threw it at Jamie. His aim was off, though, and it headed directly for Robert's head.

Jamie reached out and snatched it before Robert could even process that it had been thrown.

Callendar and Jeffers leaped up and drew their guns. Jamie ran for the back door before they could pull their triggers, and she knew that she probably looked like nothing more than a blur to Robert. It would be this and her preternatural catch of the glass ashtray that he would remember, that would undoubtedly, eventually, break through his denial about what she was.

A bullet slapped into the wall next to her as Jamie slammed into the door, breaking the locks and ripping it off its hinges, and sprinted into the backyard. The woods were only a few dozen feet away, but the bright sunlight began to burn her hair away as she ran. She put her hands over eyes, trying to protect them, and felt the skin sloughing off. Her bare feet seemed to be falling apart with each pounding tread, and her exposed neck and backs of her legs felt like they were on fire.

She heard another shot and something slapped into her shoulder, but the pain was almost inconsequential compared to the agony in the rest of her body. She heard Robert shouting "NO!"

No more bullets came her way and she made it into the woods, where she kept running until her legs gave out and she slammed face-first into the dirt. She couldn't move. It was going to take time to heal, especially without fresh blood. When they followed her, she'd be helpless against them.

As she waited for the inevitable, she considered crawling into the patch of sunlight she could see ahead of her and putting an end to it all before Robert could find her.

But the day wore on and dusk fell, and she finally began to

feel herself start to heal. She staggered to her feet, and even in her diminished condition, she managed to catch a stray cat, which she consumed from tail to head.

It was nearly morning before she felt well enough to start looking for shelter, which turned out to be a cave littered with empty beer cans and potato chip bags. She stayed there for the entire day, wondering why they hadn't come after her.

***

"You're going to leave her alone," Robert said firmly.

"She's a fucking vampire, Robert!" Callendar exclaimed. "Don't you understand that? How much evidence do you need?'

Robert's face showed both confusion and a kind of resoluteness that Callendar recognized. His sister had fallen in love with this idiot because he'd been so naïve and yet so strong.

"A vampire," was all Robert said.

"Yes, Robert. They exist. Tell me: How many times did you and your girlfriend go out during the day? Did she tell you she was a late sleeper? Did she keep you up till all hours of the night?"

"Nothing wrong with that."

"Come on, Robert." Callendar was growing exasperated. "You're not that stupid. You saw her move—did that look normal to you? We all saw her run across the yard on fire. How do you explain that?"

They were on the back patio. Robert collapsed onto one of the lawn chairs and put his hands to his face. "How can this be happening?" he groaned.

"I've got something to tell you, brother," Callendar said. "Something I'm legally not allowed to say but I've always thought was unfair for you not to know. I've been tempted a thousand times to tell you, so to hell with the law.

"Brenda didn't run away. She was killed by a vampire. A vampire who was trying to get back at me."

Robert stared at him, mouth open. He obviously wasn't processing this information.

"Too much, partner," Jeffers said gently.

Robert began to cry. He put his head down on his arms and bawled. The two FBI agents just watched uncomfortably.

After a while, Robert stopped sobbing and raised his head, and his tearstained face was serene, as if he finally understood, finally accepted the truth. "Thank you for telling me, Bill," he said calmly. "I never understood why Brenda left. It was as if everything I thought I knew turned out to be wrong. Now I know the truth."

Callendar got up and Jeffers followed suit. "So you'll let us kill her, this Jamie," Callendar said.

Robert stood and went into the house. Jeffers and Callendar looked at each other blankly. Robert came back out with a pistol in his hand.

"Stop," he said in a flat voice when Jeffers went for his gun. "I *will* shoot you. We'll see who the local authorities believe: me or Bill. Sure, your FBI colleagues will probably arrest me in the end, but you'll be dead and Jamie will be long gone."

Jeffers and Callendar sat back down. Robert kept the gun trained on them. They watched the day go by. After a while, to pass the time, the two FBI agents started telling the local cop everything they knew.

CHAPTER 20

Stuart came home right before dawn to find his mom and dad's heads on the mantel and Greg standing in the middle of the room, covered in blood and grinning.

Stuart was across the room in what seemed the blink of an eye; certainly Greg wasn't ready for him, for he went flying across the room, landing on the back of the sofa and breaking it in half.

"I'll kill you!" Stuart shouted.

"I'm sorry, man!" Greg cried. "I didn't know you cared! You used to bitch about them all the time!"

"Care? Shit, no! But both my parents work, and when they don't show up for a few days, their bosses are going to send someone around."

"I'll clean it up, Stuart. I promise."

"Besides, they've got the money for gas and stuff. I'll be damned if I'm gonna get a job."

"No problem, Stuart," Greg reassured him. "We've got all the money we need walking around outside at night!"

"Dude. Don't you get it? The more people we kill, the less chances we'll get. Hell, I was out all night and didn't see a soul outside the bars, and everyone in the bars looked ready to fight anyone who looked at them weird."

Even as he spoke, Stuart realized it didn't matter. He was getting out of this town. His parents had a stash of money that he'd occasionally plucked a dollar or two from when he was desperate. It was about five hundred bucks: enough to get him to fresh meat markets.

He'd wanted to leave for years. He hadn't told his friends this, but he'd been told that he'd have to repeat the school year. There was no way he was going to do that. He hadn't told his parents, either. Parents, teachers—it seemed like all the adults in town had it in for him.

He laughed and thought, *Yeah, right. School. Don't think that will be a problem now.*

He would leave the next evening.

He even had a place in mind, less than a day's drive from Crescent City. Jamie, the bitch who had bitten him and Turned him vampire, had said she was from Bend, Oregon. It was in the High Desert. Stuart had had enough of the coast and the fog and the never-ending rain. Time to check out someplace new—though the idea of constant sun was a little scary. Still, as long as he stayed inside during the day, what did it matter?

He'd like to look up Jamie, say hello, maybe get a few clues about how to live as a vampire. She owed him that much, dammit.

***

Greg left his best friend's house, though it was close to dawn. He knew of a garage nearby he could hide in if he had to. Stuart was right. It was getting hard to find victims. Even the homeless population was wary of strangers these days, almost as if they'd all been told what was stalking them.

He could still break into houses and get what he needed, but the night before last, while doing that very thing, he'd been met by a shotgun blast. It had mostly missed him, though a few pellets had hit him in the arm. That had been painful, and it had taken all day for the little balls to fall out.

Fuck that. The humans couldn't touch him—and even when they did touch him, he got over it. It had occurred to him last night that if he was going to kill people, there were some beautiful girls he could do stuff to before he killed.

Greg didn't feel a twinge of guilt at the thought. He didn't want to hang around Pete, who was wild and uncouth, or Jimmy, who was always being careful. Even Stuart, who'd always been up for anything, was acting like a grumpy shithead.

Who needed them?

He saw sunlight glimmering on the horizon and realized he'd better hurry to the vacant garage.

A car came up behind him and screeched to a halt. He turned around to see two men get out, both of them holding guns.

Shit, that was going to hurt. Still, he almost welcomed the action. He was ready to kill again. The men looked at each other and then, moving almost in sync, holstered their pistols and pulled—of all things—crosses and spray bottles out of their coats.

Whatever, Greg thought. He walked purposefully toward them, in no hurry, wanting to relish the look of horror on their faces when his claws and fangs extended.

But the two men's expressions didn't change. They raised their crosses, and suddenly Greg felt paralyzed; he couldn't manage to take another step forward. One of the men approached, and Greg heard him chanting: "Behold the Cross of the Lord; flee, bands of enemies. We drive you from us, whoever you may be, unclean spirits, all Satanic powers, all infernal invaders, all wicked legions…"

Greg stopped listening and started trying to retreat, but his legs would barely move. The second man approached from the other side and sprayed Greg with liquid from the bottle he was holding.

It burned like fire, and Greg felt his skin shriveling. He heard a strange snarling sound, like a rabid dog, and realized to his dismay that it was his own voice.

To hell with this! He turned to run, but the sun came over the horizon and washed over him, and it was all too much: burning water and crosses and now the sun.

He stood on the sidewalk and went up in flames, and his last thought was regret that he hadn't thought of using his powers to get at the pretty girls before it was too late.

***

Jeffers turned to Callendar. "Do we clean up after ourselves?"

They looked down at the charred meat on the concrete. It was turning darker with every moment as the sun continued to rise.

"Nah. The dogs and cats will take care of him. Let's go."

They got back in the car, but before Jeffers started it up, he turned abruptly to Callendar. "Something's wrong here. I doubt they're having a vampire convention in town, and all these vampires appear to be very unwary—untutored, almost. Like baby vampires. But how is it possible for there to be so many?"

"Remember that case study they taught us at the Academy? About the infestation in Eastern Europe at the beginning of the nineteenth century? How a virulent strain popped up where everyone who was bitten Turned?"

"Yeah, but that was never confirmed," Jeffers objected. "It was probably just a case of mass hysteria."

"I'm starting to think it actually happened," Callendar said. "Not only that, but this may be the same strain. Remember the legends of the vampire Michael? Supposedly the oldest vampire alive? Well, his progeny have always seemed the most fertile—and if he hadn't disappeared, who knows what would have happened?"

"So you're saying the legendary *Michael* is behind this?" Jeffers laughed. "Good luck including that in your report! Next thing you know, you'll be blaming Terrill."

Callendar fell silent. Most vampire hunters thought Terrill—a vampire who didn't kill humans—was a myth. But so far, just about every legend Callendar had ever investigated had had its origins in truth.

"I'm calling for backup," he said finally. There might prove to be an explanation for what they were seeing, and then they'd look like alarmists. But if what he thought was happening was really happening, they'd be remiss not to get help.

"What do we do about Robert?" Jeffers asked.

"Robert?" Callendar echoed. "Nothing happened with Robert. Unless you want to write a report that proves we're idiots and incompetents and violated every nondisclosure rule that exists."

Jeffers shook his head. "I don't suppose it matters. He's dying anyway. Do you think he'll stay quiet?"

"I'll ask him to. I'm pretty sure he'll agree."

"I sure hated to let that vampire get away," Jeffers said regretfully. "No matter what, next time I see her, I'm taking her down. I'll bet you anything she's the Maker of all these vampires."

"Right. Well, the daylight's a-wasting. Let's get to looking."

***

Stuart heard a commotion just as he was getting ready to bed down for the day. He opened the curtain a couple of inches and stepped back a few feet, out of the sunlight.

He watched Greg go up in flames. The two men in black put the crucifixes into holsters on their belts, the spray bottles back into their coat pockets. *That's the FBI or someone like it,* Stuart thought. It made sense: if there were vampires, there would be vampire slayers.

He saw the two agents coming up his front walk and backed

into the shadows. They pounded on the door. After a while, they went away, and then he heard them talking to the neighbors: the Hansons, who were a bunch of snoops.

"No, we haven't seen Jim and Mary for a couple days now," he heard Mrs. Hanson say. "I've seen Stuart come and go a few times, though."

The FBI guys didn't respond, and for a minute Stuart was afraid they'd come back and bust in his door. But they moved on to the next house.

Stuart didn't sleep that day, and as soon as it was dark enough, he headed out the back door and into the woods behind the house.

Those two agents would pay for what they had done to Greg.

CHAPTER 21

The stray dog Jamie had caught the previous day had been on its last legs. Since then, no other animal had been as slow or unwary; the wild animals could smell her coming, and the domesticated animals were being kept inside.

She found the carcass of a dead rock chuck and, gagging at the putrid odor, consumed the rancid animal. The diseased meat closed her wounds, but she was far from whole. Where the red rash of the burns wasn't showing, her skin had an unhealthy pallor. Her hair wasn't growing back. Apparently, the limited amount of flesh she had consumed was being diverted to the major wounds while the rest of the damage remained unrepaired.

There was one animal she could count on to be easy prey. It was slow and stupid, unwary and numerous, and always available.

Until now.

Much as she tried, Jamie couldn't find any lone humans. Even the homeless were seeking strength in numbers, congregating in camps.

She needed blood. She was becoming weaker with every passing minute.

What would she have done if she *had* found a vulnerable human? She wasn't sure. Until now, she'd tried to consume only those who deserved it, but as her hunger grew, she might consume anything or anyone.

Jamie was hiding out in her cave when she heard a cat caterwauling.

She emerged into the gloomy afternoon light. It hurt but was endurable. The sound was coming from the woods, about a quarter of a mile away.

The yowling grew more intense as she approached, and she stumbled into a clearing, where she saw a boy of about fourteen or fifteen swinging a cat around by its hind legs. The cat was trying desperately to fight the centrifugal force, to claw and bite the kid. Finally, one of its claws caught the boy's arm and he shrieked.

"Fuck you!" he shouted, and with the full force of his swing, he smacked the cat into the trunk of a tree. The animal gave a short, high screech and fell to the ground, unmoving.

Jamie didn't stop to think. All the pain, anger, and hunger of the last day gave her speed and strength she didn't know she had until she used it. The boy didn't even realize she was there before she was on him. They fell to the ground with Jamie on top, her fangs already ripping out his throat.

"What's this?" she heard a voice say.

She got up, though she wanted keep on draining and eating the little monster. Two adolescent-looking vampires entered the clearing, and she recognized them as Stuart's friends, Jimmy and Pete.

As they approached, she backed away. "He's mine," she growled.

The bigger boy, Pete, laughed. "Oh? Thing is, lady, we're hungry. Everyone in this town is hiding, and they've got their shotguns out, and damn, here's a meal just waiting to be consumed. So we're just gonna have to take him from you. Sorry."

Jamie eyed them and knew that even with her superior experience, she couldn't defeat them both.

"Tell you what, lady," Pete said, "since you seem to be one of us, we'll let you live. As a courtesy."

"I can help you," she said. "I'm older than you. I can teach you things."

Pete stared at her, then started laughing again. "Riiight. Looks like you're doing *such* a good job for yourself."

Jimmy sidled up to him and whispered in his ear. Pete's eyes grew wide. "You're right, that's her! What the hell happened to you, girl? You look like shit!"

"Can I just have a bite?" she pleaded, eyes fixed on her kill.

"Nope. All ours." He went over to the cat and kicked it toward her. "You can have that, though."

Jamie took the carcass of the unfortunate animal and retreated back into the cave. The cat was more skin and bones than meat, and barely paid for the energy she had just expended.

She ventured into town as night fell, sticking to the alleys and vacant lots. Even so, she had to pass some bars, and the disgusted looks the men and women gave her before they turned away made her look into windows to try to catch a glimpse of herself.

She grimaced and snorted. *As if there would be a reflection.* Once she'd become vampire, she'd had to use human reactions as her mirrors, and most often, she had seen appreciation or desire. Now she had to try to imagine how she looked: barefoot, with a tangled mass of unevenly shorn hair, wearing a dirty bathrobe with nothing but a nightie underneath, her skin covered with red and white blotches.

So much for the idea of making her way in the world with her feminine looks and wiles.

Instead, Jamie made her way to the thrift store that Billy had shown her. The first thing she needed to do was get shoes and a coat, maybe a hat. For once, she was feeling the cold and damp of the coast.

The clerk was the same guy who had been so kind to her and

given her clothes before. He glanced at her and quickly looked away, concealing his revulsion.

"I have no money," she said. "If you'll give me some shoes and a coat, I'll pay you later."

The clerk gave her a stilted smile. "Ma'am, take anything you need, and don't worry about paying. That's why we're here. In fact, let me help you..."

He came out from behind the counter and walked over to a table that was heaped with coats. He plucked one out as if he knew exactly what he was looking for and draped it over her shoulders.

Jamie started crying.

"Ma'am, do you need help?" the clerk asked gently. "Do you need to see a doctor?"

"No," Jamie said, hiding her face in the clean-smelling cloth of the coat. "But thank you anyway."

"I'm not supposed to do this, but we have an outbuilding with running water that I can let you use," he said. "You can wash up a little, if you want. The water is cold, but it's clean."

She let him lead her out the back and over to the outbuilding. It was bare concrete, with a showerhead at one end and a toilet at the other. She locked the door, turned on the water, and stepped underneath it. It was freezing. She shivered and thought about getting out, but as she saw the darkness of the water sluicing off her skin, she realized how dirty she was.

Jamie took a long, cold shower. She left her bathrobe and nightie in the corner and put on the coat.

There was a stack of clothes on the picnic table between the main building and the outbuilding. She started to get dressed, finding the right size shoes among several the clerk had laid out, along with a wool cap to cover her hair. She felt almost human—with all the aches and pains that implied—as she walked through the thrift shop's back door.

The clerk lit up upon seeing her. "There you are!" he exclaimed. "Are you hungry?"

She was hungry enough to eat him, but she didn't tell him that. He was holding out a plate of vegetables and fruits. She couldn't tell him that he might as well be offering her a plate of wood or rocks.

"Wait a minute," he said. "Aren't you the same girl who came in with Billy the other day?" Jamie nodded. He seemed to be struggling to find something to say other than "What the hell happened to you?"

"What's your name?" she asked.

"Marc," he said. "With a C."

"Marc-with-a-C, you are a saint."

He blushed and tried to wave off the compliment. "No, no. I've been there, is all. Been all the way down..."

"You're still a saint," she said. *Not only that,* she thought. *You probably saved someone's life tonight.*

She'd been hungry enough to eat a human, any human, even an innocent—maybe even him—but now her resolve had returned. She would follow Terrill's example, not Horsham's. She wasn't as strong as Terrill—she couldn't ignore the hunger completely—but she wouldn't kill innocents.

Marc grabbed a couple of big black garbage bags and filled them with more clothing, some blankets, a pillow, and a few other sundry items that he said would make her life easier. Jamie didn't refuse. She thanked him again and left, though she sensed his blood mere inches away.

She was as hungry and weak as ever, but her determination had returned. She'd find a way to get through this. Within a block of the thrift store, she'd grown tired from carrying all the stuff Marc had given her. There was a shopping cart in a vacant lot next to the street, and she put the two garbage bags in it and wheeled the clunky cart onto the sidewalk.

Always knew I'd end up as a bag lady, Jamie thought.

With sudden clarity, she realized she needed to return to the hideaway and rest. As soon as she could, she'd venture out and try to find some flesh. Whether she had to break into a butcher shop or kill an animal, something would come along.

As soon as she entered the enclosure, she could tell that others had been there. And they had left a mess, as if they had been searching for something. She felt guilty even though it wasn't her fault and tried to straighten up the place.

As the day wore on, Jamie's weakness increased, but so did her resolve.

As soon as it grew dark, she scooted out of the hideaway and started walking toward the downtown area, where—except for a few bars and restaurants—most businesses were closed. As she walked by the bars, she tried to gauge people's reactions to her. They were mixed; no one looked away in disgust, but no one whistled at her, either.

She forced open the door of a small bookstore and stole the fifty dollars in the register. Then she made her way to the nearby Burger King, where she went to the back door, knocked, and asked the girl who opened it for some raw hamburger patties.

The pimply-faced teen stared at her as if she didn't understand.

"Give me three raw patties and I'll give you fifty bucks," Jamie repeated.

The girl closed the door. Jamie was afraid she was calling the police, or at least the manager. She got ready to run toward the tangle of bushes that grew alongside that stretch of highway.

The door opened a crack and the girl put out her hand, palm up. Jamie placed the fifty dollars there. The door slammed again, then opened a minute later. A paper bag was extended.

Jamie took the bag and walked away. The beach was only a few hundred yards away, and she managed to hold back her ravenous hunger until she was sheltered out of sight behind some rocks.

There were five patties, quarter pounders at that. Blessing the pimply-faced girl, Jamie took a tentative bite out of one, then consumed the rest of the patty in one gulp. She devoured all five before her taste buds could even get a message to her brain about what she was eating. They were the best things she'd ever eaten—not counting the time she'd consumed Richard, her old abusive boyfriend, in Bend.

She could almost feel the burns disappearing from her skin. She lay back in the sand and let the healing begin.

CHAPTER 22

The wet, drizzly weather in London made Terrill and Sylvie feel right at home. Instead of the prison cells they'd half expected, they were put up in a luxurious suite in a hotel at the center of the city.

"We are invested all throughout England," Fitzsimmons said. The portly vampire was their genial host, though it seemed he couldn't help but pepper his conversations with little reminders about how he was in control. "We Old World vampires were a little slow to make the transition to the New World, but we have our hooks pretty deep in the EU."

This was all for Sylvie's benefit. Terrill was a far older vampire than Fitzsimmons. Strangely, Terrill couldn't remember the other vampire at all, which was unusual, because he knew most of the vampires who had influence. Time was the best accumulator of money and power, so their host was one of those rare young vampires who had amassed both.

Fitzsimmons was guiding them down to the hotel restaurant. Vampires stood aside as they walked by, afraid of Fitzsimmons and in awe of Terrill. He was already a legend among them. Now word had apparently gotten out of the silver crucifix that was fused to his chest and, most astonishing of all, that he had turned human and could walk in daylight. He tried to smile at the bystanders, but they looked away—whether because he was the mythical Terrill or because he was human, he couldn't tell.

There was an Old World ambience to the hotel; though it was new, it had replicated the look and feel of a Victorian mansion.

"We're holding a Council meeting tonight," Fitzsimmons was saying. "You should be honored, Terrill. I can't remember the last time the full membership has been in attendance. Usually it's just the English, plus maybe a Frenchman or a German."

"So it's worldwide?" Terrill asked. "The Rules of Vampire are in place everywhere?"

"Not quite, but close. Within a few more years…"

"All voluntary?"

Fitzsimmons looked at him mildly and shrugged. "Of course not. No one would follow the Rules if they weren't mandatory."

Terrill kept quiet. This wasn't the time to challenge their host.

While he hadn't locked them in their room, Fitzsimmons had managed to isolate Terrill and Sylvie effectively. They had no money of their own, and wherever they went, bodyguards accompanied them. "For your own protection," they'd been told.

Even so, Terrill had already heard a few rumors that not everyone was happy with the new order. And the night before, a vampire who had brought them a room service tray had handed Terrill a note while putting a finger to his lips and looking around at the walls as if to say, *You're being listened to.*

Terrill had taken the note and said, "Thank you for the meal."

He'd waited until he was in bed and had a book in his hand before reading the message:

Please destroy after reading.

Be aware that not all vampires are in league with the Council. Indeed, the majority of us oppose them. The Council is using your Rules to enforce its own viewpoint. Worse, it has become a tool for certain vampires to gain power. You must resist, Terrill. You must fight them. Know you are not alone, and when the time comes, you will have allies, both near and far.

It was, perhaps, a trap. Perhaps he was supposed to mention it in the morning.

At breakfast, he took a chance and didn't say anything about the note, watching Fitzsimmons for any sign that he knew. The meal passed uneventfully, and then they were given the opportunity to sightsee, but Terrill could tell that Sylvie was tired and jet lagged.

"I think we'll just rest, if you don't mind," he said.

"That's a good idea," Fitzsimmons opined. "You'll be fresh for the meeting. Everyone is excited to meet you—or see you again, as the case may be."

***

Sylvie slept most of the day, but Terrill paced the huge suite, trying to decide what to do.

Michael had advised going slowly: getting the lay of the land, discovering who the different factions were, finding out where the real power resided, gathering allies. But Terrill's instincts were to strike fast. Unless he was very much mistaken, the power already resided in one vampire: Fitzsimmons. If the portly Englishman was a figurehead, he was an effective one. Terrill's sense was that if he went one on one with Fitzsimmons, he could remove the guiding force behind the Council.

Fitzsimmons wouldn't be expecting it. He'd be completely unaware of Terrill's returning powers.

But Michael was the oldest and, if not the wisest, certainly the shrewdest vampire Terrill had ever met. And it was hard to disobey one's Maker, even for a vampire who had been on his own as long as Terrill had.

He decided to go to the Council meeting and meet the other members, the movers and shakers, and then figure out what to do.

***

London's nightlife was vibrant. It made Terrill's blood run faster. To a vampire, such a place was almost irresistible, and indeed, Terrill had spent most of his existence in this very city. But this was modern London, unlike anything he'd seen before. It reminded him of New York in the '60s, but was both flashier and more reserved.

He looked at Sylvie. Her face was flushed; her eyes were glittering with excitement. They'd found a gown laid out for her in the dressing room that fit her perfectly. It was dark blue, almost black, to match her hair, and low-cut to show off her cleavage. It shimmered in the nighttime lights of the streets. Terrill had forgotten she was a small-town girl and was glad that she was enjoying herself in the big city—for as long as it lasted. That thought sent a chill through him. He became more subdued, and started paying more attention to what was going on around him.

Fitzsimmons was watching him, he realized. They were being carefully managed, shown all the special sights, so they'd be more inclined to be favorable toward London and those who lived there, and the Council that ruled the city from the shadows.

After dinner, they were given a private tour of the Tower of London, and then led to Buckingham Palace, where they were quietly introduced to some of the younger royals. Sylvie nearly fell over at that. This was the life, all right: a life of pampered privilege.

But Fitzsimmons decided where they went and how long they stayed. It was a gilded cage.

By the time they made it to the Council's meeting room, Sylvie was nearly floating. She was given a chair at a side table where the assistants to the Council members sat, and the young-appearing vampires greeted her as if she was a long-lost sister.

Fitzsimmons was seated at the head of the long, strangely shaped table. Terrill looked at the concave middle, the gentle slope, and immediately understood what it was and what it portended.

Terrill was placed at Fitzsimmons's right-hand side and Clarkson was in the next chair over. Across from them sat Hargraves, his little body on a raised seat, and Peterson. Other vampires were milling around or just arriving, and all of them were sneaking glances at Terrill. A few were openly staring. Terrill ignored them.

"Where's Southern?" Clarkson asked.

"Oh, you didn't hear?" Fitzsimmons said casually. "He was caught eating one of the Council secretaries in his flat. Broke at least two of the Rules. Still, he might have gotten off if he hadn't been stupid and tried to escape. Unfortunately, the enforcers used a little too much force."

Fitzsimmons shrugged. "He's gone."

Clarkson was even paler than most vampires at the best of times, and as Terrill watched, she grew paler still. Her eyes flicked worriedly to Terrill. Fitzsimmons caught the look and smiled.

Assuming that Southern was to be replaced on short notice by someone sympathetic to the hardliners, it would split the balance of power of the ten-member Council of Vampires down the middle. A tie went to the nay votes, so it was still enough to block any power grab.

Fitzsimmons called the meeting to order, ringing a small silver bell. "First order of business. As you know, we need to vote in a replacement for Southern."

The other Council members looked uneasy. They'd all heard the news.

"Ordinarily, we'd call an election, but that would take months, and in the end I think I know who we'd elect. So I'd like to skip all that and propose that we elect Terrill forthwith."

"Wait," Terrill said.

"It'll be fine, Terrill," Fitzsimmons said soothingly. "You'll see."

Terrill looked up and down the table, but no one objected. Most of them looked almost excited.

"All in favor, say aye."

The vote was by acclamation, and it was so clearly unanimous that Fitzsimmons didn't bother to ask for nays. "And while we're at it," he said, "I'd like to ask for an exemption to Rule One when it comes to Terrill and his lovely friend, Sylvie. After all, you have to admit that this is an extraordinary situation."

Again, the vote was unanimous. There was a moment of silence as the momentous event sank in. The other vampires all smiled at Terrill; it appeared that everyone thought he was on their side.

"This calls for a celebration!" Fitzsimmons announced. He rang the little silver bell again and liveried servants entered the room, bearing champagne in crystal glasses. Etched on the goblets was a blue flower, the Royal Sigil, once the crest of the Southern family and now apparently appropriated by Fitzsimmons for the Council.

Terrill glanced over his shoulder at Sylvie and smiled reassuringly. There were two bodyguards standing behind her. They didn't know about his speed, his strength. It wasn't too late to attack, get Sylvie away from them, and declare his independence. At least half the Council would back him up. But he'd promised Michael he would wait, so he tried to calm himself.

It reminded him of being at the court of Henry the Eighth.

This was the aristocracy of the vampire world, many of them centuries old and extraordinarily rich.

"I, for one, am delighted that Terrill has chosen to join us," said a dapper man at the other end of the table. He had a French accent and looked no older than twenty. Terrill knew him as Fontaine, one of the oldest and most powerful vampires in Europe and, according to Clarkson, the leader of the opposition now that Southern was out of the picture.

"Yes, indeed," Fitzsimmons agreed. "Everyone knows of Terrill's integrity. That's why I'd like to ask him straightaway…" He turned to his right and patted Terrill on the arm familiarly. "Do you agree with the enforcement of the Rules of Vampire?"

Terrill glanced around the table again. Everyone was staring at him; each faction was probably expecting him to confirm their viewpoint. "I think the Rules are a good idea, in principle," he said.

"In principle?" Fitzsimmons echoed. There was a warning tone in his voice.

"Yes, I believe they should be enforced."

There was a gasp from the opposition members of the Council. *Look behind me,* Terrill wanted to shout. *See the human girl? Why do you think she's here?*

As if in answer, he saw Fontaine's eyes go from him to Sylvie and back. He nodded grimly. There was another moment of silence. Terrill had mentally compared this meeting to the court of Henry the Eighth: it had been a more apt comparison than he'd realized. He remembered the sense of dread that had pervaded the court as the king searched for Catholic traitors.

Fontaine cleared his throat. "Perhaps if…" he began, then faltered and gulped. He looked pale and confused. "Perhaps…" he said again, then fell silent.

Across from him, Kruger, the German representative, spit

his champagne onto the table and clutched his throat. He tried to stand, jerked backward, then forward, slammed into the table, and rolled to the floor with a thud.

Fontaine turned to Terrill, his eyes frightened but determined. "You must resist, Terrill. You must fight them."

They were the exactly the same words as in the note.

Then the Frenchman, too, clutched his throat and tried to stand. He staggered, grabbed for the back of his chair and missed, then fell to his knees and slowly toppled over.

The room erupted into chaos. Several of the opposition members scrambled for the door, but the liveried servants had produced crossbows and were motioning them back into their seats. Terrill looked at Clarkson, who was regarding her wine glass with a fatalistic calm. In the midst of the uproar, Fitzsimmons got up and strolled over to Sylvie, stood behind her, and put his hands on her shoulders.

"I have executed the two ringleaders of a plot against the Council," he announced loudly. The room grew quiet at his words. "If you aren't disloyal, you have nothing to worry about. But just to be sure I've done the right thing, I'd like to ask for Terrill's endorsement. What say you, Terrill? Do you agree with my actions?"

It was too late. They'd been outsmarted, outmaneuvered. If, early in the evening, before the champagne had been served, he'd freed Sylvie and asked for the opposition's help, everything might have turned out differently. But the putsch was over and done. Even if Terrill fought the hardliners, he'd have no allies. Just a glance at the remaining opposition councilors made it clear that they were completely cowed.

"The Rules must be followed," he said, and his voice sounded dead to his own ears.

CHAPTER 23

Robert Jurgenson went to work each day, did his job, smiled at the jokes, and kibitzed about the weather. But he was hollow inside, as if Jamie really had drained him of blood and left him for dead.

He also felt strangely calm. His wife, Brenda, hadn't left him: she'd been taken from him. He had been given a chance to start believing in himself again. When she'd disappeared, he'd been so gobsmacked that he hadn't trusted his instincts about anyone after that. For years, he'd questioned his feelings about every suspect, every co-worker. Going on dates was impossible because he couldn't be sure he was reading the signals right.

Now his former certainty had returned: his old ability to tell instantly if someone was guilty or innocent, to know where the office politics were leading, to know whether a woman was interested in him.

What had happened with Jamie? He tried applying his newfound clarity to the situation, and the answer was always simple and always the same. She'd loved him, he was certain of that. And he had loved her. The feelings had been genuine and deep.

She was a vampire, the same kind of creature that had taken his wife. Jamie had almost certainly killed people. Robert understood that. If anything, he should hate her, or at least fear her, and yet, he still wanted to see her again. Worse, he wanted her back in his life.

What did that say about him and his vaunted integrity?

"You with me, Jurgenson?"

"What?"

His partner, Jerry Smithson, was talking to him in a theatrically loud voice, as if Robert was deaf. They were sitting in Robert's office. Robert had been going through the pile of case files on his desk that, the week before, he had been certain he was making steady progress on—certainly, he was clearing as many cases as any other officer in the Crescent City Police Department.

But now, the legendary Robert Jurgenson of old had reappeared. He'd gone through the files one by one, clearing half of the cases by making connections that he'd missed before. With others, he'd been able to pluck the most salient fact out of the files, the hidden clue that merely needed to be followed up on with some legwork to crack the case. The other cops were starting to look at him the way they used to look at him, when he'd been a young officer rapidly climbing the ranks.

He should have been police chief by now.

All that career progress had stopped when his wife had left him and he had started to doubt himself.

Now his mind was working better than ever, but his heart was a lump in his chest, and at night the hollow feeling got worse as he lay awake and wondered if any of it mattered, and if, when he was gone, there would be anyone to miss him.

For a week or two with Jamie, he'd felt fulfilled. Because he'd fallen in love. With a vampire.

Robert snapped out of his reverie. "You were saying?" he said to Jerry with as much enthusiasm as he could muster. He wasn't even sure which case Jerry was referring to.

"I said, the kid from the beer kegger died. He seemed to be recovering well, then they found him on the floor of his hospital room, all twisted up as if he'd been having convulsions."

Robert frowned. "That's a real shame. Did Callendar and Jeffers get a chance to question him first?"

"They were there just an hour before," Jerry said. "Callendar said the kid seemed perfectly fine. He was cooperative but clueless as to what happened to him."

Suspicion flared in Robert's mind. Had Jeffers and Callendar dispatched the poor young man? He thought it was likely. They killed vampires, as weird as that sounded. And the kid had been bitten.

"What did the K9s find at the crime scene?" he asked.

"Nothing. Not a scent. It was like no one was ever there but the vics and survivors." Jerry sounded frustrated. This was the biggest case of the year. The national news media had even shown up. But the FBI, in the persons of Callendar and Jeffers, had taken the case away from the Crescent City Police Department, except for the some of the grunt work.

If there was one thing that still shocked Robert, it was the revelation that not only were there vampires, there were also vampire hunters—and some of them were people he knew personally. It was as if his entire reality had shifted sideways. There was a whole nother world he hadn't known anything about.

About Jamie, he had no confusion at all. He'd take her back; he'd hide her, cover for her, anything that she needed. If she needed his blood, she could have it.

Having cleared a month's worth of cases in an hour, Robert stood up. He decided to reward himself for his hard work by getting in his patrol car and searching for Jamie again. He'd been making the rounds three or four times a day, exploring every nook and cranny of the town that he'd discovered over his long career. Jerry fell in step beside him and accompanied him out to the car.

Robert had only told his partner that his girlfriend was missing. He could tell Jerry thought Jamie was weird and that Robert was better off without her, but like a good partner, Jerry kept his doubts to himself.

Robert found that he had already compartmentalized the information that vampires existed. For one thing, he'd promised the FBI he wouldn't tell anyone. He also realized that the two realities needed to be dealt with in two different ways. He now had to look at his police work from two different angles: the regular, humdrum crimes of small-town America, and the vicious supernatural crimes that underlay them.

And Jamie was a third reality, which superseded both of the others.

"Have you checked out the homeless camps yet?" Jerry finally asked after they'd driven in silence for most of an hour.

"No," Robert said. Why would he do that? He'd met Jamie in the best bar in town. In his wife's clothes, she'd looked classy. But once Jerry said it, Robert realized he'd been looking in all the wrong places.

"Partner…I know you like her," Jerry said. "But—don't take this wrong—when we first met her, I think she was staying in a dive. And I didn't want to tell you this before, but there were reports of a new call girl in town who met Jamie's description."

Robert flushed, gripping the steering wheel tight. "People do what they have to do to survive," he growled. Why was he angry? Was being a prostitute any worse than being a vampire?

"Uh, sure," Jerry said. He was obviously trying to keep the disgust out of his voice. Robert had long known that his partner was as conventional and straitlaced as they came: fat wife and three fat kids, Little League baseball, church every Sunday. But he was also a cop, and he'd been exposed to a lot of different lifestyles over the years, so Robert thought he should know by now that people were, underneath it all, just people.

Jerry was wise enough not to say anything more as Robert turned the car toward the spot near the railroad tracks where the largest contingent of homeless stayed.

CHAPTER 24

"We shouldn't have let her go," Pete said as they finished eating the boy who had been torturing the cat. That psycho had deserved it. Pete felt nothing for humans anymore, but he still kind of liked cats—carnivorous little bastards. He could relate.

"Who?" Jimmy said, covering his mouth politely as he spoke. Pete almost laughed. That was Jimmy: always polite, even when it didn't matter.

"You know, that lady vampire—what's her name."

"Jamie?"

"Yeah…" Pete mused. "She was smokin' hot that first night, and now she looks like some skanky old bag lady."

"Why shouldn't we have let her go?" Jimmy asked.

"You ever wonder what it would taste like to drain another vampire?" Pete said, raising his eyebrows.

"That's *disgusting*," Jimmy said. But when he thought about it for a minute, it didn't actually seem disgusting at all. Vampire, human, what did it matter? In fact, not only was it not disgusting, it was exciting. Besides, it was becoming harder and harder to find live prey of any kind. It was getting more dangerous to break into houses, and some of the homeless were armed with stakes. Even the wildlife had grown exceptionally wary of them.

Ever since the massacre at the kegger, the cops had been out in full force, and it was rare that Jimmy and Pete could walk down a street without seeing a police car cruise by. To the cops, they just looked like teenagers out and about the town, and they always smiled and waved. But getting caught in the act of bloodsucking was getting to be more and more of a danger.

After their meal, Pete and Jimmy walked out of the woods and down the side of the highway south of town. Before long, they came to a restaurant that had been burned out, sitting next to a motel that had been damaged by a tsunami. A teenage boy was sitting on the steps of the abandoned restaurant staring at them.

"Isn't that Hoss?" Pete asked.

"Yeah," Jimmy said. "I don't think I've ever seen him outside of school." The little ninth-grader had been called Hoss as a joke from the moment he had arrived at the high school, and no one knew his real name.

"Hey, you little nerd," Pete called out. "Out past your bedtime?"

Jimmy expected Hoss to run or at least act frightened, but the runt sat calmly, waiting for them to approach. He stood up when they were a few feet away.

They all started sniffing each other, walking in circles around each other.

"We sound like a pack of dogs," Hoss said, and the other two started laughing.

"When did you become one of us?" Pete asked. "*How* did you become one of us?"

"Well, I was asleep the other night when Jodie Fergus climbed in my window and crawled into bed with me. I thought I'd died and gone to heaven. Instead, I died and…well…"

"She drained you?" Pete asked wonderingly.

"Yeah. Right before I died, she looked down at me and smiled. 'You're such a cute little guy,' she said, and left."

Jimmy turned to Pete. "I thought you ate Jodie."

"I planned to, but then her dad showed up and we had a

fight, so I ate him instead." He looked to Hoss. "So after she sucked you, you became a vampire?"

"I think the term is 'Turned,' " Hoss said. "Believe me, no one's read more vampire books or seen more vampire movies than me. I'm an expert."

"What do you mean, expert?" Jimmy asked. He sensed this was important. He knew that he and Pete weren't necessarily the smartest kids around. Even Stuart wasn't that much of a student, though he was the only friend Jimmy had who read books. But Hoss—he was known as the smartest kid in school. He was small for a ninth-grader, but that was because he'd skipped at least a couple of grades.

"Haven't you wondered *what* we are?" Hoss asked, sounding exasperated.

"We're vampires," Pete shrugged. "What's to know?"

"But what *kind* of vampire? For instance, we not only suck blood, we eat flesh, too. So that makes us vampire-ghouls, kinda. Obviously, we can't fly or shapeshift."

"So?" Pete said dismissively.

"So what kind of rules are there? What are our powers?" Hoss looked at them with an intensity that almost made Jimmy step back. He thought, *Hoss always was a creepy little kid.*

"It's important, don't you see?" Hoss asked intently. "For instance, what can kill us? Didn't you hear what happened to Greg Foster?"

Oh, yeah…Greg, Jimmy thought. Now, why hadn't he wondered where Greg was? Maybe it was because he didn't give a shit. Greg had always been a shallow person, and being a vampire hadn't made him any deeper.

"I live on the same block as Stuart, right?" Hoss continued. "I saw Greg leaving his house early this morning, just before dawn, and then two men in black jumped out of an SUV, and they whipped out some big crosses to hold him back and sprayed him with something that seemed to hurt him, and then the sunlight hit him and he went up in flames."

"Wow," Pete said, after a short silence. "He's gone?"

Hoss nodded solemnly. "He's a black scorch mark on the sidewalk."

"Wow," Pete repeated.

"So I've been experimenting," Hoss said. "My parents are Catholic and they have crosses all over the place, so my room is the only comfortable place in the house. Crosses not only hurt, they also keep me from going toward them. I tried to pick up a Bible, but it repelled me, too. I had my sister say some prayers out of The Book, and it hurt. I went down to St. Francis and tried to go inside, and I couldn't. I'm betting that the two men in black sprayed Greg with holy water."

"I'm betting that a stake in the heart would do the job, too," Jimmy contributed.

Hoss nodded. "But we have advantages, too: like, we're super strong and fast. Oh, and we have blue blood. And direct sunlight kills us, but we can stand daylight as long as we're covered or in the shade, though it's painful. So obviously, UV rays don't hurt us."

"Anything else?" Jimmy said dryly.

"We turn into vampires if we're bitten and drained, but not if we're physically damaged beyond restoration. Once vampire, we seem to be able to take some serious damage, though it hurts and takes time to mend, and…" He trailed off and frowned. "That's all so far," he said. "But I'm sure we'll learn more as we go along."

Pete laughed. "So what you're saying is that we're, like, Catholic ghoul-vampires who can walk in the shade?"

Hoss's face turned kind of blue, which Jimmy guessed was

the equivalent of a blush in a human. "Well, if you put it that way…yeah. I guess."

"Great. I'm not sure how that helps us, but good to know."

As they'd been talking, dawn had been approaching. Pete looked up in alarm, noticing how light it had gotten. "We'd better get back," he said. He turned to Hoss. "Want to come along?"

Hoss looked delighted, as if no one had ever asked him to join them before. Then he looked crestfallen. "Well, actually, I've been staying here," he said, waving at the abandoned restaurant behind them. Then his face lit up again. "You're welcome to stay here, too!"

Pete and Jimmy looked at each other and shrugged. It was too late to find anywhere else.

They followed the little guy into the boarded-up eatery.

CHAPTER 25

When Jimmy woke up the next afternoon, Hoss was already awake, bent over his phone, texting like crazy. His small fingers flew over the tiny keyboard.

"You've been up all day?" Jimmy asked.

Hoss didn't look up. "I don't think we need sleep at all."

"Yeah, well, sitting around all cooped up with nothing to do ain't much fun," Jimmy said.

Hoss looked at him and frowned. "I find quite enough to keep me busy. For instance, I've been finding references to vampires all over the Net. Most of it is made up, of course. But some of it was obviously written by other vampires."

Pete wandered into the room, yawning. "Who's for breakfast?" he asked, and laughed.

Without looking up, Hoss waved his hand at the sink, and Jimmy and Pete went over to it to find a huge crab, still half-alive, its shell broken open and some of its innards removed. They glanced at each other, then each of them reached in and broke off one of the crab's legs. It was surprising filling, and not disgusting at all.

"Listen to this," Hoss read as they ate.

"*Rules of Vampire:*

Rule One. Never trust a human.

Rule Two. Never leave the remains of a kill, or if you must, disguise the cause of death.

Rule Three. Never feed where you live.

Rule Four. Never create a pattern. Kill at random.

Rule Five. Never kill for the thrill. Feed only when necessary to eat.

Rule Six. Never steal in the short term; create wealth for the long term."

"Rules?" Pete echoed. "What do we need rules for? We're vampires."

"No, no," Hoss said excitedly, "this is exactly what we need! If we don't start controlling what's happening around here, we're all going to be hunted down and destroyed."

As if on cue, they heard a loud banging at the boarded-up front window. The sun had dipped into the ocean only a few minutes before.

They fell silent. Pete walked quietly to the door and looked out through a crack.

"Huh?" he muttered. He opened the door and Jodie Fergus walked in.

Jimmy started getting turned on as soon as he saw how she was dressed. It was the same way she always dressed, but more so—or, more accurately, less so.

She'd always had a sexy style, even at parochial school. Like everyone else, she had to wear a uniform, but it was the little extra touches that made her stand out. Her dress was always an inch shorter than the other girls'—not so short that the nuns would send her home, but always close to the edge. Her blouse was always little tighter than the other girls', too. Once, in seventh grade, she'd worn black stockings, and Jimmy had had to spend the whole day trying not to stare at her legs. Jodie had been told not to wear them to school again, but for Jimmy, it was too late: now all a girl had to do was wear black stockings and he was goner.

Jodie's effect on Pete was equally obvious. His mouth had dropped open and he was looking up and down her lush body. She was short and perhaps a little chubby, but she wore her curves well. She had on a dress so short you could see the tops of her black thigh-highs, and was wearing a red bra outside her torn black t-shirt. She'd put on heavy makeup, with eyeliner that made her eyes look huge and almost tilted. *It's cosplay,* Jimmy realized. She looked like one of those anime characters.

No one dressed like that in Crescent City.

She ignored them both and walked over to Hoss, who stood up and looked her calmly in the eye.

"Hey," he said.

"Hey, baby," she purred. "You're just as cute as I thought you'd be."

Hoss took Jodie's hand and led her to a chair next to his. Then he hunched over and started playing with his cellphone again, ignoring her.

Pete glanced at Jimmy and threw up his hands as if to say, *What the hell just happened?*

There was another knock on the door, and when Pete opened it this time, a strange vampire was standing there. It was some guy he'd seen around town—the guy who rented kayaks down the harbor, that was it. The blond hunk looked freaked out of his mind. "I've heard it's safe here," he said nervously.

"Let him in!" Hoss shouted. "I put the word out. We're going to have guests. *Lots* of guests."

***

The vampire was hiding in the basement of her own house. It was relatively easy to smoke her out. Callendar tossed in a tear gas canister and it bumped down the stairs. Then there was silence; then the hiss of gas.

She came screeching up the stairs and Jeffers shot her with a bolt from the lone crossbow they'd brought with them, a last-minute addition they'd tossed into the trunk on their way out of town. The girl, who looked to be about eight years old, tumbled back into the darkness. They waited for the gas to clear, then carefully descended the stairs.

Her parents were dead in the living room and had been partially consumed by the little vampire over the preceding few days. It was the smell that had alerted the neighbors, who had called the police, who had called the FBI.

The girl was dead at the base of the stairs, the bolt in her heart and her innocent-looking little face smashed into the concrete, her neck at an unnatural angle.

"Hey, have you noticed the vampire population boom is starting to slow down?" Jeffers asked, prodding the body sadly with one foot. "Do you think we got them all?"

"Doubt it," Callendar said. "The strain is too virulent."

They'd confirmed that it was a maliciously potent strain of vampirism by sending some of the blue blood to the FBI office in Portland. Uncharacteristically, the results had come back quickly. This was something new—or at least, something they'd never seen before. Anyone bitten who died would come back as a vampire if the body wasn't too far gone.

Not so quick to respond were their backup squads from New York and L.A. There were only a few specialized two-agent teams like theirs, and they were mostly based in the biggest cities in the U.S. Vampires were relatively rare, and they were extremely good at hiding themselves and their crimes. They were also extremely dangerous and difficult to kill. A major task force was usually created for each identified vampire, and it sometimes took years to track down a single target, if they managed to do it at all. So the vampire hunters weren't used to mobilizing quickly, and even though Jeffers and Callendar had warned their superiors—repeatedly—that this was an epidemic, they were still on their own.

In truth, they were both kind of glad that help hadn't arrived yet. It was fun and refreshing to find and kill so many vampires in such a short time, from that first idiotic baby vamp who had challenged them on a public street mere minutes before dawn to the kegger victim who had looked at them with wide, innocent, trusting eyes as they put holy water in his IV.

Most of the other vampires had been equally easy to track down. What was surprising, even with a virulent strain, was that so many had been created, because even newly Turned vampires usually tried to consume their victims. Jeffers thought it was because the baby vamps were so inept that they were letting many of their prey get away. Callendar thought it was because these vampires thought they were only supposed to suck blood, because that's what the movies had taught them.

In any case, the new vampires were untutored and unwary. And they were so strong and fast compared to when they'd been human that most of them didn't believe they could be killed. It was like shooting fish in a barrel for Jeffers and Callendar, who had more notches on their crossbows (or crossbow, as the case may be) than any other team.

Jeffers is right, Callendar thought. *We're running out of vampires.*

"We haven't still found the vector of the infection," Jeffers reminded him. "You know, Jamie—your brother-in-law's girlfriend.

"I suspect she's long gone."

"Well, Robert doesn't think so," Jeffers said scornfully. At first, they had assumed that Robert's obsessive search was all about finding and killing the vampire who had deceived him, but after a while, it became clear that the cop was pining for his lost love. "Does he have any idea how dangerous vampires are?"

"Well, he lived with her for nearly a week with nothing bad happening," Callendar said. "You know, over the years, we've heard rumors of vampires who don't kill people. Urban myths, for the most part; but then there's Terrill."

"The biggest myth of all," Jeffers said.

"I wonder," Callendar mused. "There are so many stories, and the vampires themselves seem to believe them. Maybe it's true. But I sure wouldn't put my neck under the fangs to test it."

They took the little vampire into the backyard and watched her burn in the sunlight. Live or dead, the blue blood was flammable under the direct rays of the sun.

Then they conducted the usual canvas of the surrounding houses, interviewing the neighbors. It was clear that the child hadn't left the house since Turning. Her second-grade teacher had been Turned, but only this little girl had suffered the same fate. All the students were now accounted for.

For the first time since seeing Jamie in Robert's living room, the agents had no more leads.

"What the hell is going on?" Callendar wondered out loud.

***

Hoss was holding court. Jimmy, as second in command, was gazing imperiously at the ten or so minions currently in the room. The motel was now completely filled with vampires, nearly two dozen of them in all, of all shapes and sizes and ages. Word had gotten out that it was a safe place for them to hide. They'd knocked out the walls between the motel rooms so they could move around easily, and most of them spent the daylight hours in the restaurant when they weren't sleeping.

The first rule Hoss had insisted on, with Pete and Jimmy as his enforcers, was that no one was to leave without his permission.

His charges were getting more and more antsy, and he had expressed concern to Jimmy that he wasn't sure how much longer he'd be able to maintain control. But for now, as long as the hunting parties he sent out came back with fresh meat, most of the vampires were willing to listen to him. They'd seen too many others of their kind get snuffed out by the vampire hunters.

It had proven to be ridiculously simple to find a ready supply of fresh meat. It turned out that the cold of the ocean waters didn't affect them, and they could hold their breaths for extraordinary lengths of time and could see a long way, even in the murky water. Even when one of them drowned, he simply needed to be dragged onto the beach, and in a few minutes he'd spew up water and start breathing again.

Best of all, practically no one noticed them. The few humans unlucky enough to stumble across them were added to the food supply. So they had a steady diet of seafood, and just enough human victims to keep most of them happy.

Hoss sat on a raised dais, in a large overstuffed chair that had been accidentally left behind when the motel had been abandoned. Pete and Jimmy were perched on barstools on either side of him. Jodie sat at his feet. Jimmy laughed at how it must look. *It's like a Frank Frazetta cover on a Conan book,* he thought.

At first, the dais had been used because Hoss was so small that it was hard for everyone to see and hear him when he gave his talks. Later, it had seemed natural that he be raised up. Without meaning to, he'd become the leader of the vampires. Pete thought it was funny that the "little turd" was bossing them around, but they usually did what he asked. In fact, a bit of a power struggle was developing between Pete and Jimmy over who would be Hoss's right-hand vampire.

"Why don't we just kill the vampire hunters?" Pete asked. "There are only two of them. I bet Hoss could come up with a clever plan to trap them. Right, Hoss?"

"Yeah, right," Jimmy said, trying to gauge Hoss's reaction to Pete's suggestion. "I'm sure Sitting Bull thought the problem was solved once he snuffed out Custer."

Hoss just sat there thinking. He did a lot of that. He'd get an intense look on his face, then not hear anyone talking to him or see anything happening in front of him for a while, but when he finally smiled, he always had a solution to whatever problem was bugging them.

"Too many vampires," he said quietly.

"What's that, Hoss?" Pete asked.

Hoss looked up at them. The shrewd intelligence in his eyes made him seem like a 100-year-old trapped inside a 13-year-old body. Sure, he was slender and small for his age, but he projected authority. "What I'm trying to say is, we have too many vampires. There's no way to control them. They're bound to get us all killed. Whereas if there were only, say, a dozen of us, max, we could remain hidden."

"So what do we do?" Pete asked. "Kick them out? Go somewhere else? Leave them behind?"

Hoss stared at them.

Jimmy smiled. "Well, Pete…you *were* wondering what vampire tasted like."

CHAPTER 26

Jamie ventured out of the hideaway for a couple of hours every night. She'd find a small business to break into, steal what cash she could, and then go to the Burger King, where the same girl was waiting with a bag of raw beef for fifty bucks. The pimply-faced teen was getting a nice bonus.

Jamie had hit the jackpot on the third night, finding over three hundred dollars in the cash register of a clothing store. It only took her half an hour to walk to the hamburger joint, get her food, and scurry back to her new home. She didn't want to do anything else. She just lay in the blankets and waited—for what? To die?

Easy to do—just crawl out into the daylight, she thought.

But she didn't.

One evening, she saw a police car approaching, and she hid behind an abandoned building and watched as Robert drove by. Her heart ached at the sight of him. He looked pale and wan, and she wished she could reach out and hold him. She almost stepped out under the streetlamp, almost let him see her, come what may.

But she didn't.

She wasn't sure what would be worse: that he'd reject her and arrest her—maybe even try to kill her—or that he would accept her back into his life. The second alternative was far too dangerous for him. It would be the end of his career, and the vampire hunters wouldn't let her live peacefully with him. Even if they tried to flee, they'd be followed.

And yet…Robert was dying. Did it matter what happened to his career? Did it even matter what happened to her, as long as they could be together one more time?

She dreamed every night that he was lying beside her, and when she woke in the morning, she reached for him. And every time it happened, she had the same thought: *We could be together…forever.*

Jamie wouldn't Turn him without asking first. But was it so crazy to think that maybe, just maybe, he'd say yes? She'd convince him that it was possible to survive as a vampire and not kill anyone. It had been done—once. Terrill had gone for decades without killing a human.

Yeah, she thought. *And how did that end?* Her own Turning was proof that even the most disciplined vampire could fail.

But if anyone can do it, she thought, *it's Robert.*

As the days passed, Jamie got stronger. After a week, she ventured out late one overcast afternoon and visited the thrift shop where Marc-with-a-C worked.

He almost didn't recognize her at first; then his eyes lit up. "You look great!" he said. "You look completely recovered!"

She hadn't said anything about being sick, but she could understand his confusion. "Hi, Marc-with-a-C. How you been doing?"

"It's been kinda slow, actually," he said.

The big building was empty of people. Jamie realized that the last few times she'd visited, there had always been at least few customers browsing the aisles.

"I'm not sure what's going on," Marc said. "I mean, some of the street people usually head north this time of year. But some of the folks are here year-round, and I haven't seen any of them, either. I wonder if they're laying low because of the massacre."

Jamie felt a chill. Since she'd run away from the two vampire hunters, she hadn't thought about anything but losing Robert. Now the memory of the vampire attack in the woods returned in full force. She had smelled four vampires at the crime scene that night: Stuart and three others. At the time, because of what Horsham had told her about the difficulty of Turning people, she'd thought that was impossible.

It hadn't been impossible: it had been a warning sign, but she'd been so miserable that she hadn't thought any more about it. Now Jamie remembered the two vampires who had stolen her kill—Stuart's friends. They'd probably been Stuart's first victims.

"And then there are the others," Marc was saying.

"Others?"

"Don't you read the newspapers?" Marc asked, then looked chagrined. "Don't answer that. I always forget most people don't read the papers anymore. Anyway, there's also a bunch of people missing. I've heard conflicting stories: a gang war over meth territory, or an epidemic of some new disease that they're trying to keep quiet—or both."

"How many are missing?" Jamie asked.

"No one knows, but I'm guessing quite a few."

Again, Jamie felt a shiver down her spine. In a way, Marc was right. She *had* been ill—or at least, not thinking straight. This "epidemic" was her fault, clearly. At the very least, she should have checked on Stuart, and then taken him under her wing. Maybe if she had done that, none of this would have happened. Now there were at least four vampires running around town without any tutoring at all.

She remembered how hungry and confused she'd been when she'd first Turned; how she'd killed indiscriminately, putting herself in danger. Hell, if it hadn't been for Horsham's tutelage, she might have been standing in the middle of a field when the sun came up that first morning. She'd been that confused.

It was almost cruel, what she'd done through her inattention and inaction. It was time she started venturing out into the world again, time to find out what was happening.

"The cops come around here every ten minutes, it seems like," Marc said, "which could be another reason folks aren't coming in. Street people always think they're in trouble even when they aren't. I keep asking the cops what they're looking for, but they won't tell me."

"Local cops?"

"Yeah, and a couple of FBI guys. Real scary dudes."

Jamie had been there for at least half an hour, and unless Marc was really exaggerating, another visit from the cops could take place at any moment. *Time to get moving.*

"I want to leave a donation," she said, pulling out her last hundred dollars. She hadn't intended to give the money away, but now that she was here, it seemed like the right thing to do. She felt strong, capable of taking care of herself again. If she was going to return from exile, she'd find another way to feed herself.

The pimply-faced girl was going to be *so* disappointed.

***

After she left, a slender young man with black-rimmed glasses came out of the dressing room, where he'd been listening to the whole conversation. He walked up to Marc, who turned around with a shout of surprise when Stuart tapped him on the shoulder.

"Jesus, Stuart! I forgot you were here!"

Stuart held up a long coat with a hood. "I'll take this."

"Sure. That'll be five dollars."

"No," Stuart said. "That'll be a hundred dollars."

"Excuse me?"

"I'll take that hundred dollars the nice lady just gave you. I'll need it to buy gas to get out of this stinking town. And by the way…I'm really hungry. Sorry about this."

Marc must have seen something in Stuart's eyes. He backed away and pulled a baseball bat from behind the counter, then swung it at the advancing vampire, but Stuart barely felt the blow on his forehead before the blood started to heal him. It was too bad: Stuart had always liked Marc. But it was getting harder and harder to find any prey in this town, and he needed to regain some energy before he headed up the highway to Oregon.

Even when he was firmly in Stuart's grasp, Marc kept struggling, but he wasn't getting away: Stuart's fangs were sunk deep into his throat. Still, he got hold of some scissors and managed to stab Stuart in the chest. That hurt, and Stuart almost ripped the spine out of his victim, but he held back.

As a favor to Jamie, he didn't eat Marc. Let the nice vampire lady teach him how to be a proper vampire, if she liked him so much.

Stuart's stolen Corvette was outside, loaded up with what few possessions he still wanted. He was leaving Crescent City forever.

CHAPTER 27

"What do you mean I can't go outside?"

Slatter was the town drunk. He was also a bully: huge, loud, and constantly throwing his weight around. He was mean when he was drinking—which, until recently, had been all the time. He'd been fuming for days that as a vampire, he could no longer get drunk. Sober, he was meaner than ever.

The night before, he'd accidentally discovered that if he gulped down the blood of an intoxicated human, the effect was like the best drunk he'd ever had. He couldn't wait for night to fall again.

"It's against the Rules," Hoss said. He was calm and measured and sounded like the adult, while the older and bigger Slatter sounded like an aggrieved teenager.

"What rules?" Slatter shouted. "We're fucking vampires!"

"The Rules are for your own protection," Hoss repeated.

"What are you, ten years old?"

"I'm thirteen, but that doesn't matter now," Hoss said.

"I'm not taking orders from some damn kid," Slatter said. "You can just try to stop me."

Pete and Jimmy had both stood up and were facing off with Slatter, but Hoss looked undisturbed. "All right, all right," he said soothingly. "I'm not your boss; it was only a request. However, I'm going to ask you to carry one of our cellphones so that we can keep track of you."

"It's none of your business where I go!" Slatter snarled. Hoss's giving in so easily had only emboldened him. *There is no way we're going to control him now,* Jimmy thought.

"Please, Mr. Slatter. Take a cellphone. That's all I ask." Hoss leaned down to Jodie. "Babe, show Mr. Slatter where the programmed phones are."

Jodie stood up and walked toward Slatter, who watched her appreciatively. She brushed past him, looked back, and smiled. When she walked out of the room, he hesitated, then followed her.

"Jimmy," Hoss said. "Go with them."

Jimmy went after them, not sure what was going on. He hadn't heard anything about programmed phones, but Jodie seemed to know what was up. Jimmy had been angling to become Hoss's go-to guy, but he'd seen Jodie and Hoss cuddling and whispering, so it was clear that he was no better than third in line. Pete was clueless, unaware he could have been in the running.

The first three rooms they passed through were full of vampires waking up from the day's slumber. Jimmy caught up with Slatter and Jodie by the fourth room. Now the connecting holes were rougher and smaller, barely big enough to squeeze through. There were fifteen rooms in the motel altogether, but Jimmy hadn't explored past the fourth room. In fact, he hadn't realized the walls had been breached in the others. *What else don't I know?* Jimmy wondered.

They went through room after room. "You sure you aren't just trying to get me alone, girl? You want my body?" Slatter laughed, and Jodie laughed with him. Jimmy was starting to get a creeped-out feeling.

They reached the final room. The last two rooms had a real connecting door between them instead of a hole in the wall. They were the two biggest rooms in the motel, and inside the last one, Jimmy saw a small table with a pile of cellphones on it.

Jodie ushered the big man in. "Take your pick!" she said cheerfully.

"Whatever," Slatter said, stepping inside.

She slammed the door behind him and locked it.

"What are you doing, girl?" He was pounding on the door, which shook under the onslaught. "You think you can keep me in here?"

"That door won't hold up for long," Jimmy said. "This is stupid."

Jodie smiled at him and went to one corner of the room. There was a string dangling down through a small hole in the wall. She pulled on the string, and through the tiny aperture, Jimmy saw daylight flooding into the other room.

The cry that came from the next room wasn't made up of words; it was a shrieking sound, rising steadily from a low bellow to a scream of disbelief and denial to a mindless wail. Even through the wall, Jimmy thought he could feel the sudden blast of heat.

The vampire in the next room seemed to be pounding on all the walls in turn, as if trying to punch through them with his bare hands. Then the pounding and wailing stuttered and weakened, and finally stopped altogether after one last whimper emanated from the death chamber.

Jodie went back over to the corner, and Jimmy saw that there was a second string, which she now pulled. The little bit of sunlight that was infusing its way through the hole disappeared.

Jodie didn't even bother to open the connecting door to check the results. She turned and started walking back to the restaurant. Jimmy shuddered and followed her.

"You were in my seventh-grade health class, weren't you?" she said casually, as if they were having a chat on the street. "I thought you were cute, but you were so quiet. You're smart; I like that. Maybe not as smart as Hoss. Still, maybe we could, you know, hook up sometime?"

Jimmy was tempted, but…

"I think you belong to Hoss now," he said.

When they got back, Pete looked at him questioningly. Jimmy supposed he was looking a little pale. He pulled Pete to one side. "You need to quit making fun of Hoss," he said.

"What are you talking about? The little freak likes it."

"Listen to me, Pete. You need to leave him alone. Quit calling him names. Treat him with respect."

Pete fell silent as he studied Jimmy's face. Then he said quietly, "What happened?"

Jimmy told him what he had seen—and heard. He was just finishing the story when Hoss called them over.

"So," Hoss said. "Anyone else been giving us trouble?"

"Nothing we can't handle," Jimmy said.

"We've got it under control, boss," Pete echoed.

CHAPTER 28

"The infestation seems to be contained," Callendar said to the first team of vampire hunters to arrive as backup. It was Feller and Abercrombie: the B team who thought they were the A team. Well, technically, they were ranked the number-one team, but everyone knew that was only because the real number-one team had a problem with authority. "There have been no new cases reported in forty-eight hours."

"What was the infection rate?" Feller asked. He was big, beefy man who was serious all the time. Abercrombie, on the other hand, used a steady stream of quips and asides as a way to survive being attached to such a humorless partner.

"As far as we can tell, if the body was left untouched, a one hundred percent Turn rate."

"Jesus," Feller said.

"Jesus Christ on a crutch," Abercrombie elaborated.

"We're lucky this didn't get out of control!" Feller continued.

Callendar nodded. How nice that the new guys were saying "we" now that the operation was a success. Undoubtedly, it would have been "you" if the operation had been a disaster.

"Everyone is accounted for?" Feller asked.

"No," Jeffers said, annoyed. "We're still finding bodies in the woods, washing up on beaches. Who knows how many have burned up? Besides, there's a large homeless population around here, so it's hard to know for sure. But there have been no new reported cases of violence."

"The homeless move around," Feller said.

"And around and around and around they go," Abercrombie said.

Feller ignored his partner, as usual. "Did you think of setting up roadblocks?"

"We didn't have the manpower," Callendar answered pointedly. If these jokers had shown up a few days earlier, they might have been of some help. They'd rolled into town with a caravan of trailers and an army of techs. The state police had finally arrived as well. They taken over the county fairgrounds, where they were bustling about self-importantly, but not one of them had actually hit the streets yet or accomplished anything worth mentioning.

Then again, Callendar thought, *if they had arrived earlier, they probably would have also tried to take credit.*

"This strain is really virulent," Jeffers said. "So all it will take is one surviving vampire to set the whole thing off again."

"Speaking of which, did you find the vector? The vampire named Jamie?"

"Jamie the vampire?" Abercrombie echoed. "The vector vampire?"

Callendar saw Jeffers flush. Those two had been getting on each other's nerves since the academy. "Dammit, Abercrombie! Will you shut the fu-"

"No," Callendar interrupted, before his partner could say something he'd regret. "We think she's left the area. But we also believe she's a mature vampire who doesn't leave bodies intact. It was apparently an accident that she let one of her victims get away. She was interrupted."

"Accidents happen all the time," Feller said.

"Yeah, you know: 'Oops, I accidentally created a vampire,' " Abercrombie muttered.

"We need to find this Jamie and put an end to her," said

Feller. "We've been charged with the task of tracking her down while you two mop up."

Mop up? Callendar thought. *MOP UP?* He glanced over at his partner, who looked ready to explode. "Come on, Jeffers. Now that we've fixed things, let's go get our mops."

***

Stuart was roaring out of town in his stolen Corvette—the car had tinted windows, which was why he had chosen it—when a thought struck him. He pulled over as he reached Jedediah Smith Redwoods State Park. The huge redwoods were like a cathedral: a pagan cathedral that welcomed wild things, uncivilized and untamed creatures. Even through the shade of the giant trees, he could see that dawn was approaching. Still, he couldn't stand to leave his hometown without making one last statement. He did a U-turn and headed back through town until he got to the strip of beachfront motels.

He'd followed the two FBI agents for a week, hoping to catch them off-guard. But the agents were always cautious, and every night, before they went to sleep, they put crosses on their motel room door and poured a line of what Stuart guessed was holy water across the entrance. He'd never caught them unawares.

Their room was in the middle of the second floor of the Comfort Inn. Stuart knocked on the door of the room next to theirs on the right. He put on a small smile and tried not to look like a vampire. To the room's occupant, he hoped, he would appear to be a mild-looking young fellow, with black-rimmed glasses and nicely cut hair. A studious type.

A middle-aged man—his face sunburned, with a strange-looking white stripe on his forehead from where he'd worn a cap—opened the door, seemingly unsuspecting. "Yes?" he said curiously. "Can I help you?"

Stuart had planned to talk his way into the room, but dawn was only minutes away, so instead he rushed the man, threw him to the floor, and drained him of blood. Otherwise, he left him untouched. The shower was on in the bathroom, and when it turned off, he heard a woman humming. *Bonus!* Stuart thought. He opened the door and sank his teeth into the woman before she could turn around. At first glance she looked younger than the man, but even in her fright she couldn't really move the muscles of her Botoxed face. When he was finished, he laid her carefully in the bathtub.

He hurried past the crosses on the FBI agents' door and knocked on the door to the left of theirs. This room held three teenagers, only one of whom woke up to answer the door. The kid was at that awkward age where he almost passed for a cool dude, but couldn't quite pull it off. His cool-dude clothes, which he had clearly slept in, looked like a costume. Stuart had always hated phonies, and this sealed the kid's fate.

The wannabe asked sleepily what the hell Stuart wanted. Stuart put his hand over the kid's mouth and drained him, then followed the same procedure with the other two, taking just enough blood to kill them, no more. Even so, Stuart had never had so much blood. He felt bloated, like a tick, and queasy. He went to the bathroom and threw up.

But he wasn't done.

Stuart methodically killed the occupants of every room on the second floor. Dawn was breaking as he finished. He rushed out of the last room, jumped over the balcony railing, ran to the Corvette, and threw open the door. His skin was smoking and a fire had broken out on his hand before he managed to dive inside the car. He put out the flames, then leaned back in the seat and sighed.

He had so much blood in him, he had healed almost instantly.

Stuart started the car and retraced his route out of town. It had felt good, gorging like that, despite the queasiness, but he doubted he'd ever do it again; at least not anywhere he actually lived. Though, come to think of it, going somewhere else to do it was always an option...

No. He wasn't going to create another epidemic of vampires if he could help it. That had been his mistake, though it wasn't something he could have known was going to happen. He'd created too many vampires too fast, and then he'd lost control of them. That wasn't going to work in a place he wanted to keep living in. It made it too dangerous for every vampire.

No, he wouldn't do that again. He would find a new place to live. He would create one vampire at a time. He would teach his progeny everything he knew before he moved on to create another. Each new vampire would be his, beholden to and trained by him. They would follow his commands, or he'd kill them.

Eventually, he'd have a little army. When that happened, he'd return to his hometown and finish the job of destroying it.

CHAPTER 29

Feller was pissed. Those two idiots, Callendar and Jeffers, had stumbled across the case of a lifetime: the kind of case that made your career, pushed you up the ladder of promotion, and made you the envy of all your rivals.

It wasn't too late to take credit. He'd just have to hope that they'd missed one of the vampires, who hopefully would start up the epidemic again. Frankly, the more victims, the better—which would be tragic, of course, but if it happened, he and Abercrombie would be the heroes who cleaned up the mess.

He didn't say anything to Abercrombie, who wouldn't understand. The big guy—even bigger than his partner, and Feller wasn't a small man—played off of everything Feller said, but he had completely different motivations for doing what they did. Abercrombie was always concerned about the victims. Of course, Feller was too. But you didn't advance up the ladder without tracking down and destroying vampires, and the way you found vampires was to follow the victims. The bigger the vampire, the more victims there were.

Abercrombie didn't care about advancement, but he was a good agent, and whatever their individual motivations, they were an effective team.

They'd been living in a trailer on the road for days. Feller had talked Callendar and Jeffers into letting them use their motel room while they were on alternating shifts. Feller thought it was weird that those two had been sharing a motel room when they were supposed to have been on vacation, but he didn't dare say anything because of all the political correctness going on these days. He didn't want to have to go through sensitivity training again.

Of course, he was now sharing a room with Abercrombie, but that was different. That was from necessity, not by choice.

They'd gotten in about an hour before dawn to find Callendar and Jeffers already gone. All it took was a real shower and two real beds, and they'd slept most of the day away.

Feller got up and swiftly got dressed. He threw open the curtains to watch the sun descend into the ocean, then kicked the frame of Abercrombie's bed. "Wake up, AC! They'll be back any minute. They let us have the night shift, the dummies. Time to go hunt vampires!"

Abercrombie just groaned and rolled over, but Feller knew from experience that he would hop out of bed in a couple of minutes, fully awake. Sure enough, ten minutes later, they were both dressed and ready to go.

They stepped out onto the balcony just as the parking lot lights were going on and breathed in the humid coastal air. It was going to be a cool night, and Feller was kicking himself for not packing a heavier coat.

The door to the left of them opened and a naked middle-aged woman, her face frozen but her eyes bugging out, stumbled onto the balcony.

For a moment, Feller couldn't process the sight. Luckily, Abercrombie reacted by drawing his pistol and shooting her three times in the chest. She fell backward, then struggled to get up, but by then Feller had pulled a stake out of his coat lining and slammed it into her heart. He heard movement behind him and quick-drew his gun—a motion he'd practiced a thousand times but never actually used before. A sunburned, middle-aged man with a white stripe across his forehead emerged from the room, and Feller shot him in the head. That put him down, and would keep him down for hours—even a vampire took time to recover from a bullet to the brain. Feller staked him, never giving him the chance.

"Where the hell did they come from?" he said, turning to Abercrombie. But his partner was busy facing down three snarling teenagers, dressed like suburban gangsta wannabes, who were advancing on him from the other side. Abercrombie shot twice, knocking down the first two, but by then, the third vampire was almost on him. Feller shot that one in the head.

They didn't have time to stake these three vampires, because doors were opening all up and down the balcony, and every single person who emerged from those rooms was a vampire, all of them running toward the first red-blooded humans they saw. Grandmas and grandpas, parents and kids, husbands, wives, and lovers, single businessmen: all of them were converging on the two FBI agents.

Abercrombie and Feller kept firing, missing half their shots in their haste. Feller clicked on empty, reached for his extra clip, and realized it was in the glove compartment of their car. Abercrombie had already shot off most of his second clip.

Cursing, Feller and Abercrombie retreated to their room. They hadn't brought enough weapons, Feller realized, or enough ammunition. They were trapped.

The door nearly gave way under the mass of creatures, even though crucifixes protected it. The vampires who were pushed against the door were screaming and burning, but the ones behind them ignored them. Abercrombie hadn't said a word. Feller saw that the big man was holding a bottle of holy water up to the hallway light. It was only half full. Feller had zero bullets left in his gun and three stakes, and he'd lost count of how many vampires had surged toward them. At least a dozen;

maybe twenty or more.

Luckily for the agents, the door held. After half an hour or so, they heard shots outside and the sound of bodies hitting the balcony, the thuds shaking their room, then silence.

Abercrombie and Feller both trained their guns on the door as it opened.

"Hey, boys," Feller heard Callendar say. "You still here?"

Feller stepped over the pile of bodies at the door and onto the balcony. Backup units were arriving, staking the head-shot vampires and moving bodies into the shade before the sunlight reached them. He did a quick count and arrived at eighteen bodies, though there might have been one or two more disguised by the tangle of limbs.

"Real funny," he said.

"Funny ha ha, not funny strange," Abercrombie clarified.

But inside, Feller was elated. Sure, he was embarrassed at having to be rescued, but he'd get over it. No one had witnessed the fight: all they would know was that four FBI agents had killed eighteen or more vampires in one blazing gunfight. It would go down in FBI history, the Bureau's version of the OK Corral.

Feller had learned a long time ago that it wasn't what actually happened that mattered, but what people thought had happened. It was one of the reasons he'd become the highest-rated vampire hunter in the Bureau. Callendar was an indifferent writer; his reports were bland and matter-of-fact. He'd get all the facts right, and anyone who read between the lines would see what had happened—that Feller, helped by his bumbling partner Abercrombie, had, through great effort, overcome the mistakes of the first two agents on the scene.

But by the time Feller was done telling the story, no one would even look at Callendar's description. He might even be able to spin it a little, make Abercrombie and him the heroes who had saved their fellow agents from a trap.

Feller was thrilled for another reason.

He looked up and down the balcony at the carnage. "This was planned. It was an ambush. We've got an Alpha vampire on our hands."

CHAPTER 30

Terrill and Sylvie were never left alone after Fitzsimmons's power grab, except within the confines of their heavily guarded suite. There was never a moment when Sylvie wasn't threatened by the proximity of armed guards, all of whom made it clear that their first reaction to any sign of resistance would be to hurt her. As a human, there was no way Terrill would have been able to kill all the guards before they killed Sylvie—and even as a vampire, it was going to be difficult, even if he caught them by surprise.

Terrill bided his time, hoping that the sentries would relax their vigilance or that he could find some other way to escape. He also hoped that the opposition would contact him again, since he was certain that Fontaine and Kruger, the two murdered councilors, couldn't be the only ones chafing under Fitzsimmons's regime. But either the opponents were lying low or the coup d'état had been more thorough than he'd realized.

They were cut off from outside communication. Even Clarkson was staying away. Terrill assumed that her sympathies were with the resistance, but he didn't know that for sure.

And anyway, what could he do if he escaped? He had no money, no contacts here anymore. Though he had lived in London for hundreds of years, it was so changed that it seemed like a strange city. By himself, perhaps, he could have pulled it off. With Sylvie, he suspected they'd be tracked down within days, if not hours.

That was the whole point: they didn't have to keep him

trapped. They only needed to keep Sylvie under their control.

After a week of being cooped up—they were allowed to go for walks in the park, but not much more—he caught one of the day guards sneaking admiring looks at Sylvie. The vampire appeared young; he was blue-eyed and had floppy blond hair, and looked as if he belonged on the beaches of California instead of the streets of London. Of course, there was no way of knowing a vampire's real age, but this one had the manner of the newly fanged. He stuttered when he spoke to Terrill, as though starstruck.

His name was Cory, and according to him, his Maker was one of Fitzsimmons's chief lieutenants. Cory didn't have any political leanings, himself, one way or the other—though of course, he thought Terrill's Rules of Vampire were wonderful. Was there anything he could do for Terrill and Sylvie? "I wouldn't say anything to anyone," he promised.

"Can you see if we can't visit more of London?" Sylvie asked, and sure enough, they were given permission to go out more, as long as they were accompanied by enough guards.

Terrill didn't buy Cory's friendly act. He quit talking to Cory, and after a few more days, the blond vampire stopped showing up on guard duty. The next time Fitzsimmons dropped in on them, Cory was one of his bodyguards. He shrugged and winked when he saw Terrill glaring at him.

Terrill's old cynicism and caution were returning. He'd spent years by himself and, without meaning to, he'd lost much of his wariness. Now, back in the big city, it was coming back to him. The bright lights were rapidly losing their glamour.

He started noticing the contrast of Sylvie's youth and his age. He'd been attracted to her because of her freshness and optimism—the same reasons he'd been attracted to her sister, Jamie. He'd let his years drop away to live in the present with someone who was seeing everything for the first time. It hadn't seemed odd.

Now, living among these old, decadent vampires once again, the differences between him and Sylvie were becoming glaring. Sylvie didn't seem to notice. She knew they were in danger, and she sometimes apologized for being a burden, but there was no disguising the fact that she loved the adventure: new restaurants every night, sightseeing and visiting tourist traps on cloudy days. She wanted to visit the nightclubs, too, but most evenings, Terrill just wanted to go home and go to bed. She went back reluctantly, but once there, she made love to him every night and every morning as if each time was their last time.

He loved her more than his own life, but he was starting to get annoyed with her.

"You must be ready to run at any time," he said quietly into her ear one night when they were in bed. "When I say 'Go,' you need to follow me without question."

"I understand," she said. "But come on! I've never been out of Bend in my whole life. This is all so interesting to me. I want to explore the whole city. I want to meet everyone here!"

"I know," he said, his heart softening. *What is wrong with me?* he wondered. Then the full extent of the danger they were in sank in again, and his smile faded away. "But you must understand, they are trying to seduce you. They want you to stay."

She sat up and looked him in the eye, then kissed him. "Don't worry. I'll be ready."

He stared back into her eyes and saw there was no guile there, only love. At times like this, he felt as if she was the old one and he was the one who'd been newly hatched. She had the wisdom of an old soul in a young body. He felt like a boy in an old body.

"You think I don't know what they're doing?" Sylvie said. She punched him playfully in the chest.

He laughed, but couldn't hide his uncertainty.

"Terrill, it's my fault. I didn't want to tell you until it was absolutely necessary, but I can see how it is." She took his head in both of her hands. "Listen to me, love. I won't allow them to use me as leverage against you again. Ever."

Twice more, they had been called to the Council chamber to denounce "traitors." Twice more, Terrill had voted as Fitzsimmons asked.

"Never again," Sylvie said. He knew that tone of voice, and had never seen Sylvie fail to follow through on such a vow. "I will die first."

She rolled on top of him. "That's why I've been so insatiable. That's why I want to live every moment, to see and feel everything I can. Because soon I will be gone."

"No, Sylvie," he protested. "They would execute their opponents with or without me. My vote changes nothing."

"You don't see how much power you have, Terrill. Others are going along because you are. Oh, sure, they see you're being coerced, but in their hearts they don't believe you would vote against your own views just to save a human."

"None of these vampires are worth your life!"

"I can't judge them," Sylvie said. "But even if that is true, there is another, even more important reason. I've seen what it's doing to you. It's diminishing you with every minute that passes. I can't bear to watch it."

"Don't do anything rash," he said. "If it comes to another Council meeting, I'll fight them. We'll lose, but at least we will dispel the illusion. But let me try to figure out an escape plan first. We'll get out of here soon, I promise."

"OK," Sylvie said. She'd follow through on her threat,

he knew, if he didn't come through. She wouldn't wait for another vote.

They began to make love, and this time he felt the same desperation she did. Each time really could be their last time, he realized.

Later, as they drifted toward sleep, her head nestled in the crook of his arm, Terrill said softly, "There is another way." There was a question he had wanted to ask her since he first met her. But he knew what her answer would be.

"No," she murmured. "I will not become one of *them*."

He didn't say anything. She had said "*them*," as if he wasn't one of them. But to her, he probably wasn't.

And that was that.

CHAPTER 31

Terrill realized he wasn't going to have time to wait for the perfect opportunity to escape. He was going to have to pick among some weak options. He was on guard now on two fronts: on one, he was watching for the slightest weakness in his opponents; on the other, he was watching Sylvie, making sure she wouldn't make good on her promise.

It was as if the guards could read his intentions. They ramped up security at every point—loopholes he had discovered were closed; gaps in their rotation were filled in; weaker guards were replaced by stronger guards—not so much around him, but around Sylvie, which was both distressing and reassuring. They didn't want her to come to harm (by other than their own hands, of course) any more than Terrill did.

Terrill overheard one of the guards mention that a Council meeting had been called for the next day. He glanced at Sylvie, but she showed no sign of having heard. Still, she'd know soon enough, and if he understood her at all, she had already figured out a way to put an end to her life.

Yet he was still reluctant to force the issue. Once he revealed himself, the element of surprise would be lost forever. Never again would the hardliners be so relaxed around him. They thought they only needed to control Sylvie, and that by controlling her, they controlled him.

Certainly, they had no clue about his real powers. He and Sylvie spent time every day on the balcony, basking in the sun. The balcony was fitted with a grate, but enough sun came through that they were both getting tan. To Terrill, the feel of sunlight on his skin was a miracle, something humans took for granted but that he had not felt in centuries.

When he looked in the mirror, he could see his own reflection. Another miracle. Instead of a pale wraith, he saw what appeared to be a healthy, sun-worshipping human. But he could feel the vampire blood coursing beneath the surface. He was something new, something that was neither human nor vampire.

That morning, Terrill had cut himself shaving. He didn't think anything of it; it would heal with minutes. But Sylvie was using the same mirror, and she gasped.

"What is it?" he asked, looking around. If there were vampires behind them, he wouldn't see them in the mirror.

There was no one else there.

"Look at your blood!" Sylvie said, her eyes round.

He reached up and swiped his fingers across the trickle of warm blood. He expected to see red, though he wouldn't have been surprised to see blue. Instead, there was a yellowish sheen on his fingers. He looked in the mirror and saw blood droplets that appeared to be molten gold oozing from his wound.

He caught one of the drops on his fingertip and held it up to the light. It seemed to glitter under the glow of the bulb.

"That's…different," he said. "Never seen that before."

"You aren't vampire," Sylvie said. There was a certainty in her voice that seemed to decide the issue.

"Yes," he said. "But what am I?"

She didn't have an answer for that.

***

Terrill and Sylvie got dressed, though it was clear they weren't going anywhere that day. The sun was shining brightly outside, and they would not be allowed to go where the guards couldn't follow.

They settled in for the day, Terrill with a book and Sylvie doing crossword puzzles. Terrill sat with the book open in his hand, but the words blurred. He'd have to make an escape attempt today or risk losing Sylvie forever. There was little chance of success, but at least they would die resisting. Maybe word would get out to the opposition. Maybe their deaths would serve a purpose.

Terrill couldn't come up with a plan that involved anything other than a frontal attack, perhaps made toward the end of the shift, when the guards would be the most relaxed. He could probably overwhelm the two guards right outside the door, but it was the escape route he was worried about. The hotel was filled with vampires, on every floor and in every room, all of them hardliners.

Terrill doubted they'd try to kill him and Sylvie without orders, but there would be more than enough of the hardliners to slow them down, and if word came down that they were not to be allowed to escape, all hope would be gone.

No, some form of stealth would be required, to get them as close to the exits as possible before he made his move.

Terrill prayed for rain, for cloud cover—anything that would make the guards comfortable with going outside. Once outside, he would take his chances with the human population.

If it were just him, it wouldn't have been a problem. But all it would take would be one guard taking initiative to stop Sylvie forever.

She's going to end it herself if we don't escape, he thought. *We have to at least try.*

Terrill walked out onto the balcony and saw roiling clouds moving in. Before long, the sky was dark. His heart lifted. He felt a drop on his forehead, then another. Soon the rain was pouring down.

"Let's go for a walk," he said to Sylvie. He kept his eyes on hers for a little longer than normal and she got the message. Now was the time.

The guards didn't object to a walk. It was clear that there'd be no more direct sunlight that day, and they were under orders to accommodate Terrill and Sylvie whenever possible. After all, it would take but a moment to recapture the two prisoners— or so the guards thought, assuming they were both humans, weak and slow.

Terrill and Sylvie were getting ready to leave when they heard a loud boom outside the building. One of the windows shattered and the entire structure shuddered as if struck by an earthquake. A guard ran for the balcony. Terrill followed. There was a cloud of debris rising from the street below. Both guards' cellphones rang.

"Yes, sir," Terrill heard them say, almost simultaneously. One guard grabbed Sylvie and pulled her out the front door; the other motioned for Terrill to follow. They ran down the corridor to the stairs and up one flight.

There were several more guards waiting for them on the next landing—or so Terrill thought at first. But these vampires were pointing their crossbows not at Terrill or Sylvie, but at their guards, who put up their hands.

A tall, stringy man stepped forward. "We've been sent by the resistance to help you escape," he said. "We have a helicopter waiting on the roof. Let's go."

Terrill and Sylvie followed. Below, they could hear fighting.

"Who sent you?" Terrill shouted above the sound of the helicopter.

"You know," the man said. Then he stared at Terrill as if waiting for him to respond.

"Actually, I have no idea," Terrill said.

"Clarkson."

"Clarkson?" Terrill repeated. It made sense…and yet, something wasn't quite right. Their rescuer was again staring at him expectantly, evidently waiting for him to supply more information. Terrill didn't say anything.

They reached the helicopter and clambered inside, but had barely lifted off when the motor started sputtering. "We've been hit!" the pilot shouted.

"Can you put her down?" their rescuer asked.

"If you see another building with a helipad," the pilot said. "But it better be lower than this, because we're losing altitude!"

"There!" The tall man pointed. A helipad was visible on the roof of a three-story building next to a public park near the Eye of London.

They were dropping fast and their approach was rough, but at the last minute, the pilot straightened out the helicopter and they landed gently. The engine sputtered and died with a high whine.

"I don't know this part of London," their rescuer said. "None of my men are nearby. We'll need to go to ground." He turned to Terrill and asked, "Do you have any contacts in London? Any resources we can use?"

Terrill shook his head. "None. It's been too long since I lived here. The vampires I knew who might have helped me have already been executed."

The man's face transformed. He smiled at Terrill and pulled out his phone. "Did you catch that, boss?"

"Good job," Fitzsimmons's voice said. "Bring them on back."

Terrill looked around. The pilot was holding a gun on Sylvie, but he'd probably never have a better chance. He was ready to act as soon as the gun wavered in the slightest. He'd take out the pilot first, then the tall man.

No more than a half a dozen yards away, the door to the roof opened and armed guards came pouring out. They soon had the helicopter surrounded.

The moment of opportunity was gone.

***

Fitzsimmons was waiting for them in their hotel room. He looked completely smug. "A couple of flash bombs and some loud banging: that's all it cost me to deceive you," he said. "I've been wondering who your confederates were. Frankly, it didn't occur to me that you didn't have any. I was certain you would implicate Clarkson. No wonder you haven't tried to escape before."

Terrill didn't say anything. He hadn't been completely fooled: the whole getaway hadn't felt right. But he also hadn't lied about not having any friends or resources in London, and if it would help the hardliners relax their guard, there was nothing wrong with letting them think he had no options.

"Don't look so surprised,' Fitzsimmons laughed. "I've been watching you on the security monitors for days, and you couldn't have been much more obvious about your intentions. You tighten up, dear boy. Like you're getting ready to do battle."

"The Council meeting?" Terrill asked.

"I had that little tidbit dropped within earshot, thinking it might spur you to action. But sadly, no, there is no meeting planned in the near future. I've run out of known enemies…for now."

Terrill looked around for Sylvie to see how she was taking this latest setback. She wasn't in the room. "Sylvie?" he called.

He and Fitzsimmons spotted her at the same time. She was on the balcony, lifting up a corner of the grate that she had apparently managed to loosen. Then she climbed out onto the ledge.

If Fitzsimmons hadn't reacted so quickly, Terrill would have been forced to reveal himself. He'd never in his life had an instinct stronger than the one to rush over to Sylvie right then. But it was as if time slowed down and he had an extra moment to observe Fitzsimmons and make a decision, so when he saw a blur of movement from where the other vampire was standing, he held back for a fraction of a second.

Fitzsimmons caught Sylvie just as she was leaping off the ledge and pulled her, screaming, back onto the balcony. The guards had reacted more slowly, but were there to take her out of their boss's arms.

He marched back to Terrill. "That was foolish. Now I'm going to have to put guards on you at all times, inside and out."

Terrill felt himself sag with defeat. But at the same time, he was relieved. *They'll keep Sylvie alive*, he realized.

"I came here personally to tell you something," Fitzsimmons said. "There has been a development in America. Apparently, that town that Clarkson picked you up in is having an epidemic of vampires. Crescent City has produced more vampire sightings in the last week than all the sightings in the world in the last decade. I'm going to investigate, and I'm taking you two with me."

Terrill didn't respond, but he felt a surge of hope. Getting out of London and back into the territory he knew couldn't help but be to their benefit. His thoughts went to Jamie. She'd be there, too. The time might still come when he could get them out of this trap.

"Your progeny, Jamie, seems to be an extraordinarily Maker," Fitzsimmons said. "And she's breaking every Rule there is."

CHAPTER 32

Jamie's gone, Robert thought as he drove through the streets of Crescent City. *She's left town—or she's dead.*

He'd searched every alley, every vacant lot, and every uninhabited house. He'd explored all the parks, all the beaches, and every thoroughfare. She could be living in the woods, he supposed, but she was nowhere where he could find her.

The disappearances and murders had overwhelmed the police department, and the FBI had taken over the entire town. The cops were at the FBI's beck and call, but Robert had stopped reporting in.

On the second day after the arrival of the caravan of vampire hunters and other FBI agents, he'd been pulled aside by the leader of the group, an agent named Feller.

"We don't have time for personal missions," Feller had said sternly.

Robert couldn't even get angry. It didn't matter what this agent said; he wasn't going to change what he was doing.

"I mean it, Jurgenson—Robert, is it? Look, Robert, this could make you or break you."

Robert had nodded. "Sure."

"Listen, this is the chance of a lifetime. Promotions and honors and a hefty raise in pay await if you just follow instructions."

Robert had walked away and forgotten the conversation five minutes later.

After that, it seemed like Feller had it in for him, assigning him menial tasks—getting coffee, buying printer paper, collating files, and so on—which Robert did if it was convenient and ignored if it wasn't.

They had a huge blowup on the fourth day—or at least, Feller did. Robert just walked away again, and this time, he didn't go back.

He still listened to the police scanner, hoping for and dreading the words "female perp." Each time, he held his breath until it was clear it wasn't Jamie.

The FBI had insisted they not use the words "vampire" or "kill." Murders were referred to as "accidents" and vampires were "perps." Ordinary crime was being ignored—not that there was much of it. People were staying inside, behind locked doors, and many of them had guns. The police and FBI had to make it very clear who they were before they dared knock on a door.

After being shot at a couple of times, Robert was yelling "POLICE!" every time he turned a blind corner. Once or twice, early in his search, he had come across vampires, and he'd shot them in the head and called it in. He hadn't waited around to see what the FBI did with the bodies. He'd dragged the first body into the sunlight to get a good look at her and had nearly been scorched when the vampire burst into flames.

Robert had been ordered to come in to the police station but was ignoring the command. He didn't care about his career anymore. He'd only been working because he didn't want to sit at home and rot away. Now, what did it matter? He was dying. He just wanted to see Jamie one more time.

Part of him hoped she had left the area. He was pretty convinced she had; otherwise, he was certain, she would have tried to get ahold of him. His phone was charged and on the passenger seat next to him. He checked it—again—to make sure it was on. *Why wouldn't she call?* he wondered. *Does she think I hate her?*

He picked up the phone and called her number again. The first few times he'd called her, it had gone to voicemail. Now it was saying that no such number existed.

Was she dead? Had she been caught up in the vampire holocaust?

Robert pulled over and put his face in his hands. After he had been alone for so long, she had come into his life and become part of him. When she ran away, she left a lonely, aching void. Nothing could fill that void: nothing but her face, her voice, her smell.

A deep, throbbing pain wrenched through his gut, and he clenched the steering wheel until it subsided. It was always there now, in varying degrees of intensity. He had pain pills the doctors had given him. His oncologist had made a point of saying something like "taking five at a time is too many," hinting at a permanent solution if the pain got too bad. But Robert wasn't taking even one at a time. They made him foggy, slow to react. He'd taken one the other night when the pain was so bad that he couldn't sleep. Instead of his usual six hours, he hadn't woken up for twelve. He'd groaned, immediately checked his phone, and anxiously listened to the scanner until he was sure that Jamie hadn't been caught.

He needed to be alert, ready to respond to any sighting of a female "perp" who matched her description.

Robert had loved his first wife: she had been his high school sweetheart. But his feelings for her had settled into a comfortable, middle-aged appreciation. With Jamie, it was as if it was the first and only time he'd felt real love. Every waking moment was filled with the thought of her, and he could call up her ghost, almost see her, almost hear her laugh—but that only made her absence hurt more.

He didn't know what they would do if he found her and she still wanted to be with him. Hide? Run away? He didn't care. He just wanted to know if was possible for them to be together again. He was certain it *was* possible, that they'd find a way.

Hadn't she felt the same way? Didn't she want to know if they had any chance at a future?

So he kept driving around the small town, up and down the highways and the lanes and the dead-end streets, day and night, looking for any sign of her.

Vampire sightings had grown scarce, and then one day the scanner had come alive with agitated voices, and the massacre at the Comfort Inn had reignited the search for vampires. But the excitement had soon died down as vampire sightings again dwindled.

He'd seen his former brother-in-law once. Callendar had flagged him down as he was passing a crime scene, and he'd reluctantly stopped. It was clear, though, that the FBI agent was only checking to see if Robert had seen Jamie, and as soon as he ascertained from Robert's unhappiness that she hadn't made an appearance, he had seemed to lose interest.

"Don't be fooled, Robert," Callendar had said before waving him on. "Call me the minute you see her. Don't approach her. She's a vampire, and all vampires are dangerous. They have no conscience—and no soul."

Callendar was wrong. Robert had lived with Jamie long enough to know she had both conscience and a soul: more so than most humans, in fact. But he didn't argue; he simply drove away.

***

Jamie had packed to leave town. Packing had consisted of putting one change of clothing into a backpack. She'd break into a business to get some money before she left, she decided, and she'd try to steal a car. It was time to go.

She'd seen Robert in his patrol car again on her way home from the thrift store. She'd barely hidden in time. It hurt to see him, to even think of him. No one had warned her that she could fall in love again—and with a human, at that. In fact, Horsham had intimated that it was impossible, that vampires didn't suffer from such feelings.

It was clear she didn't know anything about her own nature. She needed to find Terrill.

It was also obvious that she'd made a mistake in running away from Bend. At the time, she'd been confused, ashamed of what she was, afraid of hurting her sister, Sylvie. So she'd run.

Now, she intended to track down Terrill and ask him, as her Maker, to teach her. Perhaps when she finally understood who and what she was, and knew that she could control herself, she would return to Robert.

If he was still alive.

That was the worst part: to know that their time was limited, that their few remaining moments together had been taken away from them.

The same thought kept breaking through the hurt. Jamie thought it every morning when she woke up, and every night when she went to bed. She could Turn him. He'd become immortal, like her, and they'd spend the rest of eternity together. What would be so wrong about that?

But what if he didn't want that? Would he curse her through eternity instead? Would she turn kindhearted Robert into a vicious vampire? She didn't think that was possible, but what did she know?

It was wrong to Turn him against his will. She didn't trust her own feelings, so, if the chance ever came, she'd have to rely on his.

***

It was nearly morning by the time Jamie was ready to go. She decided to wait one more day. The hideaway was safe and comfortable, and now that it was time to leave, she was reluctant. Robert was out there, looking for her, and somehow that thought was comforting.

She was about to fall asleep when she heard a rustling at the entrance. She thought about escaping out the secret back exit, but then thought, *What if it's Billy or one of the others returning?*

So she waited. After a minute, a young man poked his head into the clearing. At first, Jamie didn't recognize him. He was so out of place and so distressed that he looked nothing like the smiling clerk from the thrift store.

"I don't feel so good," said Marc-with-a-C. "Please help me."

***

Robert hadn't slept in more than a day. With dawn breaking, he decided he'd go home and catch some sleep. Wherever Jamie was, she was holed up by now. Maybe he'd cut one of the pills in half and see if that helped with the pain without knocking him out for too long. The time was coming when the pain would be too extreme for him not to take his medication.

As he accelerated down the coastal highway, he caught a flash of silver out of the corner of one eye. He'd driven by the rundown parking lot a hundred times, and he'd recently noticed a shopping cart sitting there, but hadn't thought anything of it. This time, as he glanced over, it seemed to him that the cart had been moved. He pulled into the lot.

As he drove up to the cart, he saw the hole at the bottom of the thicket of blackberry bushes for the first time. He held his breath and his heart seemed to skip a beat. The pain in his gut receded under a surge of excitement. *She's here*, he thought. *I'll bet anything she's here.*

He got out of the car and removed his gun belt. Whatever happened would happen. However she reacted, he would accept it. If Callendar was right, that she'd been pretending, that she was evil, then she'd kill him. So be it. At least it would end his suffering.

He got down on his hands and knees and crawled into the hole.

***

Jamie helped Marc up. She could tell at once that he'd been bitten. "How did you know I was here?" she asked.

"Billy showed me this place once. He brought me here on my birthday and they had a little party for me. I remembered you came in with Billy that first time."

She put her hand to his pale face and felt despondent. He'd been a good man, and somehow, though she didn't know how, she suspected that she'd brought this fate down upon him.

"I don't understand what's happening to me," Marc said. "I wasn't feeling well; I passed out or something. I was talking to Stuart, and then…I don't remember anything."

Jamie flushed. It *was* her fault. Stuart was on her.

"I woke up and went home, but I wanted to…" Marc swallowed and stared at her in shock. "I wanted to kill her—my mother. To…I can't believe…I wanted…"

"Shhh, shush," Jamie hushed him soothingly. "But you didn't, did you?"

"No," he said. "I ran away. I kept running until I found myself here. What's wrong with me?"

You're a vampire, Jamie almost blurted out, but she stopped herself. How do you tell a person that they have Turned, that they'll never again bask in the sunlight, that they'll be hungry for blood every day for the rest of their life?

Before she could speak, she heard someone else coming through the bushes.

"Go—over there," she pointed to the chairs and tables on the other side of the enclosure. "Hide."

Marc hid.

Jamie stood over the entrance, holding one of the kitchen knives. She looked down at the dull blade and wanted to laugh. Her fangs were so much sharper.

She recognized Robert from the first inch of him that showed—dark hair with strands of silver in it. She put down the knife and dropped to her knees at his side as he began to emerge. He looked up in alarm, then relaxed and smiled when he saw it was her.

What was I doing? Jamie wondered when she saw that smile. *Why was I avoiding him?*

She heard snarling and turned to see Marc hurtling across the enclosure, his fangs extended. She grabbed him in midair and slammed him onto his back. She stared into his eyes. "Stop!" she commanded, and he did. "Go to sleep," she ordered, and he fell asleep.

She turned to Robert. "I didn't know I could do that."

Then they were in each other's arms, and everything else in the world disappeared.

CHAPTER 33

"Come in with us, Jill." Billy was almost begging. "I guarantee you a bed, and I promise no one will bother you."

"Get away from me, Billy. I said no and I mean no. I won't be shut up in some room with a bunch of bums."

You're a bum yourself! Billy nearly said, but he knew that would be a mistake. To Jill, a middle-aged, formerly middle-class woman who still tried to keep her fingernails polished and saved and scrimped for real haircuts, she wasn't a bum. She wasn't homeless. She didn't have a drinking problem. She just liked to camp outside with her friends.

"It isn't safe out here," Billy protested. "There are *monsters*."

Jill snorted. "Yeah, what a laugh. That might work on some of the crazies in the next camp over, but I'm not buying it. Monsters…LOL."

That was the other thing about Jill: every dime she managed to scrape up that didn't go toward grooming, she put into her cellphone. Her kids, who lived far away in another state and, from what she said, probably didn't care all that much about her, seemed to believe she was living in a nice condo.

Billy didn't know all the homeless folks in Bend, not the way he knew everyone in Crescent City. He wanted to get back to his hometown, but he couldn't leave Bend until it was safe.

Billy knew firsthand that the homeless were all too often the victims of violence. They were easy prey; sadly, sometimes they preyed on each other as well. Even worse, the local authorities didn't take crimes involving the homeless seriously unless they resulted in death or dismemberment. Billy had kicked the alcohol—mostly—a few years ago, and after that, he'd taken it upon himself to save those he could. Most wouldn't accept help from civilians, but from another bum? That seemed all right.

This time, when the citizens of Bend started to disappear, the homeless weren't the victims. Of course, in a sense, they were already the disappeared—in the eyes of society, anyway. But Billy and his friends knew most of them, and Father Harry and those who worked at the St. Francis shelter kept a rough count.

Billy was a little surprised that he had managed to talk as many of the homeless into coming indoors at night as he had. All the shelters were making room, quietly breaking capacity regulations until the emergency was over. Some of the operators were told the problem was marauding gangs, others that there was a serial killer active in the area, and a select few—mostly those who had spent earlier lives on the streets—were told the truth.

Monsters.

The only advantage the homeless had over the stalwart citizens of Bend was that they believed in monsters. They'd *seen* monsters. When Billy told them there were vampires on the loose, they believed him—except for a few deluded souls like Jill, whose mind-set was still that of a middle-class woman, even as her body resided in a tent on a dirt lot.

"Well, then, lady, I'm staying with you," Billy told her now. He could count on Perry and Grime to get the other homeless folks in town into shelters. They were locals; they knew their way around.

They had taken Billy aside and told him the story of Terrill, the vampire who had turned human, and about his love for Sylvie, the human girl.

"Not all vampires are bad," Perry had concluded.

"Gud…'uns," Grime had added in his muddled way.

Billy wasn't sure he believed it. Until then, he'd thought all vampires were evil and the only good vampire was a dead one. He was still going to act as if that assumption was true.

In the backpack slung over his shoulder, he had an anti-vampire package that Father Harry had assembled: a spray bottle filled with holy water, blessed that morning; a couple of sharp wooden stakes; a giant silver cross, valuable enough that, if he pawned it, he could afford to live in a motel for a few months, but he'd resisted doing that so far. The priest had also taught him a few Catholic prayers for banishing demons.

It was all untested, but Billy was halfway looking forward to being able to use his vampire hunter's arsenal.

Best of all, Father Harry had thoughtfully included a bottle of sacramental wine. Billy put the backpack on the ground and pulled out the bottle.

Jill's face lit up. "Why, Billy, I think you're trying to get into my pants!"

Billy suppressed a shudder. Jill weighed at least three hundred pounds, and while she always sported a nice hairdo and a manicure, she wasn't so punctilious about her bathing. "Nah…I know you like them young, Jill," he said, laughing.

He built up the fire and put one of the stakes and the holy water within easy reach. He stuck the cross in the ground just behind where he and Jill were sitting.

He let her drink most of the wine, taking only a few sips himself. For once in his life, wine had little appeal. He couldn't afford not to be vigilant. In fact, he'd never stopped being vigilant since the moment he'd watched his friends torn apart by those *things*.

It was about midnight when Billy sensed the monster approach. He could feel the hair on the back of his neck rising.

He reached down and shook Jill, who was snoring, her head in his lap.

"Wha…" Jill started to say; then she, too, sensed the danger and fell silent.

Billy stood up, the fire at his back, the crucifix in front of him. He had the spray bottle of holy water in one hand, the stake in the other. Jill scooted back in the dirt, nearly going into the fire, and peered out between his legs.

He started to chant the prayer that Father Harry had taught him. "Glorious Saint Michael, Prince of the heavenly hosts, who fought with the dragon, the old serpent, and cast him out of heaven…"

The vampire had been striding confidently toward them, but once he saw the cross, he began to creep to one side. Now, as Billy started chanting, the vampire hissed and backed up a step. Billy wasn't religious, but seeing these results was going to make him question his skepticism, that was for sure.

"I earnestly entreat you to assist me also, in the painful and dangerous conflict which I sustain against the same formidable foe."

The vampire stopped and stared at him as if confused. Under other circumstances, he might have looked like an ordinary guy, but fangs distorted his face and his eyes glowed red in the firelight. He wore black-rimmed glasses, which was strange, because from what Billy had learned from Father Harry— who thought of himself as an experienced vampire hunter— vampires could see better than any human. *Either camouflage or habit,* Billy thought. There was a look of hate and hunger on the vampire's face that transformed it from that of a young man to that of an ancient evil.

"Be with me, O mighty Prince! That I may courageously fight and vanquish that proud spirit, whom you, by the Divine

Power, gloriously overthrew…"

The vampire had stopped hissing and was wavering. Billy held the holy water and stake at the ready.

Then the creature simply disappeared. He fled into the darkness so fast that Billy lost sight of him in the blink of an eye. Behind him, Jill was cowering on the ground and whimpering. Billy's legs went weak all of sudden. He sat down heavily on a nearby log.

"Now will you go inside with me, Jill?" he asked softly.

She didn't answer, but he knew she was convinced.

***

To hell with those bums! Stuart thought. *Who needs them?*

He'd had a busy and successful week, having already Turned and then trained three vampires. He had them all convinced they wouldn't survive without him. He'd embellished the truth about himself, drawing on all the vampire movies and TV shows he'd ever seen to concoct a background of hundreds of years and thousands of victims.

Having spent so much time on his disciples, Stuart was a little tired and just wanted an easy meal. Bums tended to taste pretty bad, but they'd do in a pinch and were usually easy prey.

The sensations he'd felt when the homeless guy was chanting his prayers had been strange. The crucifix in the ground had repelled him, and the wooden stake and spray bottle had scared him a little. He'd watched as Greg had burned outside his house, killed with similar implements.

It was weird: he'd never been religious, and yet here he was being forced away from a perfectly good meal by the symbols of religion. Maybe he was damned. Hell, *of course* he was damned.

And he didn't care.

He settled for a teenage girl who was sneaking back into her house after a night of partying. She started to scream when he grabbed her ponytail. He wrenched her head back and tore into her neck, cutting her off in mid-cry. She tasted better than any bum would have, anyway. As a bonus, she was drunk. Stuart drank the alcohol-infused blood and got one of the best highs he'd ever had.

He sat on the darkened front porch and ate the girl's flesh, down to the bones. He tossed the bones, one by one, out onto the lawn. He wasn't ready to take on another new disciple just yet. Well, now that he thought about it, it was time he Turned a girl: a good-looking girl. He'd been concentrating on the muscle and had forgotten how nice it was to have a female around, especially one who was in his power.

So far, he'd managed not to start a panic in Bend. He could still operate with impunity, though the homeless population seemed to be on alert. He probably shouldn't have thrown the girl's bones on her own lawn, but maybe some stray dogs would carry them off or something.

It didn't matter. Stuart didn't plan to stick around for long.

With each new vampire, he was learning how to bend them more quickly to his will. In a week or two, he'd have enough of them to really accomplish something. He couldn't wait. He'd pile them into a few vans and they'd invade Crescent City, and he'd show his hometown what he really thought of it.

CHAPTER 34

It hadn't gone as Feller had planned. After the ambush at the motel, they'd found only a few straggler vampires. They hadn't located either the vampire named Jamie, who was the vector of this outbreak, or the Alpha vampire who had set up the ambush. Without them, the victory was incomplete.

Nor had anyone spotted Clarkson since the sighting at the restaurant by Callendar and Jeffers. It was as if she'd disappeared—and yet, not long after that sighting, the vampire attacks had begun. Was Clarkson the cause of the outbreak, and not this Jamie? According to reports, the blonde vampire belonged to the Council of Vampires, the enforcers of the Rules, and this epidemic of new vampires was diametrically opposed to everything the Council stood for; still, it seemed like a strange coincidence.

So far, the FBI had only managed to kill Wilderings, vampires who were vulnerable because they were controlled by their instincts and desires and not by reason; vampires who hadn't been taught how to survive.

The whole campaign had been a boost to Feller's career, but without the death of one of the major players, it wasn't the surefire promotion engine that he'd envisioned. Callendar and Jeffers were going to get too much of the credit. Though Feller had convinced his superiors, through his reports, that he and Abercrombie were the heroes of the Massacre at the Comfort Inn, as it was being called in the Bureau, to his great annoyance, the rank and file were mostly applauding Callendar and Jeffers.

Feller continued to search for vampires, day after day, until even Abercrombie had had enough and stayed back at the motel, watching Judge Judy, and Judge Brown, and Judge whoever else while he waited for Feller to call him for backup.

Feller started patrolling by himself, though it was against regulations. When he wasn't patrolling, he was poring over the maps and reports of vampire sightings.

He was driving past the abandoned motel and restaurant on the beach for the hundredth time when he suddenly realized that there had been no reports of vampirism in this part of town. He pulled into the parking lot and eyeballed the buildings. They were quiet and dark.

He pulled out the map and checked it. Sure enough, there was a nice, wide empty zone radiating out from the nearby beach and stretching about half a mile inland. Everywhere else in town showed at least a few of the red marks that denoted attacks.

Feller scanned the surrounding terrain. Across the highway from the motel was some thick shrubbery, perfect cover for vampires. The abandoned buildings themselves were the kinds of places a vampire might find irresistible. Had they been checked?

He looked over the reports. There'd been a search in the early days of the epidemic, after Callendar and Jeffers had first gotten into town. Nothing since then. Since there had been no attacks in the vicinity, no one had thought to check again.

A feeling of dread came over him. He could almost sense a vampire lurking within the abandoned motel. Should he call Abercrombie? His partner would come, but if there wasn't anything here, Feller would never hear the end of it. He could call for backup from one of the other FBI units, but they'd naturally wonder why Abercrombie wasn't there. An agent who couldn't get along with his partner didn't progress far up the ranks.

He had no evidence whatsoever. In fact, there was an absence of evidence. While to Feller the absence of evidence was suspicious, to just about anyone else in the Bureau, it would be the opposite.

But the biggest reason he didn't call for backup was that Callendar and Jeffers were still in town, and they'd never let him forget it if he called out the troops for no good reason.

Feller pulled the big crucifix he wore around his neck out from under his shirt and draped it over his chest. He loaded his crossbow and checked to make sure he had an extra clip for his pistol, then sprayed himself with holy water. It would take ten or fifteen minutes to evaporate, and even then, it would leave a residue.

But his biggest defense was his caution. He'd approached a thousand buildings like these in his career. He knew how to be quiet and unobtrusive. If there was a vampire in there, he'd probably catch it before it even knew he was there.

The sun was high in the sky when Feller got out of the car, and it made him feel safe.

He crept over to what had been the motel office and peeked in through the slats of the boarded-up window. Inside, it was empty and dusty.

The first motel room was boarded up tight. Feller tried the door, but it was locked. He tried the next three doors, but they were all locked, too. No vampire had entered or exited any of these rooms, as far as he could tell.

Finally, he approached the restaurant. As he was gingerly reaching for the doorknob, the door flew open and several arms shot out and grabbed him. The arms burst into flames, but before he could even shout, they'd dragged him inside.

Rule of Vampire

There wasn't just one vampire in the room; there were over a dozen. Feller tried to struggle, but his arms were being held tightly behind him. Standing in front of him was a boy, probably in his early teens, who looked up at him and smiled.

"I've been reading your reports, Agent Feller," the kid said. "My name is Hoss. Welcome to the local branch of the Council of Vampires."

What does that mean? Feller wondered. These were Wilderings if he'd ever seen one. The kid had a measuring look in his eyes.

"If you kill me, every agent in the Bureau will come after you," Feller said.

"Oh?" the boy said. "I thought they already were." He turned to a tall kid next to him. "Get his keys. The minute it turns dark, drive his car across town and leave it near the Comfort Inn."

"OK, Hoss."

Feller's heart sank. This was an Alpha vampire—an untrained one, perhaps, but a natural. "Did you set up the ambush?" he asked.

"Not me, though I read about it. Sounded like fun." Hoss turned to another boy, who was probably just a couple of years older than him. "Hold him down, Jimmy."

"You heard Hoss! Hold him down!" Jimmy said, delegating, and several vampires rushed forward, grabbed Feller, and dragged him to the table at the center of the room.

"Wait!" he shouted. "I can help you! I have information you need—who's after you, our numbers, our tactics! Whatever you need!"

"Oh, I'm sure," Hoss said. "And once you've been Turned, I'm going to expect you to tell me all about it."

"But…" Feller tried desperately to think of way to save himself. "I can be your spy! You need someone who can move

197

around in the daytime. I'll work for you!"

Hoss walked over to the table and looked down at him. "I'm sure you would, but see, I'm a great believer in the Rules of Vampire. I intend to follow them in all cases. And Rule One is never trust a human."

He reached down and exposed Feller's neck. The agent thrashed his head back and forth, but Hoss reached out with one hand and took hold of his forehead. Feller felt the cold breath of the vampire on his neck, then a sharp pain.

As he felt the life drain out of him, his thoughts went to his fellow agents. They'd never liked him. They'd always made fun of him behind his back. Now they were going to know that they'd been right: he was a failure. A joke.

He closed his eyes as the room went dark.

CHAPTER 35

Once Hoss knew where to look, it was surprisingly easy to find information about vampires on the Internet. It was all there. Since practically no one really believed in vampires, it was all couched as fiction, but after a while, Hoss got pretty good at figuring out what was fantasy and what was reality.

The Rules of Vampire, created by the legendary Terrill, and the Council of Vampires, led by the newcomer Fitzsimmons, especially fascinated him. He responded to those ideas. They made sense. Rules and logic had always been his touchstones, had always guided his actions and kept him safe.

And the fact that his little group of vampires had managed to survive, to stay hidden during what was probably the most massive vampire hunt in the history of vampire hunting—well, that was a testament to the utility and wisdom of the Rules.

Some of the other information—the inner workings of the Council, for example, and especially the FBI reports—had been harder to obtain, but Hoss had always had a natural ability to find out what he needed to know, and the clarity that vampirism gave him made him feel as if no secret could be hidden from him for long. If it had ever had a presence on the Net, he'd find it.

That morning, he'd intercepted a message that the leader of the Council, Fitzsimmons, was flying to Crescent City. Even more exciting, Terrill was coming with him.

There was some politicking going on between the two that Hoss didn't understand. Apparently, there was a human girl in the middle: Sylvie, who, as Hoss understood it, was the sister of the vampire who had started the epidemic, Jamie. How this Sylvie had managed to survive Rule One, he didn't know.

As soon as he joined up with the Council, Hoss was sure they'd tell him all about it.

He'd let each of his followers have a sip of the FBI agent. There were twenty-five in his group now, all of them firmly under his command. A half dozen more had been told they could leave, but only if they carried a GPS-programmed phone. These traitors had been led to the far room and shut inside, and the curtains had been pulled back and they had burned.

Hoss had put the rest to work, turning part of the motel into a factory for making weapons. The day would come when the Council of Vampires would have to fight other vampires, those who wouldn't abide by the Rules. Hoss intended to be ready for that day. He'd have the same weapons that the vampire hunters used.

Though he was pretty sure that neither Jimmy nor Jodie had said anything to the others, except perhaps to Pete, who had suddenly begun to show Hoss some proper respect, all the other vampires seemed to sense that betraying him wasn't a good idea.

They didn't understand. It wasn't about him. It was about the Rules.

Hoss waited for Feller to Turn. He had been timing the procedure, and it seemed to take between one and three hours. According to everything he'd read, this was a new phenomenon. Historically, most people who were bitten never Turned: the figure one in twenty was used. And it usually took days, and that was under ideal circumstances.

Hoss was at the center of an outbreak, and he was taking notes. The Council of Vampires would want to know everything.

Two hours after the FBI agent stopped breathing, he sat up. Hoss had saved the flank of a horse they'd killed the night before in a pasture across the highway, and now he fed it to the newly Turned vampire. Feller devoured the raw meat down to the bone. Slowly, the Wildering look faded from his eyes.

"Can we talk?" Hoss asked.

***

When Feller woke up, he knew at once what had happened to him. He opened his eyes and stared out at the world with vampire sight, sharper and deeper than the vision he'd had as a human. He could see into the shadows. He could see the motivations in the eyes of the other vampires.

Sometimes at night a thought would drift into his brain in the form of a question: *What would it be like to be a vampire, immortal and strong?* Now he realized that the question had always been a desire, too.

Now he knew. It felt good. All the doubts, all the worries about whether he was good enough, all the guilt about the times he'd fallen short and let down his compatriots and had had to cover it up: all that was gone. He existed now for himself and only himself, and it felt good.

He looked at Hoss and knew exactly what to say. "What do you want to know?"

As he was questioned, he answered with only half his mind. The other half marveled at the strength flowing through his veins. He raised his arm to his mouth and felt the fangs extrude, and took a small nip of his own flesh. The blood that welled up was blue.

"Sorry," he said as Hoss fell silent in mid-question.

The young vampire looked annoyed, but he said, "I quite understand. I did the same thing. Now, can we get back to our little discussion?"

"What was the question?"

"How long does the FBI intend to keep searching for vampires?" Hoss repeated impatiently.

"Well, here's the thing," Feller said. "My disappearing won't help. I was the only one keeping us here, frankly. But when they realize I'm gone, they'll gear up for another door-to-door search. I don't think you'll escape their notice a second time."

Hoss gave Feller back his phone. "Call them," he said. "Tell them you're pursuing an out-of-town lead. Tell them that you're satisfied that all that can be done in Crescent City has been done."

This kid is smart, Feller thought. When he'd first woken up, he'd thought he could easily gain control of the situation. But Hoss looked to be firmly in charge, so Feller changed his mind: he'd get out of here at the first opportunity, and go off and explore his new powers without interference from a teenage control freak.

He called Abercrombie and told him what the kid had suggested he tell him. To his amazement, Abercrombie bought it.

"We're packing up," his partner said. "Leaving a skeleton crew. Callendar and Jeffers have asked to stay, but the rest of us are leaving. See you back at headquarters."

"Uh, right," Feller said. He ended the call and shook his head. He'd never thought his colleagues would buy it, but upon reflection, he realized they all wanted out of this small town, and now that Feller had all but given his permission for them to leave, they probably wouldn't question him on it.

The vampires spent the rest of the evening discussing the situation. Hoss let slip the fact that representatives of the Council of Vampires were headed this way and that he intended to meet them. Feller decided that he, too, would like to meet

Fitzsimmons and offer him his services. But he wasn't going to do that as the flunky of some teenage vampire, no matter how smart. He had to get away from here.

They talked through the entire night. It was light outside when Feller finally brought up the subject. "I want to check out the town. See what's happening."

"No," Hoss said firmly. "No one leaves here without permission."

"I understand that," Feller said, keeping the exasperation out of his voice. This kid craved respect, and he tried to show that respect on his face. "That's why I'm asking...boss."

Hoss looked at him suspiciously. Had he overplayed his hand?

"Perhaps, in a day or two," Hoss said.

That would be too late. The Council jet was arriving the next night.

"I really must insist," Feller said, exasperated. "I understand that you're in charge here, but I'm a free agent, young fellow. I've had years of experience. You really are just going to have to let me leave."

Hoss looked over at Jimmy and Pete as if wondering whether he should order them to restrain Feller. Then he shrugged.

"Very well, if you must, you must. This isn't a dictatorship. But I insist that you carry one of our GPS-programmed phones. Jodie? Will you take Agent Feller to where the phones are and let him pick one out?"

"OK, Hoss," she said cheerfully.

Feller followed the little vixen, surprised at how easy that had been. They passed through several rooms with the adjoining walls knocked out, and once again, the planning involved in sheltering this group of Wilderings impressed Feller. From the outside, it didn't look like anyone was in these rooms. Feller had thought there might be one vampire here, perhaps two, and he'd been sure he could take them. He hadn't expected a dozen or more.

Jodie opened the connecting door to the last room and Feller started to step through, but something made him stop. Later, he asked himself what had alerted him. He was an experienced FBI agent, trained to notice small clues. As a vampire, those small clues were magnified. There was the slightest odor of burned flesh. He noticed some strings hanging from the wall and wondered what they were for. He saw some black marks on the floor.

He stepped back.

"You know what?" he said. "I've changed my mind."

From Jodie's surprised expression, he knew that he had guessed right: walking into that room would have been a big mistake. He followed her cute little butt back to the restaurant and savored the looks of alarm on Pete and Jimmy's faces when they saw him. Hoss managed to keep a blank face, but Feller saw a flash of anger in his eyes.

"I'm sorry for putting you through all that trouble," Feller said. "Now I can see the wisdom of your advice. I think I'll stick around."

He moved over to one side of the room and sat down with his back to the wall, and vowed to stay awake until the chance of escape presented itself.

CHAPTER 36

Now that he had found Jamie, all the adrenaline that had kept Robert going for so long had vanished, leaving a husk of a body weakened by pain. When he stood up and took her in his arms, he almost doubled over from the sudden agonizing ache. He gritted his teeth and held back a gasp.

But the warm feeling that washed over him, starting at his forehead and moving downward over his body, cancelled the pain for a brief time. This was the most joyous moment of his life. If there had ever been the slightest doubt that he loved Jamie, it was drowned in the feelings of joy and contentment that suffused his body.

"Why did you leave?" he asked gruffly. "Why?"

She laughed a little into his neck, then raised her head and smiled at him. "I didn't have a lot of choice, what with the bullets whizzing past my head and all."

"You should've come back. I waited for you."

She didn't answer right away, just clasped him more tightly. He stiffened in her grasp as the pain returned, but he managed to ignore it.

"I'm a vampire," she said finally.

"I don't care," he replied. It was a flat statement, but it put an end to both of their doubts.

"Never again," she said. "I'll never leave you again."

***

Jamie knew something was wrong as soon as she hugged Robert. He felt—and looked—as if he'd lost ten pounds in a week. His skin had a gray pallor and his jaw seemed permanently clenched. She didn't know if it was a vampire ability, a woman's intuition, or a lover's empathy, but she could almost sense the tumor in his stomach growing.

"Robert," she said softly. "You should be in the hospital."

"Not unless you go with me," he said.

"You know I can't." She steered him over to a chair. He sat down heavily.

"I don't know what's wrong with me," he said. "It's as if finding you has been such a relief that all my strength has left me."

He's been living for the search, she thought. *It gave him strength.* "I'm here now," she said. "You don't need to do anything but stay with me."

Robert grimaced and clutched his side.

"Where are your pain pills?" she asked.

"I left them at the house," he said through gritted teeth. "They make me sleepy. I didn't want to be tempted. Oh!" He cried out the last word and closed his eyes.

He was leaning over in his chair, the gray tone of his skin had turned to white, and he seemed to be having trouble staying conscious. Jamie grabbed him as he teetered over and carried him to her blankets. She rolled poor Marc out of the way, murmuring, "Sorry."

Robert fell asleep or passed out; she wasn't sure which. Either way, the lines of pain etched into his brow faded. Jamie let him slumber. She couldn't bear to see him this way. He needed medication, and she knew exactly where his pain pills were. It was getting darker outside, and she thought she could get to his house and back again in just a few minutes, before he woke up.

After that, they'd never have to leave the hideaway again. They'd face the end together, in peace.

In the back of her mind, she began to wonder if the pain pills might make him more amenable to the proposal she planned to make. She understood him, and she knew that he'd reject being Turned, so she'd have to find every advantage she could to change his mind.

As she was thinking of leaving, Marc sat bolt upright. "What happened?" he asked.

Jamie knelt next to him. "I have to explain some things to you, Marc."

"I need to get back to the thrift store," he said, looking around wildly. His eyes took in Robert's motionless form, and he frowned as if suddenly remembering his aborted attack. "It's my shift..." He trailed off.

"You're never working there again, Marc," Jamie said.

"What do you mean?"

She took a deep breath. *Might as well just tell him.* In a torrent of words, she explained to him what he was and what that meant.

It was clear he believed her, but he couldn't accept it right away. "Can't I just keep doing the things I was doing?" he asked imploringly. "Can't I just work night shifts or something?"

"Not unless you want to end up eating your customers," Jamie said.

Marc licked his lips, reminded that he was hungry.

"We need to get you some meat," she said. "Will you promise to do as I say?" She knew the wild feelings that were coursing through his body, overriding his brain, his willpower; instincts so strong that he couldn't control them. She knew because not so long ago, she'd felt them herself.

It was because of these savage instincts that she couldn't leave him with Robert. She'd take him with her; they'd drop by the Burger King and hope the pimply-faced girl was working, then zoom over to Robert's house and get his pain medication. With any luck, they'd be back before he woke up.

Just in case, she left him a note. She didn't want him waking up and thinking she'd abandoned him again.

***

The pimply-faced girl wasn't there, but she'd apparently told a couple of her co-workers about their arrangement, because they brought Jamie a bag of uncooked patties.

"Will you take a twenty?" Jamie asked, intending the grab the bag if they said no. "It's all I have left."

One of the boys grumbled but took the cash. "Next time, bring fifty."

"Sure."

Marc could smell the raw meat coming and he almost snatched it out of her hands, but she led him to the beach before she let him gorge himself.

After that, they made it to Robert's house without incident, going through alleyways, down back roads, and across vacant lots. It was amazing how many main streets you could avoid if you tried.

The bottles of pills were on the bathroom counter. They were nearly full, as if Robert hadn't touched them. The doctor had prescribed some pretty powerful medication, Jamie noticed— and he'd done it a month ago. How much worse was Robert's pain now? How did he manage to function?

She shook her head. Putting all the bottles in a plastic bag, she prepared to leave. She'd left Marc outside by the back door as lookout.

When she got outside, he wasn't there.

Jamie frowned. *That's great,* she thought. *Just what I need.* If she had to, she'd leave the baby vampire here, and he'd have to fend for himself.

As the door closed behind her, half a dozen shapes moved out of the shadows. Two of the vampires were holding Marc by the arms. He was snarling and struggling, but they had him firmly in their control.

What looked to be a 10-year-old boy stepped forward. "Jamie, I presume?"

She nodded.

He smiled at her. "I've been looking for you everywhere! The Council of Vampires would very much like to meet you. I'm Hoss, their local representative."

"The Council of Vampires?" Jamie said. "What's that?"

The kid's smile faltered, and he cocked his head at her as if puzzled. "You're not much more than a Wildering, are you? You haven't heard of the Rules of Vampire?"

"Vaguely," Jamie said. She didn't have time for this. She needed to get back to Robert. He might wake up at any moment. If she had to, she'd flee and outrun this bunch.

As if he could read her mind, Hoss motioned into the shadows and three more vampires emerged, holding what looked like medieval crossbows, loaded with wooden bolts. A chill went down her spine.

"You may not know who the Council of Vampires is, but they know about you," Hoss said. "I'm going to take you to them as a welcoming present."

Jamie felt her muscles tense. She wasn't going anywhere with anyone. Robert was waiting for her.

Hoss took one of the crossbows and aimed it at her. Then a thoughtful look came over his face, and he turned and shot the bolt into Marc's side, mere inches from his heart. Marc cried out, and for a moment it looked as if the skin around the bolt had shriveled.

"I'll kill both of you if I have to," Hoss said.

Jamie sagged. Robert was going to wake up and she wasn't going to be there. She could only hope he'd realize that something had gone terribly wrong.

CHAPTER 37

By the time Stuart was ready to leave Bend, he had more than twenty followers. He didn't bother to count them exactly, because he intended to increase their numbers once they were on the road. As darkness fell, his Wilderings descended on a Chevy dealership and took every van they had, one follower per vehicle, and when the vans were gone, the rest of his progeny drove off in biggest SUVs on the lot. In the backs of some of the vehicles were the three car salesmen who'd been on duty, plus a mechanic, all of them dead but uneaten.

They drove down Highway 97. They passed through Sunriver and scooped up everyone on the street, then went on to La Pine, where every fast food worker, gas station attendant, and store clerk they could catch was sucked dry and tossed into the backs of the vans. The first batch of Turned awakened around then and started consuming the newly dead.

They killed and/or ate everyone who could be found in Gilchrist and Gold Hill, and by the time they reached Grants Pass, the vans were full of vampires. They descended on more car lots and scooped up more vans and SUVs, invaded all the neighborhoods lining the highway and filled the new vehicles with bodies, and by the time they reached Cave Junction, these newly Turned were ravenous. They fell upon the little town and ate everyone there but for a lucky few. They drove on, and by this time the invasion force was made up of dozens of SUVs and vans, each of them filled with vampires.

Stuart got a rush out of watching it all happen. He felt like

Genghis Khan. If his father could see him now! His old man had bugged him about making something of his life; too bad he'd never know his son was an organizational genius.

The vampires left carnage behind them, but no witnesses—and the authorities were at least a town or two behind them the whole time. They stopped under the redwoods of Jedediah Smith state park, and Stuart gave instructions to his original followers about what was to be done once they hit town.

They made it to Crescent City with plenty of darkness still left in the night, and the vans and SUVs drove to the four corners of the town and spewed their hungry contents out into the peaceful, sleeping neighborhoods.

After a nightmarish two weeks, the town's residents had started to relax. There hadn't been any attacks for days. They still kept their doors locked and guns handy, but they were sleeping soundly again.

It wouldn't have mattered what preparations they made. The vampires were too numerous and too hungry. For every Wildering who was shot, five more rushed forward.

It didn't matter to Stuart anymore who was Turned and who was eaten. He'd given his progeny instructions to seek shelter before dawn, but inevitably, some of the Wilderings weren't going to remember to do that and would burn.

But even there, Stuart was lucky. It was a cloudy, rainy day. The carnage he'd initiated continued on into the morning, then late into the afternoon. The sun peeked out from the clouds just before dusk and ignited vampires all over town, setting buildings on fire and sending roiling smoke into the sky. Stuart heard sirens wailing and guns blasting, and explosions from gas lines and propane tanks caught in the crossfire—or in actual fire.

Eventually, the humans would bring in reinforcements and would gain the upper hand.

It didn't matter. Stuart had, in one night, made up for all the injustices of his youth: all the teachers who had told him he wasn't trying hard enough, every girl who had led him on, every football player who had pushed him around.

Stuart had positioned himself in the hills above town in an SUV with tinted windows. This was like the best video game he'd ever played. It was complete warfare. He'd unleashed a ravenous plague on his hometown.

He sat back to watch it be consumed.

***

Callendar and Jeffers were running out of bullets. They'd long since used up their holy water and crossbow bolts. The number of police officers reporting in was diminishing rapidly.

When the epidemic had first broken out, they'd talked about this: What would happen if it got out of control? But then they seemed to have nipped it in the bud, and they'd thought all that was left to be done was the mopping up.

They put out an emergency call for help, but the backup units had almost reached L.A. by then, and it would take them most of the night to return to Crescent City. Jeffers shouted at them to fly up, but was ignored.

By late afternoon, it was clear to both agents that by the time backup arrived, there might not be anyone left to save. Callendar spent much of the day on the phone, calling the authorities in nearby towns, but none of them seemed to believe him and most of them were waiting for orders from some higher authority. Jeffers was on the phone, too, trying to convince their superiors in Washington to use their influence on the state police, the National Guard, anyone.

No one could get through their dense bureaucratic heads how dire the situation was. After they had called and begged and pleaded with everyone they knew or could think off, Jeffers and Callendar looked at each other and realized that, at least for the short term, they were on their own.

They'd noticed the high fences and gates surrounding the county fairgrounds and decided that they'd make their last stand there. They called a general retreat. The word went out over the radio, police scanners, and shortwaves: seek sanctuary at the fairgrounds. A National Guard Armory was at the center of the cluster of buildings, and it had thick metal doors and no windows. It would be their final stronghold.

Callendar and Jeffers were surprised by how many people began to show up: both that they'd gotten word in the first place, and that they'd then managed to fight their way through the gauntlet of Wilderings. One of the new arrivals was the quartermaster of the Armory. He unlocked the doors, and they piled guns and ammunition on the ground outside the building. Anyone who felt capable was allowed to pick up a weapon and start using it.

Callendar shuddered. How many people were going to get killed by friendly fire? How many people approaching what they thought was the safety of the fairgrounds were going to get gunned down by trigger-happy defenders?

But there wasn't any choice. By then, the vampires outnumbered the humans, and one on one, they were faster and stronger.

The guns helped even the score.

As the light of day faded, the fairgrounds' floodlights came on. On the other side of the chain-link fence that surrounded the survivors' refuge, Callendar could see masses of vampires trying to climb over the bodies of the fallen. Only a head shot put them down for long, and even then, they'd lurch back to life after a while, rising to their feet and stumbling forward.

Callendar looked around and saw a priest standing in the crowd, saying a blessing over a kneeling mass of people. He grabbed the man roughly by the arm, interrupting him in mid-sermon. "Come with me, dammit."

He had the priest bless a barrel of water, then directed the devout to grab cups, make their way to the fence, and fling the water at the heaving mass of vampires. It had some effect, though it seemed like trying to empty the ocean one cup at a time.

Jeffers found some firefighting equipment in one of the outbuildings, and they handed out axes and set some of the survivors to splintering the wooden tables in the main hall so they could make stakes.

They made Molotov cocktails out of empty soda bottles and started burning the vampires.

The humans managed to hold off the Wildering horde for hours, but by midnight, the bodies were piled so high that vampires were clambering over them to get over the fence and dropping into the perimeter. They'd run out of ammo by then. All they had was some holy water in red plastic cups and broken splinters of wood.

Callendar called the retreat. The survivors—a few hundred dirt-smudged, tired and frightened men, women, and children—ran into the Armory. The doors were slammed shut.

A few minutes later, they heard pounding on the doors, then along the walls. Then they started to feel the building shake and hear the sound of footsteps on the roof.

Callendar saw the same dismay on his partner's face that he was feeling.

They were going to lose.

***

An explosion woke Robert up. At first he couldn't figure out where he was. He looked up through a tangle of branches and saw that it was night. He smelled smoke. There was a flashlight lying next to his arm, and when he turned it on, he saw the note.

His heart sank. If it had been written not long after he'd fallen asleep, Jamie had been gone for hours. He heard another explosion, and as he oriented himself, he realized it was coming from the direction of the fairgrounds.

Robert got to his feet and winced at the pain, but it was nowhere near as bad as it had been when he'd arrived. The sleep had done him some good. The pain was unpredictable: it was always there as a dull ache, but most of the time it didn't flare into a sharp throbbing unless he was tired or overexerted himself. He laughed grimly. He couldn't remember the last time he hadn't been tired or overexerted.

Even through the thick thatch of branches, he could see flickering, as if everything outside the hideaway was burning. He heard distant screams and shouts.

He wrote a note for Jamie in turn. *Meet me at my house,* it said.

Robert crawled through the tunnel and emerged into a scene from a war movie. Fires were burning everywhere, and in the hellish light, he could see bodies littering the streets. Hastily abandoned cars had been left facing every direction. He saw a running figure, and he followed its movement as it approached what appeared to be a standing woman. He heard a shot and the running figure dropped, then got back to its feet and started stumbling toward the woman, who was now running away.

Robert got into his cruiser, which was miraculously unscathed. The second he turned on the engine, the scanner started squawking. He listened in growing disbelief to the news. He locked all the doors and looked out into the flickering darkness. Then he unlocked his door, got out, and opened the trunk. He put on his bulletproof vest, cinched it tight, and ratcheted a shell into his shotgun. He opened the glove compartment and removed the extra clips. He put his pistol on the seat next to him and propped up the shotgun.

Then he pulled out of the parking lot and wove his way through the abandoned vehicles, making his way to the fairgrounds.

***

"You got any clips left?" Jeffers asked.

"None," Callendar answered. "I've been using one of the Army Colt revolvers—I've got three bullets left."

"I've got a flare!" Jeffers asked, holding up the stick. "I plan to light these buggers up!"

Someone started shooting right outside the huge metal doors of the Armory. "Did we leave someone outside?" Callendar asked.

"I don't think so…"

"You'd better let us in!" someone shouted after a volley of shots had been fired.

The agents opened the door a couple of inches and peered out. Abercrombie stuck his big face through the gap. "You gonna let us in or what? I've got a dozen men here, along with a stray cop we picked up on the way in."

They opened the metal door wider, and a squad of fully armed and SWAT gear-bedecked FBI agents ran into the Armory, followed, to Callendar's relief, by Robert.

"I'm glad you made it," Callendar said to his former brother-in-law, securing the door behind him, then turned to Abercrombie. "Is the rest of the crew coming?"

"This is it," Abercrombie said. "We flew up on our own dime when we realized they wanted us to drive up. Hell, they weren't even hurrying."

"Thank you," Jeffers said. He and Abercrombie had never gotten along, but now they shook hands.

"No problem," Abercrombie said. "Feller has disappeared, so for once I didn't have to ask that officious horse's ass for permission."

Jeffers and Callendar laughed.

"Well, we appreciate it," Callendar said. "But I'm afraid you boys might have just busted into the Alamo."

CHAPTER 38

Smoke was billowing out of buildings in downtown Crescent City as Terrill, Sylvie, and the others flew into the airport on the Council's private jet. In fact, there seemed to be fires burning all over town. With the smoke added to the clouds and rain, it was a perfect day for vampires.

"Is this normal?" Fitzsimmons asked Terrill.

"I don't see how it could be," Terrill answered, as puzzled as the Council president was. Vampires had always been rare, and his Rules had made them even rarer. But what would happen if everyone who was bitten became vampire? What would happen if there were no Rules? What if Wilderings weren't sad, forsaken vampires left by their Makers to fend for themselves, but were instead roving free in great numbers, Making other Wilderings every time they hunted?

He could tell Fitzsimmons was thinking the same thing. A strange look came over the Council leader's face, almost as if he was thrilled by the idea, but he quickly closed that look down and replaced it with an appropriately grim expression.

"It is fortunate we came," Fitzsimmons said. He shook his head. "You see? This is what happens when the Rules aren't enforced."

The airport appeared abandoned. They landed without instructions from the tower and taxied up to the small terminal. They only had to walk about fifty feet to the entrance, but even before they left the plane, they saw several figures running toward them.

Vampires. They had a look of wild hunger on their faces, like those newly Made.

Along with Fitzsimmons and Clarkson, Peterson had accompanied them, hobbling on a cane as if he really was an old man. It was an act he put on in public, and it had become so ingrained that he now did it in private, too. Clarkson, who had stayed very quiet, was acting scrupulously neutral toward Sylvie and Terrill.

There was a six-man security crew, led by Cory, who mostly stayed near Sylvie, making it clear they were there to keep Terrill reined in. It would be a challenge to get Sylvie out of their grasp, but ever since their plane had touched down, Terrill had been watching for the opportunity.

Cory waved three of the guards forward to deal with the approaching vampires. They ducked under the clumsy swings of the Wilderings, and their claws ripped into the throats of the attackers. The newly Turned vampires screamed and thrashed and fell to the ground, where the guards finished decapitating them.

This is it! Terrill thought. *This is my chance!*

Two of the remaining guards were watching the action. Only one of them was close enough and alert enough to get to Sylvie, so Terrill decided to concentrate his attack on him.

At the last second, Terrill caught the flash of a face in one of the terminal windows, a glimpse of silver hair and alabaster skin—and a grin.

Terrill continued the motion he'd begun but slowed it down, as if it was a natural movement and not an aggressive one: a burst of enthusiasm, perhaps. He ended up beside Sylvie, who looked at him curiously.

Fitzsimmons had a suspicious look on his face, as if he'd caught Terrill's intention. He opened the door to the terminal and ushered them inside. Sylvie and Terrill went first, followed by the alert guard. Then Clarkson stepped inside. Fitzsimmons began to follow her, but the door suddenly closed in his face, as if it had been snatched out of his hands.

Peterson, who had been close behind him, walked into Fitzsimmons's back with a grunt. "What happened?"

Terrill grabbed the guard who had made it inside with them and twisted his neck until he heard it snap. He dropped the body to the tiled floor. It would take hours for the vampire to recover. Someone was pounding on the door and he heard the glass crack, but it didn't break.

The door on the far side of the terminal flew open, and Michael appeared and beckoned to them. "Hurry!" he said. "That glass is meant to be terrorist resistant, but I'm not sure how it will do against vampires."

Terrill looked back. The guards were smashing at the door and windows with the butts of their rifles. Fitzsimmons was standing there, arms crossed, glaring at him. There was a look on his face that said, *You won't get away from me for long.* But when he glanced at Michael, his expression changed to a mixture of puzzlement and awe. None of the present generation of vampires except Terrill knew what Michael looked like, but it seemed Fitzsimmons had guessed who he was.

There was a large SUV parked just outside the far door, and Michael jumped into the driver's seat as Sylvie and Terrill piled into the backseat. Clarkson got in the passenger seat. Michael tore away before the doors were fully closed, throwing Terrill on top of Sylvie.

"Sylvie?" Terrill said. "I'd like you to meet Michael."

"Michael?" Clarkson breathed. "You mean…*the* Michael?"

"The one and only," Michael said.

Sylvie, unaware that she was looking on a legend, a myth,

simply smiled at him, and he smiled back at her in the rearview mirror.

Clarkson couldn't take her eyes off him.

Michael ignored her.

"The roads are kind of hairy right now," he said. "There are vampires all over the place—vampires who don't know how to act like vampires. Wilderings in bunches. Never seen that before."

"Where are we going?" Terrill asked as Michael swerved past several vampires feeding on the same corpse. There were bodies everywhere. Houses were on fire on almost every block, and the streets were full of Wilderings, who seemed to like to travel in packs.

"The safest place I can think of is Jamie's hideaway," Michael said.

"Jamie?" Sylvie exclaimed. "She's here?"

"She might be," Michael said. "But it's been pretty crazy around here. We can only hope she's safe. If she's smart, she'll be waiting for us in hiding."

The SUV lurched over some bodies in the road and clipped a couple of car fenders, but made it safely to the rundown parking lot that led to the hideaway.

"Better let me go first," Michael said, ducking into the tunnel. After a minute, they heard him give the all-clear: "Nobody home!"

Terrill saw Sylvie's face fall. He motioned for her to go first. He looked around the SUV and saw that the keys were still in the ignition. He drove the vehicle around the side of the thicket and parked it behind some abandoned garages, then loped back.

Sylvie and Michael were reading the notes that Jamie and Robert had left for each other.

"She's alive!" Sylvie said.

"Star-crossed lovers, it appears," Michael added. He looked around the hideaway, then motioned for them to sit down. Clarkson stood guard by the entrance.

"Might as well make yourselves comfortable," Michael said. "I've got a story to tell you."

With the sound of explosions punctuating his story and the smell of smoke and burning flesh in the air, he told them how it had come to pass that Crescent City, California, had, on this day, become the center of the vampire world and the culmination of millennia of planning.

CHAPTER 39

Michael began:

"It is known among vampires that I am old; the oldest living vampire. But I am far older than anyone realizes. I am the progeny of one of the first vampires; that is, the first of the genetic mutants that evolved from humans.

"Yes…we are descended from humans. Vampires like to believe we are a separate branch of evolution. Humans believe that even more strongly. We are superior beings, or we are monsters: in any case, we are different.

"But that isn't the whole truth. Long ago, we split from the human line and became a separate species, yet we are still more human than not. When we bite humans, we genetically alter them—those who survive. Most do not.

"It is our genetics that make us vulnerable to sunlight, that make us immortal and powerful and swift.

"It is our genetics that make us hunger for blood from the moment we are Made.

"It is our genetics that still our conscience and allow us to kill without remorse.

"After a thousand years, ten thousand years—it was so long ago that I can't be sure—I started to feel something again. I would kill and feel remorse. I would look into the eyes of my victims and feel regret at the dimming of their light. I started to avoid humans altogether, hunting wild beasts instead, even though their blood was never as satisfying. I survived for millennia without killing a human. And all that time, I watched as other vampires ran wild, killing without thought.

"I started to think of guidelines to save my kind, rules that would help keep them safe. But I was also thinking of humans, for the rules would mean fewer vampires, which would mean fewer victims. Later, I told Terrill these ideas and he codified them into the Rules of Vampire.

"For a long time, I was satisfied with that. The two species were able to exist side by side, and if humans were prey, they were also often the hunters.

"Over time, I noticed two things. One, the older the vampire, the weaker the bloodthirst. Like me, other older vampires began to feel something for their victims. Two, the older the vampire, the less bloodthirsty their progeny.

"I also noticed that if the victim was already great of heart—someone who was caring, loving, and selfless—he made the transition to the more thoughtful, empathetic type of vampire more quickly.

"Without planning to, almost unconsciously at first, I began to try to protect the older vampires, many of whom, like Terrill, were of my own Making. New vampires were as savage as ever, but they were also careless and often the first to be hunted down by vampire hunters. Over time, because of the weeding out of the more vicious vampires and—thanks to the Rules of Vampire—the survival of the older vampires, our species became less mindless and brutal.

"The vampire of myth—remorseless, savage, evil—was replaced by the cautious, civilized vampire of today.

"Until recently, of course. But that part comes later.

"As time went on, I began to guide this evolution. As with generations of humans modifying their livestock, I was able to watch the change happen. I would guide my progeny toward humans who I thought would benefit the bloodline.

Each generation of vampire seemed less venomous than the last. Terrill's line was especially fruitful. Each of his progeny Turned—if you will—into empathetic vampires sooner than the last, until with Jamie, we got a vampire who was empathetic almost from the beginning.

"I had some failures along the way. Horsham began to shift in the empathetic direction before Terrill did, but that progress was derailed when Terrill killed his lover.

"Then, unexpectedly, Terrill became my greatest success... and yet, also my greatest failure, for he succeeding in dropping out of sight. For some time, I thought he was dead and gave up looking for him. Then Horsham, pursuing his long vendetta, brought Terrill back to light.

"By the time I found Terrill, something completely unanticipated had happened.

"He had become human.

"This, I had never expected. I wasn't sure, actually, that it was what I wanted. I didn't want the vampire species to disappear, only to become more civilized. I thought Jamie was the culmination of my efforts, not Terrill.

"And then a second unforeseen thing happened.

"Jamie's progeny became a new species altogether. Ever since the time of my Making, vampires had been rare. Out of every twenty victims—those left uneaten—only one would Turn. Once the Rules of Vampire took hold, there were even fewer progeny, for the Rules dictated that the prey be consumed, so it was only by accident that the occasional vampire was created. This left me free to guide my own subjects toward Making those I deemed worthy.

"But Jamie's progeny are able to Make vampires with every bite. Since they are young and inexperienced and don't know the Rules, they often leave behind untouched bodies.

"Thus we have the epidemic of today, which threatens our entire species. The existence of these Wilderings is going to be impossible to hide, and once known to the world at large, vampires will be the targets of human wrath.

"We won't win that war. They outnumber us by hundreds of millions, they can move around by day and by night, and they have developed weapons that neutralize our natural speed and strength.

"Somehow, in trying to create empathetic vampires, I have created an even more vicious and remorseless breed.

"They must be stopped."

***

There was a long silence. Terrill had guessed some of this, and the rest was like a story he'd been told once but forgotten. It sounded right.

"So you're saying that we are the results of simple biology," he said. "Genetic freaks."

"No!" Michael said emphatically. "You haven't understood me at all. I have so far told you only half the story, and not the most important part. Hear me."

***

"As the centuries passed, I began to realize something else about what it meant to be vampire.

"Genetics explained many things. But why was it that the crucifix repelled us? Why did holy water burn us? Why could we not walk on consecrated ground? What was it about a wooden stake that made us vulnerable?

"And most of all, why were we forced to walk in the shade, never feeling the blessed daylight?

"It was as if the humans were right: we were damned

creatures, condemned to darkness.

"None of this could be explained by science. It was a realm I felt unable to enter—the realm of religion.

"I never did find an answer to these questions, until one day, by some miracle, Terrill became human. But *how* did he become human? It wasn't because of anything I had done. It certainly wasn't because of genetics.

"It was because of Terrill's moral choices and his sacrifice.

"He suffered, he endured, and he resisted temptation. And he asked for redemption.

"To my utter astonishment, he received it.

"Once again, I dared meddle with nature. I thought perhaps I was defying the will of God, but perhaps I was doing His will.

"I turned Terrill back into a vampire, and he became something new: a vampire who can walk in daylight. I thought, perhaps, this was the culmination of my designs.

"But I realize now they were not my designs. They were the designs of someone far greater than I. They were the designs of the God of men, who I believe is also the God of vampires."

***

There was another long silence. Talk of God and vampires didn't go together in Terrill's experience...and yet.

"I have something I need to show you," he said.

He raised his arm and extended his fangs. From a single pair of puncture wounds, the golden blood welled out, glittering even in the dim light of the hideaway.

Michael gasped. Clarkson looked curious, but obviously couldn't make sense of it.

Michael reached out and caught a drop of the golden blood on his finger. He lifted it to his mouth.

He went into convulsions almost immediately, shaking

violently from head to toe, and Terrill got ready to catch him if he fell. Then the fit subsided and he grew still. His white skin briefly took on an almost human flesh tone, then faded to its usual pallor. He opened his eyes, and they were shining with a strange fervor.

"Clarkson. Drink Terrill's blood," he commanded.

Clarkson looked at Terrill as if asking for permission, and Terrill nodded. It felt right.

Clarkson took one sip and collapsed onto the carpets that covered the ground of the hideaway, thrashing as if she was being killed. A high, steady moan emanated from her frothing lips, and her eyes rolled back in her head.

"What have you done?" Sylvie exclaimed. She dropped down to Clarkson's side and held the vampire's head in her lap so that it wasn't pounding against the ground.

Finally, Clarkson stopped convulsing. Her eyes fluttered open. Her cheeks were flushed and her white-blonde hair had taken on a golden glow. She looked, Terrill marveled, more like a human than a vampire.

"You are God's creatures," Michael breathed. "Not mine. All this time I thought I was being clever, and I was but doing God's will."

Terrill looked inside himself and wondered, *Am I the first of a new kind of vampire? A Golden Vampire?*

Then he laughed. "God's will or nature's gift, it sure is strange. And I'm not sure it solves the problem of the Wilderings or makes us any safer. This whole thing might end in disaster if we don't do something about it."

Clarkson and Michael seemed to be in the throes of some kind of religious ecstasy. In the distance, Terrill could hear explosions and gunfire.

"Hey!" he said sharply. "*Hello?* You guys? We need to go help the humans before they're wiped out!"

"How do we do that?" Sylvie asked.

"We'll have to join them, fight on their side—if they'll have us."

Snapping out of her trance, Clarkson stared at him for a moment, then nodded. *She'd follow me anywhere,* Terrill thought uncomfortably. *I hope I don't get us all killed.* But he was certain it was the right thing to do. His progeny had unintentionally brought this disaster upon the people of this town, and he needed to do what he could to save them.

"I will not be joining you," Michael said. "I will never kill again, either human or vampire. My fate lies elsewhere."

"Then farewell my friend, twice my Maker," Terrill said. He turned toward the tunnel. He could see sunlight peeking through the hedges, and normally that would have stopped Clarkson from following him. But now?

She was a Golden Vampire. She could walk in daylight.

The world of vampires had changed.

CHAPTER 40

When Terrill disappeared behind the bulletproof glass of the airport terminal, Fitzsimmons didn't have time to get angry, because rushing toward them from all sides came Wilderings. They surrounded Fitzsimmons, Peterson, and the five remaining guards and then stopped, sniffing and milling around the European vampires as if trying to figure out whether they were prey. The smell of human was still in the air, and that was confusing them.

One of them lurched forward and tried to bite Peterson, who probably looked like an easy target. Peterson swiftly drew a sword out of his cane and beheaded the attacker. As the head rolled along the tarmac, it seemed to trigger the other Wilderings, who surged forward.

The untrained and clumsy Wilderings were easy to dispatch, and at first the guards were able to create a cordon around Fitzsimmons and Peterson. Then the sheer numbers of their opponents began to take its toll. One of the guards went down and the Wilderings tore into him. The blue blood of the vampire flew through the air and sent the attackers into a frenzy.

Enough of this! Fitzsimmons thought. He strode into the Wilderings, claws and fangs extended. He moved so fast that to him, the other vampires appeared to be moving in slow motion. Peterson followed, nearly as fast, followed in turn by the guards. They fought their way toward the plane and were only a few feet from its door when the Wilderings suddenly doubled in number. It was as if news of the battle at the airport had reached the streets of Crescent City, and those not already attacking the Armory had been diverted to this new target.

Running from Wilderings wasn't something Fitzsimmons could tolerate. Energy surged through him, and the thrill of battle. The guards were all down and Peterson was surrounded. Fitzsimmons turned from the safety of the plane's open door and waded back into the mass of Wilderings.

More Wilderings came, and then more. Amid the joy of battle, it slowly dawned on Fitzsimmons that he might have miscalculated his own strength. There were too many Wilderings: an endless number, it seemed. After a time, even their fresh blue blood failed to replenish his energy. Peterson was standing back to back with him, but the old man was breathing heavily, and it looked as though he was having a hard time lifting his saber.

Fitzsimmons heard the sound of marching feet and dared a glance over his shoulder. There, approaching in a double line, were at least twenty more Wilderings.

Fitzsimmons almost gave up then. He almost bolted for the plane, even knowing that if he broke ranks with Peterson, his back would be exposed and he might be taken down from behind.

But then the approaching lines of vampires did something unexpected. They marched into the melee and started flinging the other Wilderings aside, killing them with an efficiency that made Fitzsimmons wonder if these were reinforcements that had been sent by the Council.

But that was impossible. No one was supposed to know they were here.

Finally, the newly arrived vampires surrounded them. The Wilderings gave up the battle at that point, wandering away as if their bloodthirst had been diverted toward the humans at the center of town once again.

Out of the ranks of newcomers, a young man emerged—no, not a young man, a boy. He saluted them. "Welcome to Crescent City, Councilor Fitzsimmons."

"Who the hell are you?"

"They call me Hoss," the boy said. "I am the leader of the local faction of the Council of Vampires."

Local faction? Fitzsimmons wondered. *What local faction? This is the middle of nowhere.*

"We're not official, of course, though I hope you'll give us your sanction. But I've been reading up on you, councilor, and I want you to know I fully endorse your policy of strict adherence to the Rules of Vampire."

"How old are you, son?"

"I'm thirteen years old, sir."

"No," Fitzsimmons said impatiently. "I can see that's your physical age. I meant, how long have you been vampire?"

Hoss looked confused. "Uh...seven days?"

Fitzsimmons was struck dumb. This child had the manner of a centuries-old vampire, and seemingly the wisdom as well.

"Seven days?" Peterson laughed. "You could've fooled me."

"Shut up, Peterson," Fitzsimmons snapped. This was a prodigy, obviously. Once in a generation, there was a Wildering who understood instinctively what to do. He ought to know: he'd been such a phenomenon himself—which made this young man a potential rival. Fitzsimmons wondered if this was some kind of setup. He'd been nervous about coming back to America. He'd spent decades here late in the last century, until a particularly bothersome vampire hunter had chased him out of the country.

He wouldn't put it past Agent Feller to have set a trap for him. But, Fitzsimmons realized, he wouldn't do it through vampires. Feller would kill any vampire he saw; it would never occur to him to use them as bait.

For now, this wunderkind seemed to be impressed by the Council of Vampires for some reason.

Hoss frowned. "Where's Terrill? I was looking forward to meeting him."

Fitzsimmons ignored the question. Until he knew what this "local faction" represented, he wasn't going to talk about Terrill. "How did you know we were coming?" he demanded. "It was supposed to be a secret."

"A secret?" Hoss said. "Then perhaps you'd better improve your security."

Peterson laughed. "Clarkson would've loved to have heard that."

"Dammit, Peterson, keep your mouth shut." Fitzsimmons was thinking furiously. Perhaps these local vampires could be of use. "I've come all the way from England to track down the vampire who started this outbreak," he said.

"Her name is Jamie," Hoss agreed.

"So you know of her? Can you help us find her?"

Hoss puffed up and put on a proud smile. "I already have her in custody, sir."

"You have her?"

"Yes, sir. If you'll follow me, I'll take you to her."

"You amaze me, young man. By all means, lead the way."

Hoss turned and waved his troops into an honor guard formation, placing Fitzsimmons and Peterson in the middle. As they marched away, Peterson whispered to his boss, "What about Terrill?"

"I'm betting that if anyone knows where he's gone, it will be his progeny, Jamie," Fitzsimmons said.

"You'd better hope so," Peterson muttered. "If Terrill goes

against us, we'll lose the support of the Council. I hate to think what our enemies will do to us then."

"Our enemies had best worry about *us*," Fitzsimmons said. "The Council doesn't matter—only the power it gives us."

***

As they made their way through the town, they saw nothing but chaos. There were no humans to be seen, except the dead bodies littering the streets. Wilderings milled about in aimless bands.

There was a full-on pitched battle going on somewhere inland, but Hoss was leading them in a different direction, toward the beach. The troops marched up to an abandoned motel and stopped.

"This way," Hoss motioned.

Fitzsimmons and Peterson followed him to a boarded-up restaurant attached to the motel.

Hoss knocked on the door. "It's me," he said. "Open up, Pete."

The door flew open. A large teenager was standing there, and behind him was a smaller teen. Both of them held clubs and looked ready to defend themselves until they saw Hoss and relaxed.

The vampires inside the restaurant were a sorry-looking group. The younger people seemed to be in charge; the older-looking vampires appeared dispirited, as if not quite sure they liked being what they were. At least the young vampires looked excited.

Fitzsimmons was just inside the door when he noticed someone at the back of the group. He stepped back. "Hoss!" he exclaimed. "You have a vampire hunter in your midst!"

"Not any more," Hoss said. "Feller's been Turned."

Fitzsimmons was impressed. He wouldn't have thought it possible. Feller had been the most fanatical vampire hunter in history. It was amazing that he'd allowed himself to be Turned.

Feller stepped forward, extending his hand. "Fitzsimmons. I apologize. I had no idea what this was like—how wonderful it is. I was wrong the whole time."

Well, well, Fitzsimmons thought. *Finally, an adult.* Feller would know everything there was to know about vampire hunter operations and techniques. He'd be invaluable.

Hoss's troops came inside, and most of them continued on through a hole in the wall and into the room beyond. Feller saw a crude handwritten sign over an overstuffed armchair that was raised on a dais. On it was listed the Rules of Vampire. *How cute.*

"You've been hiding here the whole time?" he asked.

"I've tried to abide by the Rules," Hoss said. "They've kept us safe, exactly as they were intended to do."

Fitzsimmons put on as big a smile as he could summon. "Very good! Just as it should be! Now then, where's this Jamie, the cause of all the commotion?"

"This way," Feller said before Hoss could answer. Fitzsimmons saw a frown cross Hoss's young face. There was some tension there. No doubt Feller was chafing at being under the direction of a teenager.

Jamie was tied up in the last room, trussed from head to foot. She glared at him. *She'd be dangerous if she ever got loose,* Fitzsimmons thought. Next to her was a young-looking, dark-haired vampire who was also tied up, though obviously in his case it was more for show than anything else. The guy didn't look like he could move, he was so terrified, much less escape.

Fitzsimmons leaned down and grabbed Jamie by the hair. "Where's your Maker?" he demanded. "Where would Terrill hide?"

Surprise flashed across her face, as if she hadn't known that Terrill was back in town. Then her eyes widened with realization, as if she'd figured out exactly where he would hide.

Feller slapped her. "Answer him!"

"I don't know," she said. A trickle of blue blood ran from the corner of her mouth and down her chin, and Fitzsimmons resisted the impulse to lick it off.

She isn't going to tell me, he thought. His eyes fell on the frightened vampire next to her. "Who's this?"

"We don't know," Hoss said. "He was with her when we caught her."

Fitzsimmons saw concern in Jamie's eyes. *She is worse than a human!* he marveled. *I've got her. Her emotions are so easy to read.*

"What's your name?" he asked.

"Marc," the vampire whispered.

"I'm going to hurt you, Marc. Then I'm going to hurt Jamie. Then I'm going to come back to you and hurt you even more." Fitzsimmons leaned down looked him directly in the face. "You're vampire. I can torture you to the point of death and you'll come back. And then I can start all…over…again."

Marc flinched at the tone of Fitzsimmons's voice.

"But you can avoid that very simply," he continued. "All you have to do is tell me where Terrill would hide. Where do you sleep during the day?"

Marc's eyes flicked toward Jamie, who was shaking her head.

"Don't look at her, Marc. She won't want you to tell me— but you don't know Terrill. There is no reason to protect him. And believe me, you'll tell me what I want to know, one way or another." Fitzsimmons took the sword out of Peterson's hand and shoved the blade all the way through Jamie's shoulder. She cried out.

"I'll tell you!" Marc said.

"No, Marc," Jamie gasped. "Don't."

Fitzsimmons pulled the sword out of Jamie's shoulder and sliced into her leg.

"Stop!" Marc cried. "I know a place they might go!"

Fitzsimmons nodded with satisfaction. The boy was too terrified to lie.

"Get him on his feet," he said to Feller. "You're not just going to tell me where this place is, Marc; you're going to show me. We're leaving Jamie here, and if you've lied to me, I'm going to kill you and come back and torture Jamie until she gives me what I want. Then I'm going to kill her, too. Do you understand?"

"Yes," Marc whimpered.

"Feller? I want you to stay here and guard her. Don't let her get away, no matter what. Do you understand?"

"Yes, sir," Feller said. "I'll make sure of it."

"Very good!" Fitzsimmons said. This was going to work out after all! He had Jamie under his control, and he had a vampire hunter turned vampire who was calling him "sir." And soon, he'd have Terrill back.

He grabbed Marc by the shoulder and propelled him toward the door, waving for Peterson to follow. Hoss turned to his crew, ordering them to line up.

"Not you," Fitzsimmons said dismissively. "You stay and take care of your little clubhouse. When I get back, we'll discuss whether the Council wants a junior chamber."

Peterson laughed.

Fitzsimmons didn't look behind him. If he had, the look on Hoss's face might have given him pause. He might have tried harder to placate the young vampire.

Hoss sat back in his armchair, put his chin in his hand, and started to think.

CHAPTER 41

Time had never passed more slowly. Callendar was ready to throw his watch away, because it had become a distraction. It lied to him, telling him only minutes had passed since the last time he'd checked when he knew it had been hours.

The Wilderings were finding the cracks in the Armory's defenses. There was a row of skylights down the center of the roof, barely visible but just large enough for vampires to get through. The creatures squeezed through the broken glass and fell with loud thumps to the concrete floor. A few minutes later, if not dealt with, they got to their feet, seemingly no worse for the fall, and started attacking people.

It was easy enough to move everyone to the side and dispatch the wounded vampires before they could recover. But then the metal sidings of the building began to be pried apart. A few of the humans inside were grabbed, pulled toward the gaps, and bitten. Several vampires even managed to make it into the Armory.

To the horror of the trapped people, the cops inside with them killed the newly bitten before they could Turn. By now, the civilians were gathered at the far end of the building, which was flush with the hillside. So far there hadn't been any breaches there. Callendar wasn't sure if the people were more afraid of the vampires or the cops, armored in SWAT gear, who were supposed to be protecting them.

More and more vampires were falling through the skylights, and the gaps in the sides of the building were getting bigger, despite the best efforts of the vampire hunters. They were running out of bullets, even with the extra ammo that Abercrombie and his crew had brought.

Three of the dozen vampire hunters had been killed so far, taken down from behind or simply overwhelmed by the number of Wilderings. Civilians who had some training had picked up the dead hunters' weapons, but they had also been killed.

The lack of firepower wasn't the problem: bullets didn't kill the vampires, only slowed them down. It was the lack of more permanent solutions that was the real issue. Beheading was the only sure means the humans had to dispatch the vampires, and they had only a few sharp knives. It was awful work, and they took turns doing it. They were all covered in blue blood. Fire would have worked, but within the confines of the building, it was deemed too dangerous.

They had barrels of gasoline, and Callendar was getting ready to suggest that they clear a space in the middle of the floor, pile up the bodies, and take their chances with fire.

He looked at his watch. *The damn thing's frozen,* he thought. Only three minutes had passed since the last time he'd checked. Dawn was hours away, and the last weather forecast he'd heard was for a continuation of the previous day's overcast, rainy skies.

There was a rhythmic pounding at the front door and someone outside cried, "Let us in!"

Callendar sidled over to the door. It was the most secure part of the building once it was locked, so no one was near it. He opened it a crack, peeked out, and saw a slender, dark-haired woman who was obviously human; beside her was another woman, tall, fair, and blonde, who moved so fast as she fended off the vampires attacking them that she must have been vampire herself. On the other side of her was…

No, he thought. *That's impossible.*

He had studied the pictures of Terrill for decades, never expecting to actually meet the Alpha vampire. Yet here he stood. At his very doorstep. Killing other vampires.

Callendar opened the door. Later, he would ask himself how he could have done such a crazy thing. But at the time, the sight of Terrill's speed in fighting off the Wilderings decided him. Terrill, it was rumored, no longer killed humans. He was the originator of the Rules of Vampire, which forbade the very things that the Wilderings were doing.

And frankly, the humans needed the help. If something drastic didn't happen soon, they were going to lose this fight.

Terrill held the rear as the tall female vampire led the human girl into the Armory. Terrill slashed left and then right, taking out several attackers with each movement. To Callendar, he was a blur—until he appeared inside the Armory. Then, standing very still, he said, "Better close the door."

Callendar slammed it shut. Abercrombie had made his way over and had his assault rifle trained on Terrill. "Tell me that isn't who I think it is," he said.

"I'm Terrill. I'm here to help."

Abercrombie raised the barrel of his gun. "Well, I'll be damned. And Clarkson too, if I'm not mistaken."

In response, Clarkson rushed to his side and caught the vampire who was about to jump onto the agent's back just as it leaped. She beheaded it with one swipe of her claws.

"If you could help us dispatch the wounded vampires," Callendar said, "that would be a big help."

"Please make sure that Sylvie is safe," Terrill said in a calm voice.

Robert had approached by then. "I'll take care of her."

Terrill nodded and motioned to Clarkson, who followed him as he moved swiftly toward the vampires who lay, broken and battered, under the skylights. Callendar shuddered as the Alpha vampire began efficiently beheading the enemy wounded. The cops went back to firing at the invading Wilderings, trying for head shots.

Robert led Sylvie toward the cluster of Crescent City civilians, saying, "This is the safest spot." He turned and smiled at her. "If that is Terrill, then you must be Sylvie."

Sylvie looked at him curiously. There was a warm, friendly tone in the cop's voice, almost as if he knew her.

"Have we met?"

"No," he said. "But I know your sister, Jamie. She's told me all about you."

"Jamie! Is she here? Is she safe?"

He shook his head, troubled. "I'd hoped she was with you."

Half the vampire hunters were positioned between the civilians and the rest of the building, making sure that none of the Wilderings got through. Robert took up the last position, directly in front, and put a fresh clip into his rifle.

Toward the front of the Armory, Callendar checked his watch and cursed. Only ten more minutes had passed. It was as if they were the last humans on Earth and everyone outside this building had turned into vampires. The walls shuddered under the force of the attacking horde.

One minute at a time, Callendar thought. Without looking at it, he peeled off his watch, dropped it to the ground, and stomped on it. *One minute at a time.*

***

Hoss had his spies out all over town. One of them returned in the middle of the night, a couple of hours after Fitzsimmons left, reporting that there was a battle raging at the county fairgrounds, and what's more, several vampires had joined the humans in the fight.

"Describe them," Hoss demanded.

The vampire described Clarkson almost exactly, and the other vampire—the tall, dark one—had to be Terrill.

Hoss was puzzled. Fitzsimmons hadn't seemed to be concerned about the outbreak of Wildering vampires breaking the Rules en masse. No, he'd seemed more interested in tracking down Terrill, who, it appeared, had been his prisoner.

How was that possible? Terrill was the author of the Rules of Vampire; how could he be a prisoner of the organization whose very purpose was to enforce the Rules? Clearly, everything wasn't what it seemed.

Fitzsimmons had acted more like the vampires whom Hoss had sent to the curtained room to be executed: concerned only for himself, not the welfare of all.

Hoss was beginning to wonder whose side he was supposed to be on. Jamie was his grandmother, in a way. She was the Maker of all these new vampires—but it appeared that was not by choice. Indeed, from what Pete and Jimmy had told him, it was likely she had tried to stop it from happening.

Now Hoss was being told that Terrill had joined the humans in fighting the Wilderings, thus breaking Rule One: Never trust a human.

If the Rules were strictly enforced, Terrill was condemned. Yet these Wilderings were breaking *all* the Rules. Perhaps, Hoss reasoned, Terrill was joining the enemy of his enemies, for the greater good. Which was more dangerous to vampire kind: letting a few humans who already knew of their existence live, or a bunch of Wilderings who threatened to break out into the wider world and let all mankind know about the vampire species?

Terrill was right, Hoss decided. Fitzsimmons was wrong.

He made his way to the room where Feller was guarding

Jamie. Pete and Jimmy followed him.

"What do you want?" Feller asked.

Hoss examined the former vampire hunter. *Should I just get rid of him?* Hoss wondered. *He's going to keep on being a problem.*

Jimmy gave him a look, as if to ask, *Should I take him out?* Hoss shook his head slightly. "I wish to talk to this vampire," he said, nodding in Jamie's direction.

Feller clearly wanted to deny the request but couldn't think of a reason to. Hoss ignored him.

"Your Maker was Terrill?" he asked Jamie.

At first, she was stubbornly silent, as if she was going to refuse to answer any questions, but then she seemed to figure out that he wasn't like Fitzsimmons: he was only asking because he was curious. "Yes," she said.

"How is that possible?" he asked. "Terrill stopped killing humans."

"I was an accident," Jamie said. "A mistake that he has tried his best to atone for."

"So you trust him?"

She hesitated, then nodded. "He loves my sister, and my sister loves him, so I guess I do trust him. I wish I had stayed in Bend under his tutelage. All of this might have been avoided."

Hoss hesitated. He could try to free Jamie and take her with him. It would be a present to Terrill, to show his goodwill. But he wasn't quite ready to break with Fitzsimmons, which might mean breaking with the Council of Vampires. Overall, Hoss still thought the Council a very good idea.

"Hoss," Jamie said, bringing him back to the present. "There is a policeman out there named Robert Jurgenson. If you see him, please...don't hurt him. Tell him I love him."

Love? Hoss wondered. *Have I ever felt loved? Why does this woman's appeal touch me so?*

Hoss turned and, without a word to Feller, walked back to the rest of his followers. He knew Feller wouldn't leave: he was Fitzsimmons's creature.

"Form up ranks," he commanded. "We're marching to the Armory."

"Going to help kill off the vampire hunters?" Pete asked, sounding enthused.

"No. We're going to go help them."

CHAPTER 42

Stuart couldn't believe the magnitude of the cataclysm he'd set into motion. He'd expected the authorities—the freaking Army, even!—to show up and shut the Wilderings down. But either no one could believe what was happening, or in all the chaos, the communication lines were down, or it was just plain stupid bureaucratic incompetence. The only people putting up a fight were a few cops and citizens at the fairgrounds, and they were surrounded.

He'd stayed away from the action at first, catching a few unwary stragglers but not wanting to get caught in what he was certain would be a heavy response, but as hour after hour passed, he started wandering closer to the center of the mayhem. Accompanying him, he had a dozen of the first vampires he'd Made, who were loyal to him and him alone. He meandered about, watching people being chased down, seeing vampires run over by cars driven by panicky humans. It didn't matter to him who lived and who died.

They'd never forget this day. The people of Crescent City, who'd treated him like a loser, were paying the price. He only wished he had some way of letting them know who'd been responsible for bringing this horror down on their heads.

Stuart decided he wanted to be there at the end, when the last of the humans in this town were snuffed out. He started walking down the coast highway, keeping an eye on the horizon. It was a moonless night, but with his vampire vision, he could see the heavy clouds overhead. He motioned to his followers and picked up the pace.

***

Callendar thought, for a few moments, that they might even win. The addition of Terrill and Clarkson to the fight helped hold back the tide at first, but there was a seemingly endless number of vampires outside. One side of the Armory was tilting inward as the walls were pushed in by the Wildering horde.

Callendar now regretted throwing away his wristwatch. He had absolutely no idea what time it was, or whether dawn would come in time to save them. When he saw the rain start to trickle through the skylights, his heart sank. If there were heavy clouds, it didn't matter if dawn came. It might weaken the vampires and slow them down, but it wouldn't stop them.

When the corrugated metal walls finally crashed in, he expected a swarm of vampires to tumble in after them.

Instead, he saw a line of vampires facing outward, pushing back against the Wilderings trying to get in. A single small vampire faced him, a young teenager, his hands raised as if to say, *Don't shoot.*

Callendar saw Abercrombie raise his rifle, but signaled him to hold off. He walked toward the little vampire and looked down at him. "Who are you?"

"They call me Hoss," the kid said. "I'm here to talk to Terrill?"

The vampire in question walked over to them. "I'm Terrill."

"We wish to join you, at least for the duration of the emergency. As believers in the Rules of Vampire, we believe a Wildering infestation is the worst thing that can happen to our kind."

"Very wise," Terrill said. "Since you are here, perhaps you can help us prop this wall back up."

Everyone was energized by the addition of several dozen

new defenders. Some of the men and women from the pack of humans huddled in the corner came over to help pile up wooden planks, barrels, concrete blocks—anything they could find, including their own bodies—to shore up the wall against the vampires outside.

"We aren't strong enough or numerous enough to hold them back for long," Hoss said. "You'll need to take the fight to them."

Terrill nodded. He'd been thinking the same thing. Who *was* this little mastermind of a vampire? Where had he come from? How did he even know about the Rules of Vampire, much less feel such loyalty to them?

"How do you know all this?" he asked.

"Google."

It is a new world, Terrill thought, *where time and distance means little, and a 13-year-old boy can find the truth by simply looking through the information available on a machine.*

However this debacle ended, it was going to be difficult to keep it a secret, though that would probably be in both the vampires' and the vampire hunters' best interests.

Terrill looked around, but Hoss had disappeared on him. Then he saw the young vampire approaching the humans in the corner. The local cop, Robert, had his gun trained on him as he approached.

"You're Robert Jurgenson?" he heard Hoss ask.

Then he heard a huge crash and turned to see the heavy doors fly open and a car careen through. It slid to a stop. The Wildering driver's head was smashed against the steering wheel and he wasn't moving, but he was followed by a wave of vampires, who streamed toward them.

Terrill raised his pistol and shot the leading vampire, whose head disintegrated. He fired again, hitting a vampire who looked like she'd been a middle-aged housewife in the throat.

She fell, gurgling, to the floor. He pulled the trigger again and heard a click.

Terrill lifted a jagged piece of metal he'd pried from the wall and swung it at another one of the Wilderings. It was dull: the vampire's head didn't come completely off, but flopped to one side. He swung again and sent another vampire reeling sideways, but the attacker got up again and hobbled toward him. The second blow split the thing's head open.

He saw Jeffers pull the vampire out of the driver's seat, take his place there, and back the car toward the doors. Between him and Abercrombie and a few of the surviving cops, they got the metal doors closed and the car placed against them. But it was only a matter of time before one of the other vampires outside got the same idea.

Robert Jurgenson approached him. "I'm sorry, I have to leave. I know where Jamie is. I need to rescue her."

Hoss appeared at his side, as if instinctively knowing that Terrill needed to step back from the action. Terrill looked at the tall cop and didn't like what he saw. The cop was leaning to one side, wincing in pain, his hand unconsciously clutching his waist. He was pale and shaky.

"You're in no shape to save anyone," he said.

"I have to try."

"I can help you," Terrill said. "I can Turn you. You will be stronger than any vampire—if you survive my bite."

"No." Robert looked stubborn. "I will not become vampire."

"Then you will not save Jamie," Terrill said bluntly. "If you become vampire and you don't like it, I will help you end it."

Robert hesitated. Then he swallowed hard and nodded.

"If you are not pure of heart, if you have evil within you, my bite may do more harm than good," Terrill warned. "But if you have goodwill toward others, you may be turned into something new in this world. You'll be a golden-blooded vampire."

"I understand," Robert said. "Do it."

Terrill wasted no time. He scooped the man into his arms and sank his fangs into his neck. The cop was skin and bones, he realized. The uniform had hidden the extent of his decline.

Robert closed his eyes and relaxed. Terrill lowered him slowly to the floor, where he twitched once and was still. It was the quickest Turn Terrill had ever seen: almost immediately, Robert sat back up again. There was awe and determination in his eyes. "I had no idea," he said wonderingly.

"Now you must feed from me to complete the change."

Robert discovered that just by willing it, he could get his fangs to extrude. He took Terrill's offered arm and bit into it.

It was as if the sun had burst into his body, charging every cell, repairing and strengthening every muscle and tissue, making his blood course faster and more smoothly, the oxygen in the air going directly to his head. He almost fell to his knees under the onslaught of sensations, but he adjusted quickly to his new existence. It felt…right. He thought more clearly and felt more vibrant than he'd ever felt in his life.

"Go!" Terrill said. "Go, with my blessing. If I never see either of you again, tell Jamie I'm sorry."

Robert nodded. He ran toward the back of the building, where a small breach in the wall had been covered by a wooden pallet. He pushed the pallet aside and disappeared into the darkness.

CHAPTER 43

Michael stood in the middle of the hideaway as if he'd been waiting for them. Marc emerged from the tunnel first, and when he started to stutter an apology, Michael shushed him. "It's OK, Marc. There was nothing you could have done. It was destined to be."

Fitzsimmons came next, followed by Peterson. Upon seeing the gray-haired vampire staring calmly at them, Peterson drew the blade from his cane.

"I was expecting Terrill," Fitzsimmons said.

"I'm sure you were," Michael said. "You'll have to settle for me."

"And you are…?"

"Oh, come now, Fitzsimmons. You know perfectly well who I am."

Fitzsimmons cast a nervous glance at Peterson, stepped back, and pulled out his pistol. "If you are who you say you are—and I'm not sure I believe it—then why are you here? Why now?"

"One thing leads to another, to another, to another, until they lead to the end," Michael said serenely.

"The end?"

"Yes. The old world has ended and a new one has begun… though you seem intent on trying to destroy it."

"I am only following your precepts," Fitzsimmons protested. "The Rules you suggested."

"Are you?" Michael asked. "Be honest, Fitzsimmons. No one else is here besides a frightened child and one of your flunkies.

You can tell me the truth. Do you really believe in the Rules of Vampire?"

Fitzsimmons looked blank for a moment. Then he broke into a grin. "Well, well. I think perhaps I believe you really are Michael. You're the only one to have figured it out."

"But it's obvious, isn't it?" Michael said. "How better to discredit the Rules of Vampire and break apart the Council than to so strictly enforce them that you ignite a rebellion against the very things you profess to believe? I have to admit, you've done a good job of it."

Peterson spoke up, a disbelieving tone in his voice. "Fitz? Is this true?"

"Shut up, Peterson. You've never cared about anything but power."

"But without the Rules, the Wilderings will take over and we'll be doomed," Peterson said. "We'll be hunted down and destroyed!"

"Many of us, perhaps," Fitzsimmons conceded. "But those of us who survive will be *free!* Free to do as we please, when we please, to whomever we please, Rules be damned."

"Then why do you want to capture Terrill?" Peterson asked, looking confused. "He created the Rules!"

Michael laughed grimly. "He doesn't want to capture Terrill. He wants to kill him."

Fitzsimmons didn't deny it.

The vampires stood there staring at each other while outside, the sound of gunshots and explosions rose to a crescendo.

"Killing Terrill was the last obstacle," Fitzsimmons said finally. "Or so I thought. But killing Terrill's Maker, the one who helped him develop the Rules...that will be even better."

Looking nervous, Peterson raised his sword, as if expecting Michael to attack at any moment.

Michael shook his head. "Do as you will. I will not defend myself. But I don't think the results will be what you expect."

Fitzsimmons raised his pistol and shot Michael three times in the chest. The ancient vampire fell to his knees, but he was still conscious. He had a rueful smile on his face. "I have lived a long time," he said softly. "It is long past time I ended it."

"Peterson!" Fitzsimmons shouted. "Finish it!"

Peterson appeared to be frozen in place. Fitzsimmons grabbed the sword out of his compatriot's hand and raised it over Michael.

Michael looked at Marc, who was cowering in the corner. "Remember this, son. Tell the story…"

The blade slashed down, seeming to catch all the light in the room, flashing like lightning, and Michael's head rolled toward Marc, who screeched and scrambled out of the way. He kept going, diving into the tunnel and disappearing from view. Peterson started after him.

"No," Fitzsimmons said. "Let him go. We don't need him anymore." He walked over to Michael's head and lifted it by the hair. The ancient vampire's face looked calm, at peace. The legendary Michael was the easiest kill Fitzsimmons had ever made.

He tossed the head into the branches of the enclosure and turned away with a dismissive shrug.

***

Stuart was leading his followers toward the sound of gunfire when, out of the corner of his eye, he caught a glimpse of someone appearing as if from nowhere. The vampire moved fast, running around the corner and out of sight, but not before Stuart recognized him.

It was Marc, the last vampire Stuart had Turned before

leaving town. *Interesting.* he thought. *Apparently he has a hidey-hole.*

Marc and Jamie had had a strong connection, he remembered. It was entirely possible that they were hiding in the same place. Stuart wasn't sure what he'd do if he found Jamie: kiss her, or kill her. *Perhaps both,* he thought.

He left the road and approached the spot where he'd seen Marc appear. Sure enough, there was a tunnel under the blackberry bushes.

"Follow me," he said to his progeny, and crawled into the hole.

He emerged into what looked like the living room of a house, if the house had been made of shrubbery. One vampire was throwing the head of another vampire into the bushes. A third vampire, who looked like an old man, was standing nearby, looking horrified. The room was splattered with blue blood.

"Fitz!" cried the old-looking vampire.

The vampire who had thrown the head turned and frowned at him. Stuart took an immediate dislike to him. "Fitz" had the manner of every teacher, every relative, every authoritarian adult who had ever looked down on him: the pompous, smug look of someone who thought he was in charge.

"Who are you?" the vampire demanded.

"My name is Stuart. This is my town."

"Your town?" The man called Fitz laughed. "And you're welcome to it. What do you want, Stuart? We're a little busy here."

"I want to know what you're doing here. In my town."

"You do, do you?"

That's it, Stuart thought. *Vampire or no vampire, I'm killing this asshole.* The last of his followers had come in, and the room was crowded.

"Grab him," he said, and three of his men rushed forward.

The bossy vampire had a sword and he chopped at his attackers, and Stuart was interested to see how fast the movement was.

As his progeny struggled to control Fitz, Stuart motioned for Pete and Jimmy to help them. Between the five of them, they managed to secure the furious vampire. The sword hit the carpet with a dull thud.

The older-looking vampire had backed away into one corner. Stuart raised his finger at him. "Stay out of this."

"Stop this at once!" Fitzsimmons shouted angrily. "You can't do this to me! I'm Jonathan Fitzsimmons, president of the Council of Vampires!"

"Council of Vampires? What the hell is that?"

"We are the governing body of our people."

"Well, Mr. President Vampire, I don't believe in governing *anything*." Stuart reached down and picked up the sword.

The prisoner changed his tone. "Wait, young man. You've got me all wrong. I am against the Rules more than anyone. I only joined the Council in order to destroy it. I'm like you. I want freedom…"

"Make up your freaking mind," Stuart said. Then he grinned and shrugged. "I don't really care, actually. I don't like you, mister. This is *my* town, and you're interfering with my plans. I'm going to make sure you never interfere again. Hold him down, boys."

"Wait!" The foreign vampire's dignity was now completely gone. He started babbling. "I can help you! I know things that will —"

Stuart brought down the sword as hard as he could. The blow severed the connective tissue in the vampire's shoulder and his arm flopped to the ground. Blue blood splattered all over the nearby bushes. As Fitzsimmons screamed, Stuart chopped off his other arm. Then he stood back to examine his handiwork. *Not quite done,* he decided.

He brought the blade down on the vampire's right ankle and the foot dropped away; then he took off the other foot.

Stuart nodded in satisfaction. "See you around, Mr. President. Next time I'll take your head."

At the last second, he decided to keep the sword and crawled out of the tunnel with it in his hand. Within a few hundred feet, he had already dismissed the incident from his mind.

***

Peterson stared down at his boss, uncertain what to do. Fitz wouldn't stop screaming, so Peterson drew back his foot and kicked him in the head. He fell mercifully quiet.

Can he survive this? Peterson wondered. He'd never cared much for his boss. Too arrogant. But one thing he knew for sure: without Fitz, his power was gone. He'd be at the mercy of his opponents. As long as Fitzsimmons was alive, there was a chance he could recover his power.

It was certainly an eye-opener to know that Fitz's real agenda was to destroy the Council. But he'd been right: Peterson didn't care, as long as he could retain his power, prestige, and privileges. He'd have to stop Fitzsimmons before he finished the job, of course, or there would be no power left to be had.

Fitz will be at my mercy, Peterson thought. *Until a transition can take place, he can be a figurehead. Hah!* He laughed at the image. A figurehead would be all Fitz *could* be, given his new circumstances. Peterson picked up his former boss's body and slung it over his shoulder.

The private jet was still sitting on the tarmac, with enough fuel to make it to the nearest airport. It was Peterson's jet: he'd chosen it and flown it, though the Council officially owned it. One of those little perks of being a councilor, and unfortunately, he still needed Fitzsimmons for that.

Peterson didn't know what the hell was going on in this town, and he no longer cared. He crawled through the tunnel, shoving Fitz's body along before him, stood up, slung the still-bleeding vampire over his shoulder again and started trotting toward the airport.

He could be in the air within the hour.

***

Marc watched all the comings and goings, hidden in a broken-down garage within sight of the hideaway's entrance. He was in shock. He didn't know what to make of what he'd just seen.

He remembered the look of peace on Michael's face. He'd obviously been willing to be sacrificed, since he'd stood there and let Fitzsimmons kill him. It was as if he'd *wanted* it to happen.

Marc felt a kind of religious awe overtake him. This story must be told: how Michael, the oldest and most powerful vampire in history, had allowed himself to be sacrificed rather than defend himself, rather than kill again; how his progeny, Terrill and Jamie, were the inheritors of that philosophy.

In Marc's mind, the words were already flowing.

He made his way to the thrift store, which had been looted in his absence. He closed the door of his office, sat at his desk, pulled out a piece of paper, and starting writing.

The Ancient One, Michael, gave his life that we might live...

CHAPTER 44

Robert emerged from the Armory and quickly rolled a large rock against the hole in the wall. He looked around to see if any of the Wilderings had noticed, but they were ignoring him, perhaps sensing that he'd been Turned and was no longer a target.

He made his way through the mass of vampires and out onto the street. His police cruiser was still there, and he had the keys in his pocket. He wended his way through the cluttered, chaotic streets, at times being forced to drive over sidewalks and lawns, and even through a fence or two. Once on the highway, the going was easier, and he reached the abandoned motel and restaurant a few minutes later.

Robert had been ready to give his life for Jamie. But Terrill had asked the right question: Was he willing to become vampire to save her?...for his life wasn't going to be enough.

He'd thought about it from time to time, of course. What dying man wouldn't? But he'd rejected it as against God's will. We were given time on this Earth, each our own measure, and it was not for us to question it: that's what he'd always believed.

But it was no longer about him. It was about Jamie—and as a weakened, mortal man, he had no chance of saving her.

To his great surprise, his love for Jamie hadn't lessened after his Turning, nor had his concern for others. He'd always held the traditional view that vampires had no conscience—well, not that he'd ever believed they really existed. But if they did exist, he'd always thought, they would be savage creatures filled with bloodlust. That seemed to be true for the vast majority of those who had been Turned vampire, he now knew.

But there was a new breed, exemplified by Terrill, Jamie and Clarkson, and (he hoped) himself, who didn't kill unless it was necessary, who felt remorse, who controlled their bloodlust. Terrill had called them Golden Vampires.

As Robert stood at the doorway of the motel, he realized that all his youthful vigor had returned, plus a speed and strength he hadn't known was possible. The door was locked, but he broke it open with only a push.

The room was a mess, as if a band of teenagers had been camping out there. An armchair with most of its stuffing coming out was set beneath a crude sign with the Rules of Vampire written on it in colored marker. Despite his urgency, he took the time to read the six Rules.

He shook his head. They were not going to be his Rules, for they still involved the killing of innocents, and he wasn't going to do that. If he couldn't restrain his impulses, he'd take Terrill up on his offer and end his existence.

But not until he had saved Jamie.

He made his way quietly through the holes in the walls until he reached the last room. Jamie was tied up, leaning against the wall, looking as though she'd been beaten, with blue blood all down her front. She hadn't healed because she hadn't fed. Her head was hanging down on her chest.

Standing next to her, his eyes fixed on the door as if waiting for Robert, was FBI Special Agent Feller, still dressed in his SWAT gear.

"You know, when Callendar told me you'd fallen in love with a vampire, I couldn't believe it," Feller said. "Straitlaced, self-righteous Robert Jurgenson? Of course, now I understand the appeal; I just didn't expect it of you." He narrowed his eyes.

"You've been Turned? I wouldn't have thought you'd let that happen, either."

"I've been Turned," Robert agreed. "But I have no intention of living as a vampire, feeding off others. I let myself be Turned for only one reason."

"To save your girlfriend?" Feller was mocking him, but Robert didn't care.

Jamie was trying to lift her head; her eyes were trying to focus on him. "Robert?" she said softly. "Run, Robert. You can't beat a vampire."

Feller laughed. "She seems to think you wouldn't allow yourself to become vampire, Robert. I think you've disappointed her."

"Let her go, Feller," Robert said. "What does it matter to you?"

"It doesn't; not in the least. Except...the president of the Council of Vampires asked me to guard her, and, well, I think he can do more for me than some small-town cop."

"Always sucking up to authority, aren't you, Feller?" Robert shook his head. "Becoming vampire hasn't changed you a bit— you always were a petty, soulless opportunist."

That hit home. Feller's face flushed a dark hue from the sudden infusion of blue blood. "Get out of here, Jurgenson. You can't take me—you never could. I'm a trained federal agent and you're just a local cop. No contest. Being vampire? That will just make your defeat faster."

A vampire trained in the martial arts, Robert thought, *might be a very dangerous thing. But a vampire fighting to save the woman he loves is even more dangerous.*

Feller attacked, and from the beginning, it was clear that Robert couldn't match his moves. He didn't even see them coming at first. He found himself flying across the room, slamming against the wall, then flying in the opposite direction before he'd even had a chance to get up.

And then something changed. He still had no way to compete with Feller's training, but it was as if he started to see the attacks coming. He stepped aside from one, ducked underneath another, and after he dodged a third blow, he slammed his fist into Feller's stomach.

Feller doubled over, but only for a second. He straightened up, looking a little confused, and then, in a blur of motion, was on Robert again, to his left, to his right; but still Robert seemed to anticipate and block his every blow.

Robert went on the offensive. He didn't try to use any of the moves he'd been trained in, for he suspected Feller would be prepared for that. Instead, he used his anger and his fear for Jamie's safety to fuel his attack, laying into his opponent with a flurry of blows. Feller only blocked half of them. The other half opened wounds on his body, and blue blood flew about the room.

Jamie was trying to get up, despite being weak, wounded, and still tied up. She was watching Robert with an amazed expression.

Feller, too, was looking shocked. He retreated under Robert's fury.

Too late, Robert saw that he'd retreated right over to where Jamie lay. *Clever.* The agent pulled out a wooden stake and placed it over Jamie's heart.

"Stay back," he warned. "If I can't keep you from taking her, I'll kill her first."

Robert stopped. There was a curtain covering the window, and for the first time in days, sunlight was peeking through. The clouds had broken at last.

Robert started toward Feller.

"I warned you!" Feller slammed the stake into Jamie, who

let out a huff and then a regretful-sounding sigh. Robert reached them just as the stake went in and slapped Feller across the room.

He put his arm down to Jamie's mouth. "Bite," he commanded.

She looked up at him, but didn't seem to understand his order. There was a look of love and resignation in her eyes, as if she was simply glad to see him one last time. He tore into his own arm, and a surge of golden blood poured out of him and into her mouth.

Then Feller landed on his back, and Robert felt the stake go through his heart. Desperately, he reached up and tore open the curtains.

Robert felt the sunlight on his skin, and he heard screaming, though he wasn't sure if it was himself or Jamie or Feller he heard, or all of them. Then, blessedly, he passed out.

***

He woke up with the sun on his face. He felt someone take his hand, and he looked up to see Jamie smiling at him.

"I don't know how it's possible," she said, "but the sun…"

He turned his head to the side and saw blackened tracks leading out of the room. To him, the sunlight felt warm, life-affirming.

Robert sat up. The wooden stake that had been lying on his chest clattered to the floor.

"What the…?" he asked.

"It just popped out," Jamie said. "Mine did too. As if our bodies rejected them."

"Where's Feller?"

"Last I saw of him, he was running out of the room, burning."

She took his face in her hands and gave him a long kiss.

As the sunlight washed over them, bathing them in rays of warmth, she raised her head and her eyes searched his.

"What are we, Robert?" she asked. "What have we become?"

CHAPTER 45

The walls of the Armory groaned under the weight of the vampires outside, metal panels grating against each other. A roar began to build from the mass of vampires, as if they were preparing for a final push.

"We need to relieve the pressure!" Hoss shouted. "We have to take the fight outside!"

Terrill looked up at the skylights and saw a flash of blue. It was only for a moment, but it was undeniably clear blue sky. Dawn had come while they were fighting, and the clouds looked as if they were about to roll back and flood the day with light.

"You and your followers will have to stay inside, Hoss," he warned. "Daylight is coming soon. Clarkson and I are going out, along with any FBI guys who want to join us."

Hoss looked confused. "But you're vampire too."

"Yes…and no," Terrill said. "If we survive this, I'll explain it all to you. You need to know that the Rules are better than no Rules, but they aren't necessary at all if you don't kill."

"Not kill?" Hoss shook his head as if that wasn't sinking in. "That makes no sense. We're vampire."

"As I said," Terrill told him, "it ain't necessarily so…"

He turned to look for Callendar and the other FBI agents, most of whom were lined up helping the cops protect the crowd of citizens at the far side of the room. He moved quickly to Callendar and Jeffers's side and explained his plan.

"Better do something soon!" Callendar shouted. "We're

running out of ammunition!"

"Hoss! Your troops will need to take the place of these men!" Terrill commanded. "Protect these people."

Hoss motioned for half of his followers to replace the men guarding the humans. The agents and the vampires passed each other warily.

A loud crack echoed through the building as a seam in the protruding wall split down the middle. Several Wilderings tumbled into the room. Hoss's followers quickly dispatched them, then pushed the seam back together, propping the wall up with whatever was at hand—boxes of equipment, fuel cans, the bodies of headless Wilderings.

"Won't hold for long!" Hoss yelled.

Of the dozen FBI agents who'd shown up with Abercrombie, six were still alive. Terrill saw Callendar conferring with Jeffers. They looked as if they were arguing, but in the end, Jeffers lowered his head in assent.

"Agent Jeffers is staying; the rest of us are coming with you," Callendar announced.

Terrill nodded.

He looked over at the hole through which Jurgenson had disappeared. He'd been watching the opening warily, but the Wilderings hadn't found it. If they could manage to sneak out and outflank the bulk of the enemy forces, they might be able to stem the tide for a time.

Terrill moved toward the breach and heard the clatter of body armor and weapons as the agents followed him. He pushed aside the rock that Jurgenson had left against the building and poked his head out. There were a few Wilderings on this side of the Armory, looking for ways in, but it was obvious that most of them were on the other side of the building.

"Take out any of them who see us emerging," he said to

Callendar. "We don't want them finding this entrance."

They ducked into the hole and out the other side, catching the nearest Wilderings by surprise. One of the FBI guys had a silencer on his rifle, and he fired at their heads. Clarkson moved in a blur to the downed vampires and sliced their heads off with a slash of her claws.

They moved around the side of the building, slaying three straggler Wilderings they found, and then around to the front.

Terrill stopped in shock. There were hundreds of vampires, some of them climbing on others, all of them pushing against the sides of the Armory. The agents opened fire, toppling the vampires who were leveraging pressure from the top, and then firing into the dense crowd at the bottom.

The crowd broke up under the gunfire, then turned en masse and charged toward them.

Clarkson and Terrill let the agents take care of the first and second waves, but as the Wilderings grew closer, Terrill signaled the agents to stop firing their automatics and waded into the charging vampires. By then, the FBI guys had drawn their pistols and were firing at individual vampires instead of into the crowd. Terrill felt one of the bullets whiz past close to his head, and he turned back for a second to see if that had been on purpose.

None of the FBI agents were looking at Terrill; they were all fighting for their lives.

It became clear as soon as the fight started that Clarkson and Terrill were faster and their blows were harder than the Wilderings'. The Wilderings paused, as if confused that they were being attacked by their own kind, then started retreating. As soon as they did, Terrill waved at Clarkson to get behind the line of FBI agents and told Callendar to fire at will.

And then the line of agents was slammed into from behind.

A new wave of Wilderings had come out of nowhere, and within seconds, half the agents were dead. The last three were fighting back to back to back. Clarkson was surrounded and taking wounds.

Terrill didn't have time to think about what had gone wrong; he was fighting just to keep the space around him clear. These new opponents seemed more disciplined and were working together instead of getting in each other's way.

Standing off to one side, as if directing the battle, he saw a dark-haired, young-looking vampire wearing black-rimmed glasses. The glasses were strange enough—a vampire had better vision than any human—but it was the smirk on his face that made Terrill realize he was looking at the leader of these Wilderings, perhaps the one who had begun this epidemic in the first place.

The sight of his enemy energized Terrill, and he moved faster than ever. He threw off the attacking vampires and ran toward the glasses-wearing vampire, who looked alarmed for a second, then smiled. Too late, Terrill saw that he had a crossbow in his hands. He fired a bolt into Terrill's heart.

Terrill felt as though his body was disintegrating. The pain in his heart was the whole universe—nothing else existed. He felt himself falling. He was amazed that it was a Wildering who had finally brought him down.

Then he was even more amazed to find himself still alive, lying on his back, staring at the sky. He could feel the wooden projectile—which had just missed the silver cross on his chest—in his heart, but the organ kept beating. He was weakened, but he wasn't dead. He was looking up at dark clouds, and there, on their edge, he saw a patch of blue sky that was steadily expanding. He could see rays of the light behind the clouds, and it seemed to him that it would be mere moments before the sun emerged.

Too late for him, but the others would be saved. He found himself strangely content. Sylvie would live; Clarkson and Michael would carry on. It was a better result than he'd expected.

"Golden blood?" Stuart was staring down at Terrill. "What *are* you?" he asked. "Whatever you are, I want some of it."

The Wildering dropped down on top of him and Terrill felt fangs sink into his neck. "Oh… my… God," the other vampire breathed. "This is the best-tasting blood *ever!*"

After he had fed, Stuart got to his feet and wiped his mouth, smearing the golden liquid across his chin.

Terrill felt the wooden bolt being pushed out of his heart. It popped out of his chest and clattered to the pavement. He sat up.

The other vampire backed up a step, surprised. "What the hell *are* you?" he repeated. His words slurred at the end as the golden blood on his mouth and chin started to steam. He put his hand to his face and cried out as the gold liquid transferred to his fingers and began to burn.

Stuart jerked, then looked down at his hands, which were starting to curl in on themselves. He stood there shaking so violently that his image seemed to flicker in and out of focus. Then his body stiffened and his eyes rolled back in his head. He went crashing to the ground, his head hitting the pavement with a loud thump. He arched his back and screamed.

Everyone—Wildering and human alike—was backing away from him.

Then he exploded. His guts came flying out of his torso, his arms and legs split off and landed yards away, and his head shot straight up into the air and burst. The rest of his body turned into embers, then into ash, and a wind came out of nowhere and blew him into the sky.

At the same moment, the sun came bursting out from

behind the dark clouds, and the vampires who were caught in the open began to scream. The flames started in their hair and quickly enveloped them from top to bottom. They fell to the ground and curled up as if going to sleep. By then, they weren't making any sounds. Across the city, there were more explosions as cars and houses caught fire, ignited by burning vampires.

Terrill and Clarkson looked at each other with trepidation, but they felt warmth, not pain, from the sun. Clarkson's eyes were wide and frightened, but the fear quickly turned to amazement. She held out her bare hand and examined it as if it was some kind of marvel. Her hair had turned from the white-blonde of her earlier incarnation to a soft yellow; her skin was as tanned as if she was a beach girl who had spent the summer basking in the southern sun.

Terrill laughed joyously. Behind him, the door of the Armory opened and the humans started venturing out. He could see Hoss and his followers staring out from the shadows, staying well away from the sunlight.

Sylvie ran to him and he caught her in mid-leap.

"It's over," he said.

But even as he said it, he knew it wasn't true.

***

Terrill's story continues in *Blood of Gold,* the third book of the Vampire Evolution Trilogy.